Crying Out for Magic

Crying Out for Magic

P.S.C. Willis

Space Wizard Science Fantasy
Raleigh, NC
www.spacewizardsciencefantasy.com

Publisher's Note: This is a work of fiction. Names, characters, places, and incidents are a product of the author's imagination. Locales and public names are sometimes used for atmospheric purposes. Any resemblance to actual people, living or dead, or to businesses, companies, events, institutions, or locales is completely coincidental.

Cover art by Jess Montz
Editing by Heather Tracy
Book Layout © 2015 BookDesignTemplates.com

Crying Out for Magic/P.S.C. Willis.— 1st ed.
ISBN 978-1-960247-45-2

Author's Website: https://pscwillis.com

For my parents, who support me whether I'm having a crisis of confidence like Niall or jumping feet first into adventure like Draven. And for Jiji, who sat on my lap through every draft except the last.

CONTENTS

Chapter One

Given he'd wanted a romantic evening watching the fireworks, bailing on his date five minutes before midnight wasn't the smartest move. But no one had ever blamed—or praised—Draven for using his head over his heart.

He stumbled, tripping over his own feet in his haste to get up the hill to the castle. Running was not in his skillset, but he couldn't miss the fireworks. Galdorsfarne only had magic like this on show a couple of times a year. He cast a quickening charm on his feet. It was a little wasteful, and on any other day probably would have earned him a lecture about responsible magic use, but there was no one around to see.

Maybe next year would be the one where he started making plans actually involving planning. The letter he'd received that morning held the promise that, starting on Monday, he would finally be where he wanted to be.

Draven crested the hill with a whole thirty seconds to spare, leaning back against the cold, crumbling ruins as he tried to catch his breath.

Before he had totally recovered, the sky exploded. The first rocket burst into a shower of purple, and he felt that giddy rush he'd always felt as a child. The light scattered into tiny blue sparks which danced through the sky, forming huge, rolling waves. A series of smaller silver fireworks burst behind them, giving the waves their crests before the blue faded and the silver began cycling through all the colours of the rainbow.

It felt perfect to watch the display alone, and to do so from one of his favourite places. He had always loved the castle ruins. They stretched into a past so far and distant, so different to the reality he lived in, that it might easily have been a different world. Draven exhaled, his breath forming clouds in front of his face which joined the smoke streaking through the sky after the first fireworks.

The whole community of Galdorsfarne was on the lawn below the castle, stretched on picnic rugs, and wrapped in jackets lined with warming charms. Kids ran around with batons letting off little puffs of coloured smoke and sparks, not taking anywhere near enough care where they pointed something that was full of tiny explosives. Given the world only contained a few hundred people, it was easy enough to gather them together. Somewhere down there was the guy he'd been on a date with, until Draven had bailed in favour of the castle ruins. There hadn't been anything wrong, exactly—perfectly nice guy but that was it. Just nice. No spark. Draven had decided he'd prefer to spend midnight imagining someone perfect rather than kissing someone who wasn't. He smiled at the scene, enjoying it from a distance. People were happy. New Year was always such an exciting holiday, so full of promise.

Silver comet fireworks streaked through the air, whistling and leaving glittering tails. This was the world as it should be, and from Monday, he'd be working out how to generate enough magic to light the sky with dancing rainbow stars every day. It had taken long enough for him to get a shot at his dream guild. He'd almost completed his rotation, trying out every other type of magic, and now it was finally time for the thing that truly interested him. He'd looked forward to it every time the magic levels dipped too low, and he had to do chores by hand. Every endless afternoon of scrubbing ink stains out of his school uniform or peeling potatoes over the kitchen sink. He dreamt of the few old spells he'd seen passing references to—the ones that had been real once upon a time but which they never, ever got to use. How much easier his evening would have been if he could have ported up to the top of the hill—appearing there with a sudden "pop." Or would it "whoosh?" He had no idea. He'd never seen anyone do it.

His mother might have chided him for those thoughts, telling him not to be lazy or shallow. But was it shallow to want a world full of shining stars? They would make everyone else happy too. Those kinds of spells always did.

Maybe he and his friends would be able to shoot sparks for fun or give each other makeovers with glamours instead of just lipstick and powder. He didn't only want it for himself—he liked it when he made the people close to him smile. And in a place that was running short of problems, there was only one thing left to do.

The last volley of rockets went off, crashing, sparkling and swirling through the sky. He didn't have New Year's resolutions as such. He was a good guy, on a good pathway, and didn't need to fix himself. That wasn't an arrogant thing to say, because he would have said it of everyone else too. They were all good. They had to be. But he certainly had New Year's Goals:

1) Solve magekind's one remaining problem.
2) Get a proper boyfriend.

Someone who made him feel like there were fireworks, even if he didn't solve the energy crisis and make that literal. He tried to push aside the thought that he was running low on options. Yes, admittedly, he'd gone through basically everyone in the world who professed even the slightest inclination towards liking boys. And most of them he'd dropped as fast as a hot potato because they didn't give him That Feeling. But...well... He was struggling to find a suitably positive end to that thought when he heard a sigh.

"Happy New Year."

Draven jumped, looking around. But he was the only one up here. Some weird echo, somehow, from down below? He was pretty sure sound didn't work like that. The sigh had seemed to come from the bricks themselves. He was not aware of any magic that allowed buildings to talk. But hey, why not? He turned, laying a careful hand on the bricks.

"Happy New Year," he whispered back.

* * *

Niall stumbled away from the house party. Everyone there was drunk. Given he didn't seem particularly capable of maintaining a straight line, he thought he might be too. Just a little bit. He wasn't sure he was a fan.

New Year's Eve was typically spent at home with his parents. They got fancy crisps and other party snacks, drank Prosecco (of which he was allowed a glass), played board games and watched Jools Holland on the telly. He thought he was probably a freak in that he wished he'd stuck with that instead of trying to go out.

It had been his friend Ellen's idea. She had promised him fun times, cute boys and good music. These had all been lies.

Well, okay. There had been some cute boys. She had even pointed out two that liked other boys. Niall had got himself a drink and watched the guy with glasses, trying to work out how he'd strike up a conversation or whether he even wanted to, and what would happen if, by some wild miracle, the guy actually wanted to kiss him, and what if Niall was terrible at it because he'd never kissed anyone and— And he had sat on the sidelines, thinking and watching as the guy talked to someone else, and started making out with him on the sofa.

That was not fun. None of the rest of it was fun either. Ellen was off in the centre of it, happy as could be. Niall had been drinking vodka Coke. He didn't even like vodka or Coke on their own and wasn't sure why he'd thought either would be improved by mixing them together. Although, the cheap, paint-stripper vodka burnt your throat less once it was diluted. The sickly-sweet Coke was maybe better with an edge to it. It wasn't as horrible as a mixture of two things he didn't like should have been, but it was not fun. Watching everyone around him get steadily more pissed and less coherent wasn't fun either.

And the music had been drum and bass.

But leaving might have been the stupidest idea in the world. Was being outside on New Year's Eve safe? Niall crossed the street to avoid a pub, where the loud sounds of drunken merrymaking, and the people making them, spilled onto the street.

He dug in his pockets, quickly checking around before getting out his phone and headphones, putting only one in so he could keep an ear on the street. It seemed like a decent neighbourhood. The neat terraces with tidy potted plants were only threatening in that he was out, alone, at night. Some of the houses even had punny retirement names. But they nestled side by side with the kinds of people who let horrible teenagers have a house party. Better safe than sorry. He scrolled through the titles of all the Martha songs, trying to remember which was the one about New Year. Oh right "So Sad (So Sad)." Great. Fitting.

But it had a saving grace, this whole horrible evening; the sight of Tynemouth Priory, its jagged, ruined top cutting through the sky at the end of the street. He drew up to the railings and leant on them, staring up at it. Niall wasn't a rule breaker. He preferred to keep his head down, too afraid of getting into trouble. He wasn't sure exactly what force was pulling him in right now. Maybe it was the fact that he'd been stuck on the outside at the party, and the priory was the kind of place that had always felt like his. Maybe it was vodka and the fact that no one was around to stop him. But—with absolutely no athletic grace in spite of the advantage of his height—he climbed the low fence, designed more as a polite request than a real deterrent.

It wasn't like he was a bad person who was going to do bad things. So, therefore it was alright? He would be kind to the priory.

He knew better than to sit on the ground. It would be freezing. The chill of the night air was already nipping at his hands and his nose. As he leant back against the brickwork, the cold seeped into his back too.

There was a sudden screeching *"wheeeeeeew"* and a burst of bright red stars. Soon it was happening all around him, as people set off the fireworks in their backyards. He must have wandered out just in time to spend midnight by himself. Niall stared up at the sky, thinking about what he wanted to get from this year.

He wanted to stop hiding in corners. He wanted to feel like he could talk to people. He wanted to stop having horrible chest acne, oh and probably something in there about not failing exams but that wasn't much of a risk. The bigger risk was that he was going to die alone, spotty and unloved, in some dark corner because he didn't know how to relax around other people.

He was off to a great start with that, spending New Year alone in an abandoned ruin. Except he thought it was kind of cool. Why couldn't he meet someone who thought that this sounded like the perfect evening, instead of the hell that had been the house party?

"Happy New Year." He sighed to himself, to the night sky, and to the priory walls.

"Happy New Year."

He almost jumped out of his skin when he heard it coming back to him. He glanced around. No one else was here, he was sure of that. He didn't believe in ghosts. It seemed to take too long to be an echo, but maybe his brain was running things at weird speeds right now. It couldn't have been anything else, after all. Just an echo. His heart, which had initially leapt into his throat, was settling back to its usual position and slowing to its usual rhythm.

He touched his hand to the brick work. Just an echo. But even so, he felt less alone.

Chapter Two

"It's January 2nd, the time is seven AM. Today will be overcast with showers later." The chirpy voice of the weather announcer filled the room as Draven's radio alarm clicked on. *"Highs of five, lows of two. The ambient magic level is low amber so..."*

"...some restrictions apply!" all the presenters chorused. It was a running joke, seeing as it was always amber, seeing as there were always some restrictions. People were unsurprised when there was a run of low days after New Year celebrations, even though they'd been taught it didn't work that way. Magic was most consistently affected by doing good deeds—more kindness meant more magic. But predicting their own impact was an inexact science, and the results were capricious, fleeting and temporary. They could use magic while it was there, but they struggled to store it up in case of a still day—they could harness about ten percent. That let them gather emergency reserves and guaranteed some celebration at festivals. Even if they'd been able to store more, where would they have taken it from? They couldn't gather a resource that wasn't there.

Today though, Draven was starting his internship at the guild who would push them out of amber into green. He jumped out of bed, heading to the shower, where he soaped himself quickly. Low amber days meant five minutes of hot water per person. If they got a green day, how long would he be able to let the warm water slide over his skin? He didn't like to think about what would happen if they sunk into the red. Amber was okay, in theory. Everything still worked, more or less. Would he take more green days if he ended up with red ones to make up for it? Low amber days irked him, but high amber days weren't filled with wonder. Would he take days where anything was possible if the price was days where nothing was?

He shut the water off before his time was up, as he couldn't think of a more unpleasant start to the day than being doused in cold water.

His school teachers had never liked his thought experiments. *"The emphasis of our society is calm and continuity..."* blah blah blah. Sure, those things were important. But was "change" such a dirty word? The Energy Makers' Guild must want to challenge the status quo. Finally, he would be pushing the boundaries.

The guild wore green—not Draven's favourite colour, but his mother liked him in it, and it didn't look terrible on him, plus he'd treated himself to a cute cotton blazer with a floral print. He thought the guilds should choose their colours more carefully. He'd liked the Potion Makers' Guild, but he didn't want to wear orange to work for the rest of his life. It washed him out and was ugly—by seeming universal agreement with this, no one made cute clothes in orange. He'd struggled to find anything that he didn't hate, especially as colour change charms were forbidden for being too frivolous. At least warming charms were fine, as he never would have survived the pain of a season spent in chunky knitwear.

He pushed aside the detritus on his dressing table, searching for a comb, which he found under a flyer for the fireworks display. *"Happy New Year."* He replayed the voice for the umpteenth time in his head. That voice coming out of nowhere had been like nothing he'd ever experienced. There was no spell he knew of which would account for it. His mind spun, crafting a story, and a person, to go with the voice. Someone who—

"Draven? Breakfast!"

The shout punctuated his daydream. He gave his dark hair a sharp side parting and admired his reflection. If he was off to save the world, he ought to look pretty whilst doing it.

He scrambled down the stairs, finding his parents already in the kitchen, along with Yvette Lee-Miller—his school friend and neighbour who was as comfortable in their home

as her own. She was also rotating onto the Energy Makers'
Guild, and they'd agreed to go in together.

Four steaming mugs of tea sat on the table, giving off a
gentle, smoky scent. There was a pre-made breakfast roll
next to each one. The stove was gas, so they weren't ever
without the means to cook, but it was so time-consuming
without magic.

"Didn't get enough nightdreams, so have to daydream
too?" his mother asked, as he slid into place.

"No. I was..." He trailed off. His mother had hit the nail
right on the head. She was also giving his chosen attire a
definite Look.

"If you insist on making yourself stand out, you need to
make sure your behaviour fits right in."

Draven nibbled his breakfast roll, trying not to point out
how contradictory that sounded. It wasn't like he wanted to
rebel, and he knew what his mother meant. If he was going
to wear a loud blazer, he couldn't be zoning out when
everyone inevitably stared at him.

"Maybe this will finally be the guild that appreciates my
unique perspective." Perhaps if he could get her to laugh it
off, she'd stop worrying about him being an oddball.

"Try not to start a revolution on your first day." She
pressed her lips together.

"What?" Okay, sometimes he asked awkward questions,
but this was the thing he'd looked forward to his whole life.
He was going to be good. He was going to be the best so
they'd take him. But surely, that had to involve thinking
outside the box? They were dealing with a problem that no
one had ever made headway with. "Who said anything about
revolting?"

"Anyone who's seen your blazer?" Yvette smirked.

"You're just jealous I saw it first." Draven stuck his tongue
out, although Yvette usually expressed her placements in her
hair and make-up.

"Now, now—you'd think you'd never been to Assembly,"
his mother said, frowning at him.

"We're not picking on each other," Draven said. His mother fretted. She was fond of rules and order. Neither Draven nor Yvette was a rule breaker—that would have been taking things too far. But his mother wished Draven would do more to blend in, even though no one was going to punish him for standing out. She wished he and Yvette wouldn't joke around, even though they didn't mean it.

"I know," his mother said. "But imagine if people said hurtful things and meant them."

"But people don't," Draven stated, even though that was obvious—they'd had it drummed into them since birth how the magic would fail if they weren't kind. He'd heard stories about contact with a crueller, wider world. Everyone had. But even if the Others had been real once, they weren't any more. Draven didn't get how his mother didn't get it. When he and Yvette teased each other, it was a game. He felt silly being formally polite with someone he'd grown up with. But whenever he wasn't, it frightened his mother into thinking he didn't care about Yvette properly, and—for all that she fussed—he didn't want to frighten his mother.

"I'll behave," he promised. "Shall we go?" he asked Yvette, swallowing the last of his roll.

* * *

Draven and Yvette's tram shuddered to a halt outside the home of free thinkers and wild ideas. The Energy Makers' Guild was at the end of the line, and there were so few passengers left, the tram had switched to electric so as not to be a selfish use of magic. He could see the generator building in the near distance, technically under the purview of his new guild though he hadn't given it much thought. No one else had either, judging by the way it sat off to the side.

For one of the most important guilds, it was remarkably understated. But that was their jive. The Energy Makers' Guild decided what each restriction level meant, and made handy pamphlets (recyclable, of course!) detailing ways to save magic around the home. They believed in leading by example, so their building was as minimally wasteful as possible. Little podules rose out of the landscape as if they had grown there organically. Grass swirled seamlessly from ground level over the gently sloping sides of the units and onto their roofs.

Draven and Yvette made their way inside. The atrium was small (after all, what was an atrium for except showing off that you had one?) and dominated by a tall, twisting tree that burst through the roof, and which no one had felt it polite to disrupt.

Rowan Wessington, a cheerful mage with horn-rimmed glasses who'd been a couple of years above them at school, was waiting for them. She waved them over into a group with Matthias Borne and Melvin Drey from their own cohort. The combination of people on placements varied, so the apprentices could "network," as if they hadn't all grown up in the same claustrophobically small community. Matthias was the kind of person you couldn't help but notice, not always for the right reasons. He was very into sports, was good at them, and knew it. Bragging was unseemly, but you got the impression that Matthias would, if it was allowed—much like everyone else would call him big-headed if that was permitted. Melvin was...also there. That was about as much as Draven had been able to say about him in school too.

"Hi." Rowan smiled at them. "I'll be your supervisor. I'm in my first full year as a guild member, so there's a lot of overlap between what I do and what you'll be doing. We'll have a brief tour, then start some simple orientation tasks. I hope you've all got good heads for figures!"

Draven's eyebrows furrowed. He'd envisaged dramatic experiments, eureka moments. He'd easily got good grades in most of his subjects, but he'd never felt a particular affinity for maths. It was disappointing to learn that his preferred branch of magic might include a lot of it. But he swallowed the worry and smoothed out his frown, not wanting to make a bad impression.

Rowan's grin was still in place as she began their tour. Draven knew she was rarely without a smile, and he liked that. People were fun to look at when they were talking about something that made them light up. Everyone was enthusiastic about their own guild—that was a benefit of testing people out and placing them where they fitted—but the animation of Rowan's voice, and how she bounced on her toes as she talked reminded him of himself.

If she fitted in here, surely he would too.

Their tour included several rooms of people simply poring over piles and piles of paper. There were tantalising glimpses of experiments. Mages were measuring the spell-life of magically generated objects and the energy they emitted on dissolving, or testing the magical waste when using different insulating materials.

One room was dedicated to a scale model of Galdorsfarne, the entirety of their world easily encased under a glass dome. The real thing felt like that sometimes, like there was meant to be more. People told him they understood that itch, and that he was just missing magic.

In the basement was a storage room with rows of boxes, and shelves piled high with mismatched and broken objects, waiting to be repaired or stripped down for residual magic and useful parts.

Draven left all this behind somewhat reluctantly, as they followed Rowan to the data analysis lab. He tried to feel cheerful about being someone who now worked "in a lab," for all that it seemed to be a room full of filing cabinets and desks. This was the first step to solving all the world's problems, and it was a welcoming space. One of the energy-saving features of the building was plentiful access to natural light, and there were large windows through which weak winter sunlight filtered. There were lots of pale tones, to better reflect and maximise this, and a pleasant view of the surrounding fields. The room thrummed with palpable energy, and Draven realised why when their tour concluded with a room out back, where a heavy machine spat out graphs.

"Over the coming weeks, we'll teach you various statistical interpretation methods to help you analyse our data," Rowan informed them. "In a sense, Galdorsfarne is an ongoing experiment. We collect so much data, and we can easily verify results against individuals, so the solution to our energy issues might already be here—we just have to find it.

"We're going to start with something fairly unscientific during your first week. You'll be looking over your personal data to familiarise yourselves with the filing system, introduce some basic statistical analysis, and let you get to know each other better." This latter purpose seemed unnecessary, given that they'd been classmates. Still, this tapped into some deeper stuff—what motivates you as a person and all that. Draven couldn't say he knew that about everyone here. "Mage Starkweather, who heads the guild, likes to meet each of our apprentices personally, so expect to see her before the end of the week. We'll also break up the statistics lessons with shadowing some of the senior mages, and learning about our ongoing experiments and other day-to-day duties."

Rowan handed them diagrams of the filing systems and lists of questions to answer from their own data, such as which spells they used the most, and how well they'd been matched with their merit activities.

Gathering the records took time. The volumes of data were substantial, and their lack of familiarity slowed them down. Draven weaved through the tight aisles of cabinets, pulling papers from stubborn, overstuffed files until he had his primary school analysis (*historical records area, junior records subsection*), his most recent profiles (*citizen records*), and his usage and merit statistics (*accounting*).

The latter interested him the most. Usage statistics came through regularly, so people could self-monitor and reduce any overuse. They couldn't go over their allowances, but someone who was always using mending charms could learn to be more careful, or someone who used a lot of quickening charms could drag themselves out of bed a little earlier. Usage let people evaluate themselves, and work on self-improvement, but merit was done collectively. They all had regularly scheduled sessions in which they had to do enough good to balance out the energy the community used. There were times he could tell it was going well, they got it banked quickly, and it was easier to estimate his contribution in small groups. But he'd never seen all the good he'd done in the world put into black and white before.

The graphs were self-explanatory—there was a line for their expected target, and for what they'd achieved. His first month, he'd sailed happily way above the line. He was good at doing good. Good to know. As he made his way through the pages, the picture became less clear. Sometimes he cruised way above, sometimes he dipped below. He bit his lip. He tried, didn't he? He wanted to be good. It mattered to him. What if they took this into account when deciding whether he could have a permanent placement here?

"Are you done?" Yvette stuck her head around the end of the aisle, causing Draven to almost drop his papers. "Rowan has something for us to do with inferential statistics. She says it's a game." Yvette's tone betrayed a deep distrust of this probability.

"Yeah." Draven took another look at the most recent crater in his graphs. If there was anyone he could trust with that, it was Yvette, but as he followed her towards the table, he found Melvin and Matthias already waiting. He tucked the paper down to the bottom of the stack, hoping it wasn't involved in their next activity, and trying to ignore the awful, gnawing feeling in his gut that he was hindering rather than helping with the energy crisis.

* * *

"Is day one of saving the world living up to your expectations?" Yvette asked as they stowed their lunch trays.

"Day one's not over yet." Draven forced himself to smile. First days were always slow—besides, his biggest problem was his own wobbly graph, which wasn't the guild's fault. "Let's see what the afternoon holds."

"I know this is your dream job, but am I allowed to be bored?"

"It might pick up," Draven said. Yvette hadn't found a guild that motivated her, and given that this was their last placement, this had to be it. Or she could settle for something she'd found okay-ish, but that didn't feel good enough.

Rowan had asked them to meet her in one of the basement storage rooms for the afternoon. Make-do-and-mending was not Draven's forte, but it was one of Yvette's, and might sweeten her opinion of the guild. The room looked more like a second-hand store than a workroom, and there wasn't a filing cabinet in sight.

"Hello! Good lunch? Welcome to the warehouse. We've just had a delivery. As you know, Mage Gaskin passed on recently." Rowan muted her usual smile in favour of a more sombre expression. "We need to identify which of her possessions can be reused or have their powers stripped and added to our energy reserves, which are at their lowest given the New Year celebrations. You'll need to weigh each item to help us sort them." She indicated sets of brass scales on each bench with a small glowing cloud where the weights would normally be. "Items that register as green have enough magical potential to be worth reusing or stripping down. Those that glow red are the magical equivalent of eating cucumber—burns more than it gives you. Anything that's no use magically can be put into general donations and will be given or sold as needed. Anything with magical potential can be put on the orange shelf to be further sorted between repairing, reusing, and stripping. Mage Starkweather will be stopping in to meet you at some stage."

Spending the afternoon unpacking boxes wasn't a strong uptick in saving the world, but at least it didn't involve maths. Although one of the only empty spots was by Matthias.

Which was fine. Draven could not say he disliked Matthias because no one disliked anyone. He just found it challenging to relate to his competitive streak. But if Matthias wanted to turn this into who could sort the most boxes, Draven could easily let him have a win, which would probably make Matthias happy.

"Get much time to look at your stats?" Matthias asked as they started pulling things out and placing them on the scales.

"No." Draven hoped his feelings weren't obvious on his face as Matthias brought up the thing he least wanted to talk about. His answer wasn't a lie. He hadn't had much time. None of them had.

"I hope they take those into consideration when considering us for permanent positions."

Yours are good then? Draven swallowed it down, aware it invited the response *Aren't yours?* "You want a permanent placement here?"

Draven placed a woolen blanket on the scales, lighting the cloud up green. There was a flicker of something like jealousy across Matthias' face, except being jealous was frowned upon.

"Obviously."

"Why obviously?" Draven asked. People didn't all want the same things. It was why they were profiled for merit sessions and put on different placements to find their Adept. He picked up the shawl, wrapping a hand into the large, loose cable knit stitches, feeling the comfort of a warming charm seeping through his fingers. The blanket would probably end up in the recycle shop, and he was tempted to buy it if so. A lot of Mage Gaskin's things gave him that familiar, cosy feeling, and not just because she was someone his grandma had liked. While there wasn't much choice in the spells they could use in daily life, there was enough to give clues to someone's personality.

"Anyone who makes headway on the energy crisis would be a legend." Matthias swiped items across the scale—a dimly flickering lamp (red), a crystal ball (red) and a rusty self-sharpening knife (red). "Maybe you'll be happy mixing potions or whatever—"

"I want to work here!" Draven pulled a set of tarot cards (red) off the scale, admiring their art and making a mental note to tell Yvette about them. She enjoyed poking her nose into the future. Several forms of Divination were free to use, which said a lot about the magical energy it drew on, but Draven indulged her sometimes. He wasn't sure he wanted anyone to spell out all the answers for him, but it was fun to be tantalised with the promise of great romance or adventure.

"Really?" Matthias tossed divination supplies on his growing heap of rejected items.

"Why so surprised when it's so obvious?" Draven asked, earning him a sour look even though he'd meant it with genuine curiosity. That happened a lot. He would say things, and people's smiles would get tight or outright fake, like they wanted to argue or say things they weren't supposed to. He could see Matthias calculating his words, like it took time to find the nice way of saying whatever he was thinking.

"We don't overlap in many other areas. Our merit duties are very different, for example."

"Yeah... Well..." Draven couldn't imagine working side by side with Matthias every day either, but he wasn't going to imply that one of them was wrong about their dreams. Especially as his wonky graphs suggested it might be him.

"May the best mage win." Matthias' look barely concealed which one of them he thought that was, though it fell slightly when Draven placed a small, smooth stone pendant carved in a figure of eight onto the scale, and the cloud lit up green.

"That can go straight in the pile to be stripped down."

"Wh—Mage Starkweather!" Draven cut himself off as he turned and found who he was speaking to. He knew her face because the guild heads appeared regularly in the papers. And at Assembly. And in the one grocery store in town. He was not trying to estimate her age, because that would be rude, though he knew that typically the head mages were around sixty years old. She had short silvery hair held in firm flicks by some kind of product, and her green eyes were surveying him with what appeared to be genuine interest.

"We can't repair a spell we don't use any more," Mage Starkweather answered his unspoken question. "Here, we'll get our one-to-one done, and you can stack some of that on the shelves at the same time." She pointed to a cart at the end of the workbench which a handful of mages had been placing their green items into.

Draven followed her, sure that Matthias would love the fact he was going first. He pushed the cart over to the shelf for positive finds, the necklace still clutched in his hand. He was never sure how welcome his questions were—well, no, that was a lie; he was entirely aware how unwelcome most of his questions were, but he was often tempted to ask them anyway. He was supposed to be good. He was meant to toe every line toeable. But he so rarely saw evidence of the spells they didn't use any more.

"What does it do?" Draven peered at the markings. They were like the runes they traced in the air or inscribed in things for spellcasting, but he didn't know these particular ones.

"It's a spell for bringing a little good into someone's life," Mage Starkweather said, speaking slowly and carefully. "We don't have any shortage of goodness," she reminded him.

But there was one in Mage Gaskin's lifetime? He held that question back. It wasn't the first time someone had suggested they knew something outside of this world, usually something unpleasant. It never met with positive results to ask. He ran a finger over the unfamiliar marks. He could feel the magic, it was soft and warm, and unlike even the nicest of the spells he used. His spells were practical, this was loving. He performed magic for loving reasons, but it was different when it was in the magic itself—

"How was your first day?" Mage Starkweather asked.

"Uh. Fine. Thank you." He looped the necklace over the cart's handle, then began unloading, grateful for the excuse to break eye contact. She had the kind of stare that went right through people.

"I checked in with Rowan and she mentioned you in particular."

"Good things or bad?" Draven kept his tone light, like this was a joke. Luckily, she laughed.

"Good things. Why? Are there terrible ones to know as well?" she asked, matching his tone. He wondered whether hers hid the same serious intent that his had.

"Hopefully not." He tried not to sound uncertain. First days were always slow, and he trusted it would pick up. Whether his own wobbly graphs would, and whether the guild would have him...

"Rowan mentioned that you're enthusiastic about joining us. Is that still the case after day one?"

"Yes," he said, even though it hadn't been what he was expecting.

"What do you hope to get out of your time with us?" she asked.

The honest answer was making some amazing discovery, preferably by doing something much flashier and more exciting than poring over pages of statistics. However, that would sound ridiculous and ungrateful, or like he didn't value the wisdom of the methods being currently employed. Just because he didn't was no reason to say so to the head of the guild.

"To gather a thorough understanding of how the Energy Makers' Guild works and determine whether my skills are useful enough to join." It was a flat answer, the basic definition of why they went on apprenticeships. Mage Starkweather eyed him steadily, expecting more. He scrabbled for an item in the bottom of the cart.

"There's no wrong answer," she assured him. "It's my job to get to know you all and understand what makes you tick. If, from tomorrow, I gave you licence to do as you pleased, how would you use your time?"

"I..." He didn't know what brilliant solution he would offer, otherwise he would already have presented it. He would have to spend time learning the ropes, or coming up with an idea worth testing. Maybe this conversation was merely an exercise in teaching him patience and appreciation for the work he was already doing. "I'd be in the labs. I don't know what type of experiment I would run, but

I'd want to learn as much as possible about running a good experiment, so that I can come up with my own when I join."

"And come up with the grand experiment that unlocks it all?" she asked. Draven was relieved to see that, although she had read him like a book, she wasn't amused or offended by his presumption.

"Yes," he admitted.

"Why?"

"Pardon?" he asked. "Why do I want to solve the energy crisis?"

"Yes."

His brows furrowed. It was a strange question, especially coming from the head of the Energy Makers' Guild.

"Isn't that what we're all supposed to want?" he asked.

"Everyone wants an end to the crisis. Not everyone dedicates their life to finding that answer."

That was true. But not everyone was suited to this type of work. He had never stopped to think about the difference between being suited and wanting to—you presumably wanted to do the things you were suited to and supposed to do. The people who didn't work there...it wasn't, in his mind, that they didn't want to solve the energy crisis, they just...they weren't doing it because they weren't good at it.

"Well...not everyone can...I suppose... I mean, if your Adept is potions, you get invested in that but..." He trailed off. He was trying his hardest to put himself in someone else's shoes, something he was normally good at, but he couldn't imagine not caring about this. He looked up, finding Mage Starkweather regarding him with affectionate understanding, as if she could see this realisation forming, and shared his sense of it being unfathomable.

"You want to because you want to. You don't understand the idea of not wanting to," she summarised. "That's usually a good sign. Try to work out what makes you feel that way. Let me know if you do."

"I will."

"I look forward to talking more with you. Looks like you're almost done." Her eyes lingered on the necklace, still looped on the cart's handle. It saddened him to think of it losing its powers. He so rarely saw real, living evidence of the spells they didn't do any more. It was sweet, optimistic magic. The best he could do was push it to the very back of the shelf, so that it would be the last thing to be stripped down. It went further than he'd anticipated, and when he let go, the string slithered across the shelf as if the weight of the necklace had dropped. He turned to check if Mage Starkweather had noticed, but she was already heading over to talk to Yvette.

He ought to retrieve it. But at least this way, it could keep hold of its magic for longer. Besides, he couldn't even work out where it had dropped to.

Chapter Three

"I'll be going into town later, if you want dropping off anywhere."

Niall quickly hit the power button on his phone, even though his mum would need some kind of mirror or x-ray vision to read it from where she was standing. Still, being caught searching *"hearing disembodied voices"* was not something he wanted.

"Okay. Maybe." His eyes strayed to the window.

"Not a bad day, eh?" his mum said, before heading upstairs. No, it wasn't a "bad day." The clouds had cleared, the sky was approaching blue. It was cold but crisp, lovely weather for a walk. And that was the problem. Schools were still out, and he was sure the priory would be busy on a day like this. He folded his arms on the windowsill, glaring out at the sunshine. He needed the kind of weather that would drive everyone else away. Preferably on a day when his mum was out so she couldn't ask where he was going and argue against wandering around a clifftop in the rain.

"Happy New Year."

The more he replayed the voice, the less it sounded like his own. The intonation, the emotion in it, none of them had been how he had said it. But he was sure he was changing it with every repetition.

He pulled his phone back out.

"Hearing voices, supernatural." No. He'd be bound to get a bunch of ghost hunters and "psychics."

"Delayed echo." He'd tried that already. It had led to some pretty cool things about radios, but nothing that explained what he'd heard. By this point, he was sure he'd tried every possible combination of words, but he hadn't found anything to explain the voice.

A little bubble with Ellen's pink-haired head was permanently glued to his home screen. He tapped it for the umpteenth time that day. In a two-way tie between a real, actual human who was his friend, and obsessing over a disembodied voice that he may have made up, he knew what he ought to pursue. Seeing as his priory plans had been thwarted, his only other option for the day was sulking, and Googling things he'd already Googled. A large portion of his brain wanted to give into that, but another part of him knew that was pointless. That part was far smaller, but it did have the sunshine and the offer of a lift on its side.

He opened his messages.

Niall Silverstein: Want to hit the charity shops this afternoon? Might be good picks in people's New Year clear-outs?

Cos, obviously he needed to justify to his friend why she might want to see him.

Ellen Sorn: Sounds good. Where?
Niall Silverstein: Newcastle?
Ellen Sorn: Aye

"Hey," he said, poking his head into his mum's office. "I'll take you up on the lift. Can you drop me at the metro so I can go into town and meet Ellen?"

"Sounds good. I like Ellen. She's a nice girl."

Niall was aware of the pause before he answered, "Yup." He wasn't sure if that had just been a comment, or whether his mum was trying to give him an opening to say something. If she was, was she trying to get him to say that Ellen was his girlfriend, or that she most definitely was not and never would be? Sometimes he wondered whether his mum had figured him out and was gently trying to prod him into saying something. Other times, it was clear she had no idea—she defaulted to asking him about girls, or made comments which in one way or another assumed. Not that he thought she'd mind. He'd just never found the right time or the right words.

His phone buzzed, and his mum dismissed him with a wave of her hand. He clicked his messages open.

Ellen Sorn: Speaking of things getting out of closets for the new year...
Niall Silverstein: Ha. Ha.
Ellen Sorn: You said you want to date. What about Chris?
Niall Silverstein: ??
Ellen Sorn: *::glasses emoji::*
Niall Silverstein: Think he's taken now.
Ellen Sorn: Just cos they made out doesn't mean he's taken.

Niall tucked his phone away, not wanting to get into that discussion. Sure, he'd agreed the guy was cute but that was it. He wasn't sure that impression had lasted through watching him drunkenly make out with someone else. It wasn't exactly a romantic "first time I saw you" moment.

* * *

Niall gave a cheerful smile to Earl Grey atop his column as he emerged from the metro station in the centre of Newcastle. He checked his phone for any indication that he wasn't here first. He almost certainly would be. He was more punctual and more desperate to leave his little corner of the world than Ellen was. Not that where she lived was exactly abuzz with excitement. Hence visiting "The Toon."

I'll be in the bookshop he messaged, unnecessarily. This was entirely predictable behaviour, as confirmed by the response a moment later.

Ellen Sorn: Obviously. ::eyeroll:: I'll be late ::haha::
Niall Silverstein: Obviously ::tongue poke::

He tucked his phone into his pocket and turned his eyes upwards. He'd got into the habit of looking at the city from the first floor up. At ground floor level, you saw the same repetitive shop fronts that occupied any city centre. From the first floor, the character of the city shone through. Case in point, the soft sandstone in front of him with its elaborate carvings over every window, a turret on each corner for no other reason than showing off. Even when he stepped inside, to the recognisable repetition of the chain store decor, it worked around the arches of the building. Looking up, the white plaster moulding was perfectly preserved behind the shelves. It felt like a bookshop should.

He turned off his music as he entered. He knew there was no rule against it—there probably wasn't even one in the library, so long as you kept your headphones in and the volume down—but it felt wrong to him. Bookshops were supposed to be quiet, even inside your own head.

He wasn't in a browsing-with-intent kind of mood, more a browsing-to-absorb one. Drifting through, appreciating the sheer bookshoppiness of it. Judging books by their covers—seeing which drew him in. Looking for ones with velvety spines or silver embossed letters, ones which looked like they were waiting for the right person to pick them up to reveal all their magical secrets. It was a game he played with himself—pretending he still believed enough in magic that he'd somehow stumble across it, if he only spent enough time exploring the places it was likely to be. Bookshops, museums, libraries. It helped that he also liked being in those places in their own right. But it let him suspend his disbelief—sometimes, so far that he wasn't even convinced he was just playing.

He opened a few books at random, from the fantasy and science sections, to see if Fate (which he didn't really believe in) was going to guide him to a passage that would explain the voice.

Nothing did. Though he read some cool things about telescopes, and got half into a novel about a girl and her sentient tree friend. He was holding a special edition hardback—mostly to appreciate the texture of the cover beneath his fingers (because damn, those were expensive)— when Ellen arrived.

"Hey." He shelved the book and offered her a hug, propelling them both towards the exit. He loved her, but she was not a force for calm and did not belong in a bookshop.

Sure enough, she was already chattering away, telling him about some new person she was messaging online. Ellen had a knack for putting herself out there, whether it was being the centre of attention at a party, or striking up a conversation about someone's make-up on Insta. Some of those felt more achievable to Niall. It wasn't like he never scrolled #Gaymer or #LGBTQBooks, but even giving out "likes" would leave a paper trail. His participation in online communities was stacked with so many layers between it and his real life that it felt like as much a fantasy as looking for magic.

* * *

"I already see ruffles," Ellen whispered with a smirk as she and Niall entered the charity shop. "Polka dot ones."

He nudged her to be quiet, trying to keep his own amused grin off his face. He didn't want other people to think they were taking the piss, even if that was precisely what they were doing. They both loved charity shops. In some ways, they were absolute goldmines. In approximately equal measure, they were absolute car crashes. It was his and Ellen's challenge to not only find the bargains and the I-can't-believe-someone-got-rid-of-this items, but also the most ugly, the most baffling, the I-can't-believe-anyone-ever-owned-this ones. There were some seriously heinous tent-like things that had been done with floral fabric over the years. There were consistently cringey slogan t-shirts. And there were ruffles. So. Many. Ruffles.

"Did you hear?" Ellen asked, as they rifled their way along the racks. "About Jamie Swift?"

"Yeah." Niall pulled two hangers further apart to subtly point out an exceptionally lime green polyester dress. Ellen gave it a so-so head nod, and he knew that was all it deserved. He'd been trying to derail the subject from the fact that one of the out queer kids had, apparently, seen Jamie at a Pride event she'd attended last summer.

"He's cute," Ellen pressed.

"Can you not?" Niall hissed, glancing around them self-consciously.

"Are you worried those old ladies are going to come and beat us up?" She nodded at the nearest other occupants of the shop, though dropped her voice so they didn't hear that.

"No—just. Don't. Please."

"Sorry." This was offered sincerely, and Niall accepted the apology with a nod. Was he being paranoid? He knew Ellen would say "yes"—the nearest people were five feet away and chatting animatedly to each other. They weren't going to hear. If they heard, they probably weren't going to care. Why should he mind, even if they did? He and Ellen were out in the city, and part of the point was that they didn't know people here. But it made him feel exposed.

"I swear, the closer we get to the size sixteens, the more hideous things there are. It's like a personal vendetta against me," Ellen grumped. It was a familiar complaint, though she almost always found something super cool. Or at least, super cool on her. She had the confidence that let her pull off a much bolder style than Niall.

"How do we feel about diamantés on sleeves?" he muttered, pulling out something with shoulder pads that could take someone's eye out.

"Looks promising."

Niall moved along the rail, searching for more crimes against clothing. As he did so, his foot skidded on something that had been dropped on the floor. He bent down to pick it up.

It was a necklace. It looked like it had probably come from some historical site's souvenir shop. There were even runes on the inner edge.

"Whatcha got there?" Ellen asked, looking up from the jaunty eighties sweater she was evaluating for hideousness.

"Found this on the floor." Niall held up the pendant. "Dunno if it's from here or if someone dropped it." He turned it over. "There's no price tag."

He headed over to the counter, finding that his eyes kept returning to the symbols. His thumb was already making a habit of tracing between the cool smooth stone and those little notches. There was something soothing about that. He held it up to the volunteer with a brief explanation.

"Not seen that in here before," she said. "I'll put up a sign, in case anyone's dropped it, and leave a note for the other volunteers, in case one of them saw it come in. Thanks, pet." She smiled at Niall. His fingers flexed, wanting to hang onto it, but what she was saying made sense. Anyway, he didn't want it. He'd grown out of his pseudo-historical phase in year nine.

"No bother." He handed it over but his head kept turning back to the counter as he returned to the clothing racks. Though his attention was diverted back to Ellen as she held up a sweater with a kitten photo surrounded by appliquéd glitter, her expression saying that she'd won this round.

* * *

A tour of the charity shops resulted in the "winners" being the kitten sweater, a rib-knitted dress in luminous yellow with some kind of strange structural ruffle on the sleeves, and a t-shirt depicting a mash-up of two things that had barely been funny three years ago. Niall had suggested a fluffy pink skirt as a contender but it had done that loop that things sometimes did where they were so weird they were cool again. As it matched the current shade of Ellen's short hair, she'd bought it, along with a fishnet shirt that her parents were bound to hate. Niall had mostly raided the bookshelves and had come away with a selection that he hoped would allow him to convince himself, for an afternoon at least, that magic was real.

Ellen's attention/feet had been exhausted, although Niall regarded the time they'd been wandering around as negligible. Still, as she pointed out, she was about a foot shorter than him, and only had little legs, and those legs needed coffee. He'd allowed her to pull him towards a nearby café, because when had he ever said no to a cup of tea?

"Shall we get them to go?" Ellen asked, as they lined up to get drinks.

"Are you kidding? It's lovely in here." Niall had already stripped off his hat and coat in anticipation of staying in the tea house. He'd already ranked which of the unoccupied tables were his first, second and third picks, and was mentally willing the people in front of them in the line not to take the plush red armchair that he had his eye on.

"I was hoping to get to the bottom of your love life and figured you might want somewhere a bit more quiet. Are you gonna let me do it here?" she asked.

"Yup. I don't have one. There. Done." Niall ran a hand through his hair. It was probably a vain hope that it wasn't looking weird, because one of the things about having curly hair was that it was always doing something weird, even if it hadn't been jammed under a hat for the morning.

"You always say you want to meet someone," she said. "But you bat me away the second I make a suggestion. How can I help?"

"Is there any chance you're gonna let this drop?" he asked.

"Yes. Boundaries are boundaries. I'll respect yours even if they're..." She trailed off, clearly struggling to find an adjective that wasn't insulting.

"Stupid?" he suggested. "*Here or to go?*" The question was being put to the people in front of them, but it would be them soon enough. "Are they actually stupid?" he asked.

"You said that, not me." Ellen gave him a hard poke in the ribs. "There's no wrong boundaries or wrong pace. But yours are a bit like an eighteenth-century fortress. All I'm saying is that if you ever wanna date anyone, you are going to have to admit to wanting to date them. Even if it's only to them."

By this time, they had moved up to the front of the line.

"One Americano, and a...?" Ellen prompted.

"Hot chocolate," Niall decided. There was an intimidating range of canisters along the back wall that implied this place didn't understand the concept "just a cup of tea" and would look askance at him for wanting to dump milk and sugar in it.

"For here or take away?" the barista asked. Niall weighed up the facts that the chair he wanted was unoccupied and he couldn't feel the end of his nose.

"Here," he confirmed. Ellen paid and he took the wooden spoon with their order number, heading over to his chosen table. The huge glass windows made a cinema of the passing world. The café sat on a corner next to the broad concrete stairs which led up from street level to part of the university. That made for interesting passing traffic—Ellen, he thought, would blend in seamlessly with the tide of cool looking students. He would not. Across the way, the Civic Centre rose, its verdigris covered seahorses watching the city below them.

He pulled out his phone to transfer her the money for his drink.

Niall Silverstein: Okay, so you wanna "talk"?

"Seriously?" she asked, raising her eyebrows at him.

"You didn't specify out loud," he whispered with a smirk. She rolled her eyes, but co-operated in lapsing into everyone's criticism of their generation—too busy tapping away at their phones to have an interaction with the person sitting opposite them. Except that was exactly what they were doing.

Ellen Sorn: Jamie - y/n?

"It's a single letter answer." She rolled her eyes as Niall tapped away furiously.

Niall Silverstein: I heard he made out with Susan Jeffries at Rob's party.

Ellen Sorn: And?

This was accompanied by a bi flag emoji and a pointed kick under the table.

"Ow!" Niall glared.

"You deserved that." Ellen shrugged. "Don't erase me."

Niall Silverstein: It's irrelevant whether I think he's cute if he has a girlfriend.

A member of staff came over and Niall clutched the conversation protectively to his chest as their drinks were set down and they both muttered their thanks.

Ellen Sorn: He's hot.

She tilted her head at the departing waiter. Niall sent back a shrug emoji.

Ellen Sorn: Oh come on. What's a guy gotta do to impress you?

"Stop staring," Niall hissed, as Ellen turned around to blatantly eye up the waiter.

"I'm allowed."

"You are the least covert person ever."

"Yeah, well, when I'm interested in making out with someone, I tend to let them know too. It has a much higher success rate that way."

"For you, maybe," Niall muttered, picking up his hot chocolate.

"You never know unless you try," she said. Niall sunk down in his chair, holding up his mug to shield his face. "Live a little. Global warming or the zombie apocalypse is going to get us before we're thirty, so you might as well try to get laid a few times."

Niall wasn't sure it was possible to hide any more behind his mug than he was already doing, which was a definite problem, as he was sure he was rapidly turning red.

"You got homework to do tonight?" he squeaked, losing the right to critique anyone else's covertness skills as that subject change couldn't have been more painfully obvious if he'd accompanied it with a flashing neon sign.

"Some." She picked up her coffee, leaving the subject of homework to shrivel up and die.

Niall sipped his hot chocolate. On the one hand, talking to Ellen had always been easy. She had always talked about people he liked. What sort of people did you have a crush on in secondary school? Have you kissed anyone? Dated someone? Always "people" or "someone" not "girls." The fact that she didn't assume made it so much easier. She was the first person he'd come out to. She had asked things, and he'd been able to answer her questions without feeling like he was lying or having to openly correct her. She hadn't batted an eyelid when he'd said a guy's name, and they'd carried on talking.

On the other, it meant she was constantly pushing like he needed to jump on the first available hot guy he saw. Well, maybe that wasn't fair. He did want to date. But Ellen-style dating was a lot more carefree. You saw a hot person, you asked them out, saliva got exchanged. Occasionally you might call each other back to do it again.

He fiddled with his phone and saw the last message from Ellen still sitting on the screen.

"What's a guy gotta do to impress you?"

His hand tightened around his mug, and he half wished he'd chosen tea. He could feel the rich, sweet hot chocolate clinging to his mouth and throat. He wasn't convinced this was really an admission. He couldn't believe that Ellen hadn't figured this out by now, but the way she pushed, like it was easy...

Niall Silverstein: Be guaranteed not to reject me. Or laugh in my stupid freckled face.

He stared at the message for a moment, then hit send. He watched Ellen's expression as she read it. She was normally quick to tease, but a flicker of sadness passed across her face, followed by a look of concern as she typed back.

Ellen Sorn: Your face isn't stupid.

He actually laughed.

Niall Silverstein: Thanks. Now find me someone else who doesn't think so?
Ellen Sorn: There's lots. I'm sure.

Niall shrugged, unconvinced. But he returned to his hot chocolate feeling like he could swallow again.

Niall Silverstein: Thanks.

He wondered if there were any who would believe in him, and in magic as well.
He typed another message, but didn't hit send.
"I will try."
If he said this to Ellen, she would be full of follow-up help. He didn't need that, because he already knew the first place he was going to look, and that she wouldn't understand.

Chapter Four

Draven perched on a tall stool in his grandma's kitchen. It was a high amber day, so the potatoes were peeling themselves, relieving him of some of his usual kitchen duties. Still, he tended to occupy this same seat regardless. His grandma needed to supervise the saucepans, and he liked to spend the time with her, having their weekly catch up before everyone else arrived for Friday night dinner.

"So, how's your first week been?" She put the kettle on and turned to look at him.

"It was alright," he said, willing that saying it out loud might make it true. He had gone on for years about how excited he was to join the Energy Makers' Guild. How he was going to revolutionise things and save the world. He knew that even this lacklustre answer betrayed quite a lot about how badly it had gone, but he wasn't willing to write it off completely yet. He knew he could be impatient, so maybe he had to give it some time. Or maybe it was the fact that admitting he'd been wrong about the one thing he wanted to do with his life felt like too big a step to take. "We're the newbies, so you take what comes with that."

"Are the newbie jobs a whirlwind of excitement?" she teased, having noticed his tone and his slumped shoulders.

Draven occupied himself in fetching mugs from the cupboard so he could take his time answering. He pulled out a matching pair in speckled pink which started out deep and intense at the top, before fading to almost white. He ran a thumb over the flaking gold band around the top of his mug.

"Not really," he admitted. "But, that's fine. That's how things go. It's...fine."

"Is it?" she asked.

He resumed his seat, kicking his legs against a rung of the stool for a second, considering his options. He was supposed to respect the hierarchy and appreciate his place in it. But he also was not supposed to lie to his grandma, and she had always had a habit of reading him like a book and pushing him to admit things.

"Not really," he said again, only this time a rueful smile spread across his face. He often felt better after he said the thing he wasn't supposed to. It got the bitterness out, saying it out loud. On the plus side, they'd been able to pick and choose from their personal data for the training exercises, so he'd been able to keep his wonky graphs a secret. Now they were handling actual experiment data, so no one needed to find out. "But it's bound to get better. Right?"

"Maybe." She turned to reach for some spices off the shelf, so he couldn't see her face. She sounded as carefully neutral as him.

"You know me better than anyone." He hesitated, wondering whether he wanted to ask if she thought it suited him. She was full of smiles and enthusiasm when she liked an idea, and currently she was keeping her shoulders square, and her focus on the soup, giving it more attention than it needed. "What would you do, if you were me?" he asked instead.

"I always feel like the best way to change things is to do it myself. How do you want it to be?"

"That's the trouble, I don't know. I find the way they do things a bit dull, and I can't believe it's going to solve things. But I can't exactly say that, because I haven't got anything better. I'd be stabbing in the dark." He wanted to hang onto necklaces that had old spells because they were beautiful. He wanted to make more things like that, not destroy them. Even though, rationally, he knew the energy was being wasted by it not being used. With so few people, everyone's actions counted, and he was selfish for not reporting it as lost. "That makes me think... I mean, partly it makes me think they're right—or they're doing the only thing that there is to be done, even if it's tedious. Maybe there is no better way."

"You used to be full of ideas, when you were little."

"They were made up though. They wouldn't actually work."

"At least you had them though. And anything you come up with now would have the benefit of your experience. You sound like you're missing your creative spark more than anything—don't like what's going on but can't think of anything better. Well then, the solution's to think of something better, isn't it?"

"You make it sound simple." He liked that, but he had a horrid feeling it wasn't going to be.

"Normally, the things we have to do are pretty simple, when you boil them down. Find the thing that's missing. Do the thing that's right. It's working out how to do them that's the tricky part."

"Any chance you're going to tell me how I do that?"

"Same way you find anything you've lost. Try to remember the last place you had it and look there."

Draven sipped his tea, trying to decide what to make of this advice. He wondered whether his motivation and creativity really could be treated the same way as a missing piece of clothing or a school textbook. It was an oddly comforting idea. Partly, it amused him to think of himself rummaging down the back of an old sofa (*I know I had it sometime last week. Maybe it fell out of my pocket?*), but it also made his target once again solid and achievable. He didn't know how to be brilliant. He didn't know how to have ideas or save the world. Even though he wanted to, part of the problem of trying was also having to confront the possibility of failure. But he could look for a lost thing.

"Thank you." He lowered his cup to reveal a much more genuine expression of happiness than he'd worn all week.

* * *

Draven was leaving the bathroom when the little trapdoor in the ceiling caught his eye. Where was the last place he'd had whatever feeling he was missing. A sense of wonder. Of creativity. He wasn't sure it was the last place, but it was definitely somewhere he'd spent a lot of time indulging it. He snapped his fingers, and the door opened, dropping down a small set of wooden steps. He climbed upwards, flicking on the light.

His grandma's attic had been a favourite retreat of his as a small boy. He had often brought Yvette here when his mother's insistence on minding their manners was getting too much and they wanted to let loose. The room was plastered with their pictures. His had a steady theme. Flying to freedom on the back of a huge, winged gryphon. Being rescued from a tower by a handsome prince. Opening a door onto a bright land of strange and wonderful things. Yvette's were more rooted in this world, but as fantastical. They showed magic flowing freely from her fingers, turning the sky to rainbows and sparkles, filling it with bright blooming flowers, or magical beasts to keep him happy. There were a few co-drawn pictures of them together, with liberally applied hearts. The pictures around the walls tracked his and Yvette's progression through wobbly stick figures and scribbling. As they got older, there were more of hers and fewer of his. He'd realised that he could never get what was in his head replicated on the paper, and it frustrated him too much to try and to fail. Their paths had diverged, Yvette carrying on with art while he turned his attention to words.

He had dim recollections of a whole world that he had made in his head. It had largely been populated by rabbits, and he was fairly certain that the houses had been made of marshmallows. Marshmallows were both soft and wonderful, which had seemed important details in house construction to his six-year-old self. With more than ten years of hindsight and a lot more life experience under his belt, that seemed a lot less practical. He searched his memory for other details but found them hazy. He glanced around the room. Aside from the beanbags they used to lie on, it was minimally furnished. A shelf at the side held three old tea canisters, and there was a small box of junk in a corner, its miscellany of string, screws and an old magnifying glass gathering dust. A large trunk was pushed against the wall at one end of the room. He had vague memories of using all of them as hiding places as a small child.

He started with the tea canisters. The first contained tea. He supposed he had stored some, so that he didn't have to trek downstairs for more during the long afternoons spent up here. He plunged his hand into the second and recoiled sharply as his fingers sunk into something sticky. Cautiously, he turned the tin upside-down. A lone marshmallow, misshapen with age, fell from the tin and landed at his feet. He had actually tried to build the house. He reached in more cautiously, finding something solid, and pulled out several figurines coated in the sticky goop. It was in the final tin that he found the plans, maps, and stories he had written.

Escape. That appeared to have been his grand plan when he was at primary school. Run away to a different world, where things were more fun. He had little evidence that such places existed. The only other land he had ever heard of was not full of sunshine, rainbows, and marshmallow houses. It had been a place of senseless cruelty, where even the goodwill of mages could not outweigh the wickedness done by the people who lived there. The Other World was too unkind, and its people too stubborn. They didn't even believe in magic, and the little that could be done in secret was never enough to outweigh the violence, the starvation, and the anger they inflicted on each other.

It had always been a matter of speculation amongst his classmates whether the Other World was real, or just a story to frighten them into being good. Draven could never make his mind up. The story had never quite added up to him, but he couldn't articulate why. He didn't feel like it made sense. That was all he could say. But when he tried to draw people out on it, they always made excuses to end the conversation. It was what it was—there had been Others, they were bad, mages had tried, they'd had to leave. Maybe it didn't make sense because a place like that couldn't possibly exist. Maybe it was only an allegory, to make them think what things would be like without the values they were being taught.

But if there had been one other world, couldn't there be more? Ones that would be soft and gentle enough to welcome him? To let him spread his wings and go on adventures, without exposing him to any nasty, real danger? It was a comforting daydream, and one he'd never stopped indulging in. It wasn't going to save the world though. He wasn't even sure it was going to save his sanity anymore. It was starting to hurt more and more to try to believe that there might be adventure out there, when all signs pointed towards him being stuck here, ploughing through the problem, one data column at a time.

Still, he continued to turn over the room, in search of any hint of ways to improve life in Galdorsfarne. He was sure he'd turned at some point from writing fiction to more serious matters—theories, machines, whirlamagigs. Almost anything he'd turned in for credit had been gently pulled apart by his teachers, but he knew he'd filled notebooks with ideas. He turned to the trunk. In one corner was a neat little pile of notebooks. There were stories, but also *Machines by Draven (aged 7 ¾)* and *Theories of D. Montrose*. There was a notebook called *Ideas for Saving the World*. He stretched out on the beanbag, flicking through them.

> *We have to generate merit by being nice and doing good. When I am older, I will go around being nice to as many people as possible, and then there will be more magic. If I run out of people to be nice to, I will go somewhere new and find new people and be nice to them.*
> *Electricity is slow but it's okay if boring things go slowly. We could do boring things with electricity and have more parties. I would not mind riding an electric tram if I could make lollipop trees and funny shaped clouds to look at as I went by. Then the world would be better.*

He lay back, staring at the skylight. The evening had hurried in early in the day, as it always did in winter, and there was now a crisp square of night sky laid out above his head. He stared at the stars. Travelling to them would be ridiculous. It wasn't something he wanted. He was sure space was freezing, and you couldn't get a decent cup of tea anywhere up there. But the stars had always made him feel free because he had always been able to invent other people—ones he didn't know yet—who could stare up and see the same night sky as him. The more he thought about it, the more convinced he was that his younger self hadn't actually been too far off the mark. He would need to rewrite the ideas to sound like something an adult might say, but the electricity one in particular seemed sound.

He made his way back down to the kitchen, bouncing slightly as he walked. He reached to open the door but paused when he heard his name.

"Draven needs to keep his feet on the ground!" That was his mother, and it was a typical enough complaint that he thought little of it, apart from the fact that it was being directed at someone other than him.

"He needs something to believe in!" That was his grandma.

"He has that! He's just started at his preferred guild! Stop trying to turn him away from it," his mother said.

"I'm not. I'm giving him space to make his own mind up, but if he doesn't fit in there, I want him to have something to fall back on."

"A bunch of daydreams are not a reasonable life plan!" His mother wasn't raising her voice, but was close to it. Draven didn't want them arguing, especially not about him, and especially not when it was fixed. He pushed down on the door handle and went in, cutting through the argument.

"Draven. We were just..."—his mother floundered around the fact that they'd been disagreeing—"discussing how you can get on best at your placement."

"She's helping," he promised his mother. "I've got ideas for things." His mother didn't look thrilled at that. Him "getting ideas" wasn't her favourite thing.

"Okay, but be careful. Don't rock the boat? You want them to like you."

"They do. I'll keep working hard on what they want from me too, but they've said we can come up with our own suggestions."

"So, where did it turn out you'd left your fire?" his grandma asked.

"In my old notebooks. But I can apply them to what I'm doing now—what they want me to do. Happy and sensible," he assured each of them in turn.

Except, his grandma's comment stirred up something else. The attic wasn't the last place that had inspired him to think of wild magic or distant people. The last place to stoke his imagination had been much more recent than that. It felt like the opposite to keeping his head down and working hard, but if he needed more from life, he knew exactly where he should start looking.

Chapter Five

It was raining, it was cold, and that meant it was priory time. Niall just had to survive two short journeys to get there.

He folded himself as invisibly as possible into the corner of his seat in the middle of the bus. It was sort of tricky to be unnoticeable when you were six foot tall, but he'd had quite a lot of practice. Weirdly, he thought he might have been less noticeable if he was chunkier. Not fat (which would also get him picked on), but not so noticeably skinny. He was pretty sure his height attracted people's attention, and his physique made them consider him an easy target. Not that anything had ever spilt over into the physical. It was just people talking shite.

To that end, he jammed his earphones in to block out the people around him. He spun the volume down, so that the words thrummed, barely audible under the rumble of the bus engine, and hit "play" on his Queer Northerners playlist.

Each time the bus slowed to a halt, he felt his heart squeeze as if it stopped with the soft swoosh of the automatic doors and only started again once all the passengers were on, and none of them were people he'd gone to secondary school with.

The bus was warm enough that he'd pulled his coat off. He sort of wanted to roll up his sleeves but he'd gone for wearing a bracelet as his toe in the water of self-expression for the day, along with one of his favourite comedy TARDIS t-shirts. At secondary school, they'd had a uniform, but outside of that he had generally aimed for his clothes to say, *"please don't notice me."* Life was supposed to be different now. He was still working out what exactly he wanted to say with his clothes and searching for the confidence to wear all the items which, magpie-like, he was starting to collect. Especially as he still had to get the bus through Bedewell to link up with the metro lines into civilization.

The doors swooshed again, and this time he recognised the kids who got on. They'd been a couple of years below him, and he didn't think they cared enough to bother with him—they were probably too busy picking on the nerds in their own year—but he kept his eyes averted. He watched their general movements, to check where they were going, but avoided any chance of eye contact.

Their presence made him feel warmer, flushing with self-consciousness. Which was doubly unfair when they were the reason he wasn't able to roll up his sleeves or remove his sweater. He clicked his music down another few notches, but not so low that he couldn't hear Onsind calling them narrow-minded pieces of shit. He rested his head on his hand, smirking into his palm, before dropping his hands to slip his finger under his cuff. He ran his finger over the little plastic rainbow stars and felt pleased instead of embarrassed that they were there.

He was even happier when the bus pulled into North Shields. As the passengers got off, they dispersed. The people from his old life melted off in the direction of town, whilst Niall headed towards the bright yellow "M" that announced the metro station. Niall would not have said he was a big fan of vivid yellow. It wasn't a colour he wanted on his person, or his walls, or even his stationery. But he had to smile every time one of those trains slid into view—perhaps it was because they took him away from where he didn't want to be, but he somehow enjoyed the fact that they were stupidly yellow whilst doing it.

One song later, he emerged into the wrought iron arches of Tynemouth metro station. Stall holders at the weekend market stamped their feet against the cold. Niall normally enjoyed browsing the stalls, but today he had a more pressing mission, one that had occupied every spare second of daydreaming since New Year. He joined the trickle of people who were putting up hoods and brollies and venturing out into the rain-soaked streets.

* * *

"Where are you going?" Draven's mother asked, as they stepped out from Saturday's Community Assembly, and he peeled away from them.

"For a bike ride," he said.

"It's hardly the weather for it." She gave the sky a reproving look, as it continued to spit a steady tattoo of rain on her umbrella.

Between the Energy Makers' Guild being one of the furthest out, and the run of low amber days they'd had, Draven hadn't had any evenings that weren't occupied with slow trams, biking if his line was suspended, or extra household chores and merit sessions. He wasn't about to waste his first opportunity to get back to the castle because of a little rain.

He shrugged off his mother's concern, working his hands in an intricate pattern, over his head and arms. The rain began bouncing off him.

"Problem solved!" He grinned.

"I hardly think that's a responsible use of magic when you could come home. Or wear a rain jacket. It's almost like we haven't just had Assembly!"

"See-you-later-love-you-bye!" Draven called over his shoulder, as he swung a leg over his bike and hit the pedals. It was a high amber day, and not being stuck in an ugly cagoule was a perfectly reasonable use of magic. Plus the talk at Assembly hadn't even been about magic usage—it had been about something that stood half a chance of holding his attention for once. *Intent.* Magic was tricksy stuff. Words were like the hammer, used to shape it. However good the idea in your head was, the results would be shaped more by how you wielded that tool. That was why you had to be incredibly careful if you used words when casting magic, and why it was best to stick to the tried and trusted spells contained in rune patterns. Magic didn't always know not to take you literally. Still, having a good plan in mind was better than hammering at the metal without thinking, and that was where the need to be pure of heart and something and something had become the point of the lecture. That had been the point when he'd stopped listening. Blah blah, be good. Blah blah, don't be like the Others. He didn't need the reminders. His mind had spun off, to the riddles and jokes his grandma always made out of the fact that magic did what you said not what you meant. *Why did the table turn into a chicken-and-egg riddle? Because it was asked to lay itself. What glamour makes you stick to metal? Being more attractive.* By Assembly standards, it had been a pretty fun one.

The mention of the Others had caught his attention too. He was sure that what he was supposed to take away was that the Other World was bad, and this world was good. What he was focussing on—as his feet pumped the pedals so hard that he lost his breath—was that other worlds might be real. Or had been, once upon a time. He had found a chink into one, where people whispered *"Happy New Year"* in ruined castles. That didn't sound like a land of senseless cruelty.

* * *

This is stupid.

Niall, for the umpteenth time, re-stuck the ageing Velcro that was supposed to keep his hood vaguely around his head, and tried to ignore the nagging voice of self-doubt. Sure, the steel grey sky above the priory was hardly welcoming, and the steady pour coming from the clouds was somewhat more than a drizzle. But that was the point—he wasn't stuck in a full-on downpour, and it meant he more or less had the place to himself. If it had been swarming with tourists, he wouldn't have had the confidence to go have a friendly chat with a wall, or been able to hear it if it decided to talk back.

Was that really what he was expecting to happen? It sounded mad when he said it like that, but the wall had talked to him, hadn't it?

The wind tugged at his hood, the fastening making a microscopic scraping sound as it tried to give in again. He pressed it pre-emptively back down.

It was still better than being in sodding Bedewell anyway.

He walked carefully all around the ruins, not rushing right up to the place where he'd heard the voice. He'd been here all of five minutes and he wasn't quite sure what he was going to do with himself for the rest of the day if he walked over and found nothing waiting there.

For seventeen years, the world had only ever been as magical as he'd been able to make it with his own imagination. But then, there had been the voice. The voice that had probably been an echo. Except echoes didn't repeat whole words and phrases, except in cartoons. They only caught snatches, bouncing them back into your ears with the added thud of cold, damp rock. It hadn't sounded like his own voice. It had spoken with feeling.

He bounced on the balls of his feet. What if they were there now? What if he missed them by wasting time? He didn't want to confront the possibility of this not being real, but he couldn't stop the rising anxiety that he wasn't doing it right.

He circled, finding he was getting closer to the wall each time. He gave up the pretence that he was here for any other reason, and paced directly and purposefully over to it. Time to rip off the plaster and find out.

* * *

Draven dismounted, leaving his bike at the bottom of the hill. The outline of the castle stood out against the sky, and he was surprised to see figures moving about in it. Assembly hadn't been over for that long, and it wasn't the weather for being outdoors, which he'd figured would play to his advantage. There was a placard outside the castle, one that he knew hadn't been there before, though he was too far away to read what it said.

He hurried up to the top of the hill, finding that the sign said, "Unsafe Structure—Authorised Access Only." It was stamped with the logo of the Guild of Maintenance—the least exciting guild imaginable.

* * *

Niall laid a hand against the bricks, trying to remember any detail of what he'd done before, except for being tipsy, which he wasn't going to recreate at two in the afternoon. That hadn't been it anyway. That hadn't been the reason.

"Hello?"

Nothing.

"Are you there?" he asked. "I heard you before. Maybe you can't hear me?"

Or maybe this wasn't real.

What did you think was going to happen? He could already feel half of his brain calling himself an idiot, even whilst the rest of it fought back. *Believe, believe, believe.*

He laid his forehead against the wall. Was he imagining it, or was there sound on the other side? Not as clear as he'd heard it before. But mingling in with the background patter of the rain, was there a low thrum of conversation?

* * *

"What's going on?" Draven called out. The workers jumped, noticing him just as he realised that they were gathered around the exact section of wall where he had heard the voice.

"Doing some patching up." One of the workers came over, tapping the sign as they spoke. "Hopefully be open again tomorrow."

"What kind of patching up?" Draven asked. Should he mention the voice? He doubted they would volunteer that information to him, but perhaps if he revealed that he already knew, they would be more willing to discuss it.

The point was rendered moot, however, as there was a clear, echoing shout.

"Hello? I can hear you! Can you hear me?" It came directly from the wall.

The workers jumped back, wide-eyed, before one of them quickly levelled their hands at the wall.

"Yes!" Draven shouted, trying to duck past the mage who'd come to talk to him, but they caught his shoulder, holding him back. "I can hear you!"

He had no idea if his voice carried far enough, or whether he got his words out before the mages at the wall finished their gesturing. A shimmer burst through the air, rippling like a heat haze for a second. Then the world was silent.

He felt the grip on his shoulder relaxing. Around him, the mages fidgeted, clearly wondering how to address what he had heard.

"A stray bit of magic, probably," one of them said, after a sizable pause.

"Where did it come from?" Draven asked. They seemed concerned that he had unanswered questions, and he was going to press that advantage as hard as he could.

"Probably a manifestation of an old spell. Magical echo, if you will."

"I've never heard of that. Are they common?"

"Not really." The workers shifted, glancing at each other, like he was a hot potato they were trying to pass.

"What spell did you use?"

"A sealing spell. You'll have done those in your placement, aye?"

"They were talking to us. They knew we were here."

"Just an echo. Or something. There's no one there. Don't worry."

Ah. Yes. Worry. That was the appropriate reaction to things outside of the ordinary. He was more worried that nothing like that would ever happen again.

* * *

Niall waited, his ear pressed to the wall in the seconds after he had shouted. For a moment, he thought he still heard the distant voices mingling with the rain, but then they were gone. However hard he strained his ears, there was no noise that he couldn't account for. Just the rain hitting the ground, the slap of the waves against the cliff, and his own breathing. Maybe he had imagined one or other of those had been something else.

He waited. He counted. The seconds stretched out beyond the point of comfort with his own idea, and it shrivelled in the silence.

He became excruciatingly aware of how odd he must look, standing with his ear pressed against the wall.

He was too old for this. He was out, in the rain, shouting at walls. Obviously, the walls weren't shouting back cos they were *walls*. He needed to get a life. One that was actually grounded in reality.

Chapter Six

"Good weekend?" Yvette held out an empty mug in invitation and Draven nodded, to both the spoken and unspoken questions. Even on high amber days, not every tram line could run, and theirs was one of the ones suspended for the day. They hadn't had much breath for chatting whilst biking in. "Whatcha get up to?" she asked, pouring out a mug of tea for each of them.

You wouldn't believe me if I told you. "Looking for a lost thing, mostly." He slung his satchel over the back of the chair, and immediately had to steady it, as the weight of books within tried to pull the chair over. After the incident at the castle, he had cycled over to the library and pulled every spellbook, security book, and vaguely relevant history book he could find. So far, they hadn't yielded any answers, but in some ways that was better. The fewer answers they yielded, the more certain he was that this was nothing within the realms of ordinary.

"Oh, did you find it?"

"Not quite." Before she could dig too hard into what that meant, he turned the tables. "You?"

"My mums took me shopping." She gestured to some especially vivid green eyeshadow that was her nod to guild colours today, along with bright green tights. "Not much else."

"I like it."

"Thanks. I wish we could do glamours though. They've always sounded so fun."

"Yeah," he agreed. "I mean, I guess maybe we're about to crack that wide open." He gestured to the table full of files that awaited their arrival. There was a noticeable beat where they both still didn't sit down to work. Yvette drew breath, no doubt getting ready to say how much it sucked. "Let's get to it." He jumped in before she could, not quite ready to hear that yet. He had his mystery voice at the castle to follow, but there was also his notebook. He still had two different options for turning the world upside down.

The morning passed quickly. Technically, it hadn't been two whole days since he'd seen anyone because they'd all seen each other at Assembly, but that had been in passing. The time before Assembly was a good chance to chat to people he didn't see from Monday to Friday, and thus Monday was a perfect time to catch up on what people had done with their weekends. He even listened as Matthias described his coaching session in detail and tried to push down all the thoughts about what that said about his enthusiasm for the task at hand.

The afternoon felt slower. When he came back from lunch at one o'clock and realised there was as much of the day as he'd already done (only without a meal break for the final hour), four hours sounded like a very long time. About halfway through, Draven had to admit he might be in danger of nodding off. He was thinking more about the next tea break, and which books he could look at, than the columns in front of him. He was ploughing through some data from the recent rain days, where a lot of those who preferred outdoor duties had been reassigned to indoor work. Many had been paired with friends or family instead but it hadn't been possible for everyone, so he was comparing that to a group who had been assigned randomly. He stared at the ceiling wondering why he had to mathematicise the idea that spending time with your friends would make you happier. Though, after a week of trudging through numbers plucked from thin air, it was almost refreshing to be handed something that might actually work out. Almost—but not quite enough to keep his eyelids from drooping, and his attention from drifting every five seconds.

He crawled through the steps of the calculation to look for significance. After a week, they were familiar, but he still didn't quite trust his brain to get them right. He punched the final numbers into the small adding machine. He blinked.

"Check my numbers?" he requested, pushing the sheet over to Melvin. Mel looked surprised by the break of routine but bent his head over the paper, pen occasionally scribbling to keep track.

"Gosh," he said softly, as his result for the friends and family group versus the control group came out the same as Draven's. "Gosh, yes, you're right, that's—"

"Significant!" Draven shouted, finding himself amused by Melvin's degree of underreaction. He supposed a "Gosh" was pretty strong stuff coming from Mel.

"Should we wait for Rowan to come back or...?" Melvin asked.

"No way, I'm going to tell her now." She had, after all, said they could interrupt her if there was anything urgent, and how did this not qualify? He made his way through to the next room. She looked up as he arrived and announced his news.

"Okay, great!" Rowan smiled at him. "You can send that up to Mage Hurron. I'm sure she'll be excited to get it. That's part of her study, and it'll give her some guidance on how to set up for the next rain day."

"Then what?" Okay, so this wasn't quite the most dramatic eureka moment, but it was still a discovery. He had found something!

"When you index it, you can add 'preliminary finding: significant.' I don't think we have enough data on this yet for you to pull more sets, but hopefully she'll send them your way when they come in. She might ask you for some breakdown of these numbers—seeing how strong the effect is according to different variables like age, or how well the secondary merit activity was matched, but that probably won't come through right away."

"So...?" he asked.

"Onto the next one on the list. Good job."

Now that she said it, he dimly remembered things about "five more data sets" from their induction. But he'd spent so long churning through lists of numbers that it had numbed his brain. He had narrowed his focus down to this point— finding something Significant. And all that meant was some words on an index card, and more number crunching.

"Great. Thanks." He managed to plaster something like a smile on until she turned her back.

He returned to his work area, relieved to find that everyone else was already on tea break. He dropped the blank card onto his desk, wondering whether he'd be able to face filling it out when he got back. Or analysing whatever request came in. Even if this proved to be significant, what difference would it make? A slight tweak to how they handled rainy days? Once you scaled that up to the whole of Galdorsfarne, what would it mean? Would it even be enough to increase the number of high amber days? How many more a year were needed to be statistically significant, and how did that compare with actually *feeling* different? They reported annual averages on the radio—"*we're experiencing a good number of high amber days this spring as compared to last*"—but did it feel that way when you were living it? One year later, it was hard to remember what the previous spring had been like. It felt like things were kind of average, all of the time. Kind of average, with occasional irritating lows.

"Kettle's just boiled. You want one?" Yvette called to him. He shook his head, not trusting himself to speak, and made his way out through the back door, into one of the many courtyards created by the modular building system. The weather was doing a great job of proving that it wasn't linked to the ambient magic level because it was bloody horrible. It was overcast, turning the whole world grey and depressing, and there was a persistent drizzle. It could have been worse, he supposed. There could have been a raging storm, but then he wouldn't have come out. The weather could not have been any more unpleasant and still been something he could stomp through feeling sad and sorry for himself. He sat down on the roots of a sprawling yew tree. He had refused to cry inside, in front of everyone, but now, he supposed he could. Except tears were fickle creatures, and now that he had the space and freedom in which to release them, he found they no longer wanted to come quite so badly as they had before. He picked up a stick and poked savagely at the dirt instead.

"How are you feeling?"

Draven jumped. He hadn't heard anyone approach. He was even more surprised to find that it was Mage Starkweather, who presumably had better things to do with her time than take rainy walks outside to talk to apprentices.

"You don't have to tell me that you're fine when you're clearly not," she added, settling on a root next to him. "Today's supposed to be a good day. You made a significant finding."

"How did you know?" he asked.

"I keep an eye on what's going on. Anyway, you're making progress, and yet here you are, sitting on a tree in the rain, looking like you want to burst into tears. Why is that?" Her tone was kindly, rather than critical, and Draven weighed up his options. He knew the honest answer, but the honest answer did not feel like a polite one. He was torn between these two things, but decided that, since she'd already noticed that something was wrong, the honest answer was the better one to give.

"Because it doesn't feel significant." He jabbed the ground with the stick one last time, then dropped it. "It's just a bunch of numbers, and even if we do find something, it's maybe going to make one tiny chip in the problem. I wanted to make things better. And it feels like I can't. Nothing I ever do is going to be enough."

"You remind me a lot of me when I was your age. Nothing but saving the world in one fell swoop will do, right?" She smiled like they were sharing a joke or a secret. "I tend to look at it this way: If there was one miracle solution, it would probably have been found by now. Then there would be nothing left for me to do."

"Do you really think that's not out there?" he asked, because it seemed like being honest was allowed right now. "However many times people say that, I still like believing that the world's problems are finite and solvable."

"True. I think it's a good thing to believe in. It's good to have a dream, and to think that maybe things can be perfect one day. But it doesn't have to be so black and white. It doesn't mean that every other thing has to be pointless. Or, to look at it another way, if you could invent something and it would make life a little bit better in a lot of ways, or make one problem go away completely, which would you choose?"

"I don't know. I mean, it's sort of a moot point, isn't it? This is the only problem."

"Depends what you define as a problem, I suppose. Are you happy? You can give the answer you think you're not supposed to."

"Sometimes," he admitted. "Sometimes I am, and sometimes I get frustrated or feel like there isn't any point."

"Do you think you're the only one who feels like that?"

"Probably. I'm sort of odd."

"You're not. Plenty of people go up and down. Now, given that you know that, is it worth making everyone a little bit happier, some of the time?"

"I'd rather make everyone much happier all of the time." Surely if they had enough power to make life easy, everyone would be happy. It was the same problem.

"I think we all would. But that's surprisingly hard to achieve. So, if you can't achieve that, does it make it pointless to make them a little bit happier where you can?"

"Well, no."

"So, making the world a little bit better is a good thing? And one worth doing?" she probed.

"Why is it so hard to make people happy?" he asked, still not satisfied that this solution involved a level of giving up.

"As you're someone who isn't happy sometimes, I think I should be asking you that."

"I don't know. Cos I'm sixteen. Cos I never meet anyone interesting. Um, to date I mean. Cos I feel like I don't know what I'm doing and that's confusing and it worries me."

"Lots of people feel those things. I think, sadly, they might be part of being human. However perfect the world around us is, people have a tendency to go up and down. But not to an extreme. Not to the point that they tank out or are a danger to themselves. If you could trade the problem we currently have for that as a problem, would you?"

"What? No! Why? Do I seem like some kind of psychopath?" he asked, appalled by the idea of making people unhappier. She actually laughed at this.

"Just trying to show you, there are worse problems to have than a lack of problems. At least the problem we have doesn't hurt anybody."

"You mean like the problems in the Other World?" he asked cautiously. It felt like she was hinting at that. A hint was different than bringing it up directly, but people so rarely did either that he felt invited to indulge his curiosity.

"Yes," she agreed. "Like those. No one's hurting anyone else. I know when you're sixteen, everything can seem very dull here. But there are some experiences that I can't imagine wanting to have."

"No. I don't want bad things to happen. But is that the price? If you're not going to have anything bad happen to you, you can't have anything good happen to you either?"

"I think it's more like you learn to look for good in a different way. Why don't you come with me after tea break?" she invited. "I know it can get hard when you're bogged down in data all day. Come and look at the bigger picture with me."

"Aren't you too busy?" He was still surprised that she was making time for this conversation, much less inviting him further in, especially since he was being demonstrably terrible at falling in line with expectations right now.

"I've got a few things to do. The invitation is to come and watch me do them. To ask questions when I'm not too busy, and to see how things look from where I am. Maybe that will give you a new perspective on what you're doing."

"I would like that. Not that...not that I want to seem like I..." he floundered. Like he what? Was ungrateful? Like he was questioning everything? He *was* questioning everything. He was lost and none of their ways of doing things meant anything to him, and this was the one thing he'd thought he wanted to do with his life. How did you sum up having got to that point but with *"but I'm not questioning your authority, ma'am"* tagged onto the end?

"It's okay to be confused when you're sixteen." She stood up. "Come back inside."

* * *

That afternoon, he had a bird's eye view, rather than an ant's one. He followed Mage Starkweather. Her life was a lot like his in that there were lots of briefings and lots of data. Only often she was giving the briefings or meeting one on one with someone. He saw some of this firsthand and picked up other pieces from conversations with her secretary. He sat in on a meeting she had with the Head of Potions, whom he knew from his previous placement and liked. She also got feedback from the day's experiments, and added data to a five-year plan, which showed graphs snaking skywards, aiming to meet realistic and reasonable long-term targets.

"Merit's the steadiest factor." She gestured to a line on the chart. "It does its job, but well, we're pretty maxed out on making any more out of it."

Draven's breath caught. There were words that wanted to leave his mouth on the exhale, but his brain held them back for a second. He had said he would observe and not interrupt, but he had also promised himself that he would take advantage of the next opportunity he had to present his ideas.

"Are we?" he asked. This was the question from his notebook he had found hardest to paraphrase into adult language. However you looked at it *"Why don't we just try being nice?"* sounded rather naive. "I mean, we have our merit sessions but all of us aim to be good people outside of that. Could we not harness that somehow?"

"That's a common misunderstanding of the merit system. It's not so much that the merit sessions themselves are our only way of generating good will. It's the only time we measure it. Measurement itself takes energy, after all."

How much energy? Draven bit his tongue, though tracing everyone's magic usage and merit efficiency had to be a very complex spell. The machine he'd seen in the back room of the data lab was a heavy mass of metal boxes and whirring gears, punching data points into moving strips of paper. Its thrumming provided a constant soundtrack to their calculations, and it made their hair crackle with static when they were sent to help file its output on low amber days. Still, the solution of ripping out the measurement systems and using the magic that powered them wasn't going to go over well with someone who'd built their life around statistical analysis, however much it grated on him to try and quantify goodness.

"On the whole, it's believed that the good you do in your daily life is as important as the good you do in merit sessions. That's why it's so important that we have a harmonious society," Mage Starkweather continued.

"It's not important because those are basic values?" he asked. This idea that people were being good because they had to be bothered him. Weren't they being good because it was morally right, rather than because they expected some kind of reward from the universe?

"Well, yes of course. But you're asking, 'Why doesn't that count?' aren't you?" she asked.

"No. I don't think so. Not exactly. More like, why can't we make more opportunities to do good?"

"I would say we're at capacity on those. If I asked you to try to do ten good deeds a day, even small ones, would you manage it? Or would you struggle to find them?"

"I might struggle, a bit, I guess. Though I'm sure I could."

"They would be small things. Because there aren't any big problems here. So, we're talking ten small deeds, by one person, spread out across the course of a day. How would we go about measuring that?" she asked. The question wasn't phrased critically, she was taking the time to patiently walk him through his own idea, but she thought it was useless. Her insistence on measurement was irritating. Why did there have to be a science to being nice? Why did it have to be analysable in order to be worthwhile? Couldn't they all just try a little harder? But at the same time, he recognised the futility of that advice. Sometimes, he felt he was trying as hard as he could, but it was pointless. There was so little to do, and even if he did, it didn't feel like it made the world a better place.

"The targets for making more energy efficient spells are going to be the hardest to hit." She turned back to the graphs. "That's something we've put a lot of effort into but, well, the spells are the spells. You know the rituals around them, and it's hard to change those. Happily, we share the responsibility for that with the Guild of Lore. Recycling and preserving energy within the system is where we're making the biggest gains. Those are right on course, or even a little above expected."

"That's great." He forced a smile. Maybe the Guild of Lore would take him. Reinventing magic hadn't seemed like it would play to his strengths, but nor did anything that involved long-term growth projections and so many graphs. "What about energy efficiency for the electrics?" he tried. They were a constant afterthought in her graphs, and this felt like the one unique idea he'd had.

"Those old things? They're practically falling apart at the seams. I don't think they could handle doing more, even if we wanted them to."

"So, why not upgrade them?" Draven pushed.

"Why would we do that? We're trying to use less electricity, not more."

"At the moment, we can't use any more of it, even if we wanted to," he pointed out. "If it worked more efficiently, we'd be able to stabilise a few things—ones where it doesn't matter how they work, like the trams. What if we could make them run as fast on electricity as they do on magic? That would free up more to be used in daily life," he argued. Implying people could cook with it was likely to get him further than saying "fun stuff," even if that was what he hoped for. "Same with light sources—a light source is a light source. If we could light places consistently by electricity—"

"But we are mages. We do things by magic," she stated. He could tell she was trying very hard not to have That Look on her face, the one people gave him sometimes like he'd sprouted an extra head. But it was clearly a conscious effort.

"Right, but we don't have enough of it," he reasoned, equally confused as to why this was so hard to grasp.

"Which is why we're trying to make sure there's more. Mages do not like electric devices. They want a society to run reliably on magic. Trying to make more electricity isn't solving the problem."

Draven bit his tongue, refraining from saying "*Which mages?*" He didn't care how the trams ran, so long as they ran. If they could have a full tram service every single day, that was tangible. It was better than tweaking the system so that there was a statistical-but-not-noticeable increase in some reading or other. What if that full tram service came coupled with being able to have a long hot shower and cooked breakfast, or dying his hair blue with a wave of his fingers, or finally trying spells like glamours that had been forbidden for his whole life? Then maybe he'd stop wanting to sail off into the sunset because life here wouldn't be drab and colourless.

"You're full of good ideas," Mage Starkweather said, even though she had rejected everything he'd had to say. "Keep having those. Now you see how it looks from here. You create all these tiny little drops of data. I like to think that each one is like a star. The night sky wouldn't be beautiful if you could only see one, but when it's full of them, it's worth beholding. That's what I get to see from where I am."

"Yes." Draven didn't need to force back any further arguments, because he'd used them all. He realised his smile had slipped at some point during their interaction, and he attempted to hitch on a replacement, though he wasn't sure it came across naturally. "I appreciate where I fit into things now. Thank you for showing me."

"Glad to hear it," she said, and Draven was surprised to find himself being waved from her office, because he had never been a good liar. He wondered whether he'd done well at faking enthusiasm, or whether she didn't know him well enough to hear that it was slightly off. Because what he was really saying was *"but I'm still not satisfied."*

Chapter Seven

All the way down the stairs from Mage Starkweather's office, it felt like he was choking.

There was a momentary reprieve when he stepped outside, free of the building and into the cold, crisp air. But then he was pressing onto a tram full of quietly contented people, all coming from the neat little places in the world that they slotted into. What if he never found one?

"Are you okay?" Yvette asked, as they slid into seats at the back. She'd known better than to probe in front of Matthias, but they'd managed to get seats apart from him and Mel for the ride home. Which meant there was no escaping talking about it.

"Fine," he said. He had to be, didn't he? Everyone was fine all the time. If you weren't...what would this mean for his already wobbly graphs? He dreaded to think. "I don't think I belong here after all." He gestured vaguely over his shoulder, so she could take it to mean the building they were pulling away from, but did he mean that? He thought about his childhood drawings, and the solution of running away. If only there was somewhere to run to.

"That sucks. I'm sorry." She squeezed his hand. For all that she'd been down on the guild since day one, she knew this had been his dream for a long time. "Hey, on the plus side, we're on the same page now. We can be comrades in arms as we drown in statistics!"

"Yeah." He wasn't sure he was ready to joke about it or complain his way through it. He still wanted it to be something more than it was, regardless of the evidence staring him in the face that it wasn't going to be.

"So, you think you'll go potions?" she asked.

"I guess." It had been the thing that clicked most with him. Yay, a lifetime of wearing orange. But that minor disgust paled in comparison to the fact that he had *liked* potions but hadn't *loved* it. He had always thought that finding your Adept would be some soul-awakening moment, something that gave you drive and passion. But no one had ever promised that. They'd only ever promised that you'd go where you fitted best. If a six-out-of-ten feeling was the best you got, that was still your highest and was where you were supposed to spend your life.

He rested his head on Yvette's shoulder, letting her fill the silence as much as she wanted to, until she nudged him in the ribs, two stops before their usual one.

"You've got a merit session," she reminded him.

"Oh. Yeah. See you." He dragged himself out of his seat and off the tram. He crossed his arms over his chest and hunched his shoulders against the evening, even though it wasn't that cold. If there was a task that involved repeatedly beating your head against a rock or screaming at the sky, he would excel at it right now. Anything else was going to be beyond him.

The outline of the library loomed, softly lit against the backdrop of a dark winter sky. Draven felt a little of the cloud around him lifting. The building was one of the oldest in town, giving the impression that it had simply always existed. It had large columns along its front, flagged by a pair of stone gryphons. As he walked towards it, a warm feeling stirred in Draven's stomach, as if meeting an old friend. He stopped to pat the beak of the left gryphon on his way in and would pay the same courtesy to the other one on his way out. They had hard eyes and sharp beaks, and he had come to the vague conclusion as he got older that they were meant to be serious and intimidating. He had always regarded them as friends though, and been pleased to see them, meaning as it did that he was in for a pleasant time amongst books.

He stepped into the snugness. Perhaps it was the library's interior that had made him, by association, regard the gryphon statues as kindly. He'd always felt that the interior of the library wanted to make people feel welcome. The first and foremost element of this for Draven was the smell. He had never considered the possibility that not everyone enjoyed the smell of old books. How could they not? That scent of ageing paper, mingled with the warm hint of old leather, and all of it promising ideas, and fantasies of faraway worlds. It was simultaneously comforting and intoxicating—and, right now, painful, as he longed for reality to offer him what he'd only ever found in books. He took a deep breath of it as he entered the building. Perhaps he could live his dull, work-a-day existence and find his stimulation here. It was something.

The colours of the room also comforted him. Dark reds, blacks, browns. Occasionally there were dark blues or other colours, but for the most part, people bound books in warmer tones. This palette was emphasised by the rich brown of the wooden shelves and the tapestry covers of the many soft, inviting chairs. There were tables too, should someone find themselves needing to adopt a more serious and scholarly posture, but on the whole, the room extended an invitation to read, to relax, and to be comfortable.

He hoped his job that evening would be something that gave him a chance to wander—to remember the sources of contentment he had.

"Hi," he said, leaning on the volunteers' desk. The universe seemed determined to litter his path with little things that made his day brighter, as the head volunteer on duty was Mage Renaud. The library had a core of head volunteers from the Guild of History and Information, who took librarian-like responsibility when it was needed. Draven was pretty friendly with all of them, but Mage Renaud had always been his favourite. This was partially based in childhood memories, and there being nothing the tall mage couldn't fetch down for him—an absolutely mesmerising feat when everything above the second shelf was out of reach. The relationship had weathered Draven growing up, and gaining the ability to access most of the shelves by himself. Mage Renaud still stood a clear eight inches taller than him, his black hair and beard now dotted with hints of grey, but he was always gentle with the books and the people around him. "What have you got for me today?" Draven asked.

"Mostly reshelving." Mage Renaud pushed a book cart forward. "The last few low amber days plus the bad weather..."

"More people reading, but the books don't put themselves back." Draven had been here often enough to know the issues the library had. "Who else is on?"

"A couple of people are going to be working a specialist assignment, but the main floor is just you and me."

"Right. Better get cracking." Draven wasn't sure whether the people in Special Collections would be counting towards their target. He didn't ask. It would sound like he wasn't confident of meeting it. What if they were stuck here all night because of him? Was that even possible? He grabbed the book cart, hoping that working fast might make up for anything else he was lacking.

* * *

Shelving books wasn't usually mind numbing, the way that other repetitive tasks were. His eyes skimmed over each cover, taking in the title at the very least, occasionally reading the synopsis or first few pages if it looked particularly promising. Each book represented a little door into another world, and he lived for the glimpses they showed him. Normally.

Today, there were a lot of history returns. He tried to appreciate the value of every book, but he couldn't understand why people read history. There was such a select time period that people wrote about, and he couldn't believe the library had this many books on it. It felt like Galdorsfarne had only existed for a generation or two. There was evidence to the contrary, of course. Firstly, basic biology. They had not all sprung up out of nowhere. Then there was magic itself. It was referred to as an ancient force, and the runic characters that formed the basis of most spell casting were from hundreds of years ago, as was the castle on the hill. He wasn't sure how many hundreds in either case, but there were basically three time periods; things that were ancient and to be respected; the handful of decades taught in history class; and now. Whatever had happened in between the invention of ancient runes and his grandparents' generation simply didn't exist. Or wasn't worth talking about. At least, according to everyone writing books, and everyone he had ever bugged on the subject until he'd been told to stop asking awkward questions. He had learnt to shut up, more or less, but he still wanted to know.

He was absent-mindedly pushing history books back onto the shelf, when there was a mutter close to the end of the aisle.

"I hate monitoring this thing. It gives me the creeps."

The words were quiet but in the library they carried. The voice was familiar, though most voices in Galdorsfarne were, at least to some degree.

"Oh, come on. It's always the same, and it's not as if you have to go through."

"After that hoopla up at the castle the other day, who knows what's going on?"

Oh! That was where he knew them from. Draven sidled up to the end of the aisle. He peered around, wondering what mysterious assignment they were on now.

He was just in time to see them disappearing, accompanied by the resounding click of a door being snapped shut in a still and silent room.

It was a plain wooden door, set into the brickwork at the back of the building. The title "Special Collections" hung above it, written on the same wooden plaque as every other library section's header. The door itself had bold but polite white lettering which read "Restricted Access" and in smaller letters underneath "Please do not enter without permission."

Draven picked up the remaining history books on the trolley, reinserting them with barely even a glance at the covers. He watched the door. Maybe he was making all this up in his own head. Maybe there was nothing but fragile old books in there. Except that didn't make much sense. In some senses, you could go through a book, but that didn't sound like how the word had been being used. It had sounded much more physical and literal.

"Do Not Enter Without Permission."

It was calling to him. Those words, which as a child had firmly pushed him back, now enticed him. But he was pretty sure there would be hell to pay if he got caught. There might even be alarms on the door if he tried to open it, plus there were two people inside who would know he shouldn't be there. Not that he would, without permission, because that was wrong. Though technically the sign did not forbid him from trying the door, just to see what would happen, only from entering. Still, rushing it wouldn't do. If he blew this, he was likely to be sent far, far away from whatever was inside.

When he finally moved away from the history section, he reshelved the rest of the books at lightning speed. Returning to the desk, he sorted as fast as possible, piling all the history books he could find onto the cart.

"Ah, got another one ready to go?" Mage Renaud rounded the corner at exactly the same time.

"Yup. Let me help you load up." Draven nudged the remaining pile of books towards the head volunteer, and his carefully stacked cart further away. He pushed books onto Mage Renaud's cart. Haste was the same as enthusiasm, right? It was fine. It wouldn't seem weird. The door to Special Collections was like an itch though. "What are the specialist jobs?" he asked. "I know I'm not qualified, but I'm at the Energy Makers' Guild, and we're meant to be studying ourselves. Sort of." It wasn't an outright lie. That had come up a few times.

"Certain of the library's assets need careful handling and monitoring."

"Right. The Special Collections." He had imagined old books, their flaking pages needing to be touched gently or handled with the lightest of charms. That was the impression people liked to give. He tried to remember whether anyone had outright said so. Lying was bad. People did not do it. But there was a difference between lying and pointing someone in the wrong direction and letting them draw their own, inaccurate conclusions. Hadn't he just done something similar to Mage Renaud, after all?

"Something like that." Mage Renaud ran a hand through his hair and tweaked his tie. Was that nervousness? Regret? Like he didn't like leading Draven down this path of misinformation. "I'm afraid I have to get on," Mage Renaud added, and Draven nodded. Pushing this was not going to do anything except put the person in front of him in a difficult situation. Anyway, he had a well stacked cart and a history section to return to.

He unloaded the books slowly, not entirely sure what he was watching or waiting for. He had observed two people enter, neither of whom had come out yet. They hadn't had to do anything special to get through the door. They had simply walked up, turned its handle and gone in. It was tempting to try the handle. Except, they presumably had permission—whatever it was, whoever it came from. More pressingly, they were still inside, and might see the door open, if it worked. Also, he did not have permission. That thought still bothered him. He wondered whether there was no spell to it at all, but that simply writing "Please don't do this" was enough of a deterrent to the law-abiding citizens of Galdorsfarne.

He was still in the history section when he heard the door click. He tucked himself in against the shelf to reduce the chances of them seeing him. He had every reason to be here; he was shelving books. But he didn't want to look like he was looking. Plus, if they didn't know that he'd seen them come out, he'd have an excuse to check later. It would never do to leave the library and lock people in. It was strange that a plan which contained doing something he shouldn't do and lying about it if he got caught felt like the right thing to do.

At five to eight, a green light flickered through the library, letting them know they had reached their quota. Even with his excuse prepared, he glanced around before making his way over to the door. Bracing himself, he reached out, feeling the cool metal of the door handle under his fingers. He turned his wrist and...nothing. No alarms. No flashing lights.

But also no yield. His fingers moved, but the handle pressed back firmly against them.

Chapter Eight

What did "getting a life" mean? It was the resolution Niall had made to himself after the priory, but it was hard to put his finger on what he was supposed to start doing. Getting drunk? Getting on dating apps? They both sounded like hell, and anyway, who'd want him? Joining a queer book group or something was more his style, and he knew those existed but it was so public and blatant. He tended to be honest with his parents about where he was going. He wasn't a good liar, nor did he want to lie about that. He wasn't sure he was ready to tell the truth either. Not to mention that the person who'd allegedly seen Jamie Swift at Pride didn't seem to realise that wasn't something she should broadcast without consent.

He'd decided that random, ill-defined acts of bravery were the way to go. He would try harder not to tuck himself into corners. Something about needing to love yourself before anyone else would love you played vaguely through his mind. Although he couldn't help but feel he was indulging the same magpie tendency that had filled the box in the bottom of his chest of drawers—he was trying to be someone else but without the risk of anyone seeing it. Hence, he was back in Newcastle, in Oxfam, without Ellen. Bravery hadn't extended to asking her opinion on this or asking her to bear witness to it. It apparently didn't extend to telling the truth either, because as he lay the sweater on the counter, he blurted out, "It's for my friend."

He hoped he wasn't as red as he felt.

"The pink-haired girl?" the shop volunteer queried. Niall's head jerked, caught between that lie, which was convenient, but which could easily be rumbled. Because obviously Ellen was going to come and gossip about him with the Oxfam volunteer. It wasn't like he couldn't ask Ellen to lie for him in the unlikely event that this ever came up. She asked him to lie for her all the time, covering for the times she went drinking or on dates that her parents would disapprove of. But he would have felt ridiculous asking her. It would involve admitting both that he had bought the kitten sweater and that he had felt compelled to lie to the shop assistant about who it was for.

"Uh, no. Different friend," he said, hoping it was plausible that he had more than one.

"It's a fun one, isn't it?" The volunteer laughed cheerfully, holding up the sweater so its glitter caught the lights in a way that made Niall want to repeat his lie to the entire shop. "Oh, no one claimed that necklace you handed in by the way. At this point, we're assuming it's stock. Though funny thing is, no one remembers it coming in. But one of the ladies who does Wednesdays, her memory's not all that, between you and me, pet. Plus, she's worked here twenty years, and it all must start to blur."

Niall nodded. His thumbs fumbled as he rolled the sweater up, wondering whether it really was taking a ridiculously long time to turn it into a tight, anonymous bundle or whether it was just his imagination. Even with the picture part on the inside, it was still an easily ridiculed mauve colour. Once it was safely stashed in the bottom of his backpack, he had planned to get out as fast as possible—back into the cool air of the street, surrounded by anonymous people who didn't know that he had just purchased a glittery kitten sweater. "For his friend."

The news about the necklace stalled him though. Now the sweater was safely out of sight, he found his panicked brain fog clearing.

"I didn't notice it on the shelves." He always browsed carefully, enjoying the changing scenery of the shop from week to week, keen to make sure he didn't miss anything interesting.

"Oh, I guess it's still out back. But they plan on selling it. Were you interested?"

"Uh, can I have another look?" Hopefully it would have a price tag on already so he could subtly weigh up whether it was worth whatever they were asking. "If that's not an inconvenience," he added, self-conscious about making her go and get something for him that he might not want.

"It's no bother, pet," she said, calling out to one of the other volunteers. Niall tried not to tense at being identified as someone who was interested in necklaces in addition to kitten sweaters.

He bounced on the balls of his feet whilst he waited but tried to stop doing it as soon as the volunteer came out with the necklace. It was hard not to fidget given that she was watching him, waiting for a decision.

It could be magical, said the back of his mind, as he ran a thumb over one of the symbols. That was the part of his brain that he wasn't supposed to be listening to anymore. He was supposed to engage with reality, or whatever. But something about the symbols drew him in. He'd memorised a few different symbol systems (another side-effect of not having a life) and he didn't recognise these. They were a mystery to throw himself into, even if that was the opposite of what he was supposed to be doing right now.

And they only wanted £1.95 for it.

And he didn't want to have bothered someone for nothing.

"Sure. I'll take it," he said.

* * *

Niall stood waiting for the metro back to North Shields. Deep in his backpack were the contraband goods of the kitten sweater, the necklace, and a story about dragons. It was a kids' book, titled *The Field Spotters' Guide to Dragons* but it was so cute and whimsical.

He sat on the platform, relishing the last taste of city freedom, reading another one of his purchases—a respectably young adult novel, even if it was geeky and weird. His mind kept drifting to the necklace. He'd tried various searches already on his phone, but it was hard to know what to even put in. He was considering getting it out, to look over the symbols again, when a voice cut across his thoughts.

"Hey. Niall, right?"

Niall's head jerked up.

"Yeah. Hi, Jamie." His stomach twisted. Jamie, besides his rumoured appearance at Pride events, was an unknown quantity. He was in Ellen's law class, but that meant he might be a posh wanker. Ellen got a pass on taking it because it was her parents' choice of class and had been bartered for them letting her also do drama. Not that law was uninteresting, or a bad thing to study. It just had a reputation for being for posh wankers.

"Where are you headed?" Jamie asked, as the yellow metro pulled in and they both climbed on.

"Bedewell—well, Shields on the metro, then Bedewell."

"Oof, sorry to hear it," Jamie joked.

Niall smiled whilst slightly wanting to punch him in the face. Sure, he complained about Bedewell all the time. But he was allowed. He lived there.

"You?" he asked instead.

"Monkseaton."

Posh wanker.

"Nice," Niall said.

"Is that any good?" Jamie nodded to the book in Niall's hand, a sceptical tone suggesting he had a preconceived notion of the answer.

"I like it." Niall made up his mind mostly based on Jamie's tone. He'd read a chapter and had still been deciding. It was superheroes rather than magic, which wasn't his favourite brand of escapism, but he'd take it. Plus, the main character had South-East Asian heritage so he would have felt disloyal to Ellen passing it up. And yes, he did feel deeply self-conscious reading a book with a female lead character emblazoned across its cover, but he also knew that was stupid, and he was trying his hardest to care less what everyone else thought.

"Isn't it a girls' book?" Jamie asked.

"It's just a book." Niall shrugged. "I don't think it cares who reads it."

"Right. Think I'll pass." Jamie's eyes drifted to the window, and for a moment Niall thought he might be spared having to make further conversation. "Hey, you and Ellen, are you guys like, a thing?"

"Uh. No." Niall swallowed, hoping this wasn't going where he thought it might be going. Partly because they were on a crowded train, and partly because he was liking Jamie less and less every second.

"Cool. She's hot."

Oh. That was less awkward, but equally uncomfortable if Jamie was an arsehole. Though admittedly all he'd done was say he didn't want to read Niall's choice of book, and Ellen probably cared less about that than Niall would.

"Yeah. Well, maybe don't start with the fact you think books with female POCs as the lead are beneath your notice," Niall advised, glaring slightly.

"Wow, chill." Jamie rolled his eyes. "I didn't say that. I just don't want to be seen reading some girly book right when everyone's talking shit about me. Not even true, by the—" he began. "Not that there's anything wrong with that," he added, and Niall was acutely aware that Jamie's eyes were hovering on his wrist. He glanced down, seeing the rainbow stars poking out. "I'm just not." Jamie held up his hand as if Niall had initiated some kind of conversation about that.

"Right. Well. This is my stop," Niall blurted, as they pulled into Chillingham Road, in spite of the fact he'd already told Jamie where he was going. He dove away from Jamie, having to wait several agonising seconds in front of the metro doors before they opened. He stepped out onto the platform, allowing the harsh biting air to cool his glowing cheeks. At least Jamie hadn't tried to stop him. He felt like kicking something. But he would wait until the people cleared off the platform. It was already embarrassing enough that he was going to hang here, blatantly waiting for the next train.

By the time the platform had cleared though, his anger had ebbed, leaving him with the cold, and the frustration that whilst he'd jump to defend Ellen (even against imagined slights or ones she wouldn't care about), he couldn't do the same for himself.

He pulled out his phone, venting some of his frustration in a message to her.

> **Niall Silverstein**: Jamie's a wanker and if he asks you out say "No."
> **Ellen Sorn**: Okay. Take it that means you're not going out with him either?
> **Niall Silverstein**: He's straight. He just took pains to point that out.
> **Ellen Sorn**: ?????
> **Ellen Sorn**: Did you make a move on him or something???
> **Niall Silverstein**: NO! We ended up on the same metro. He feels strongly enough about the topic of asserting his own hetero broness that it came up naturally. But he saw my stupid bracelet and wanted to assure me that he has nothing against the homos. I hate my life.
> **Ellen Sorn**: Your bracelet isn't stupid ::Prideflag::
> **Ellen Sorn**: You okay?

Niall clicked off his phone, not sure how to answer that. He opened his bag, pulling out the necklace and transferring it to his pocket, so that he could squeeze it for the rest of the ride home.

* * *

As he opened his front door, Niall heard the gentle hiss of the kettle coming from the kitchen.

"Aha!" His mum grinned, sticking her head into the hallway. "You heard my summoning spell."

It was a long-running family joke that putting the kettle on made people reappear at home.

"Guess so." Niall pulled off his shoes and his winter layers. He padded through into the kitchen in dinosaur-socked feet. He tried to feel cheery that the coincidence had happened with the kettle. He tried to call it magic inside his own head. But he only felt sad and pathetic.

"You alright, love?" his mum asked as she chucked teabags in the pot.

Niall had pondered how to answer that inevitable question on his second metro ride, his bus and then his walk. What was he supposed to say? He could say that Jamie had been a jerk, but his mum would want to know what about. He could say he'd been a homophobic jerk, and she would agree that was a bad thing because she was a good person. Which made it silly that he'd never told her. But he hadn't. And now he would either say this, and she wouldn't understand why it was bothering him so much. Or she would. And that would be how he told her.

"Just tired. Been slogging around town in the cold."

"Nothing a cup of tea won't fix. Shall we see if there's a quiz or something on?"

"Uh, sure," Niall agreed. He wasn't in the mood for one but it was the usual routine, and he didn't want to rock the boat. And he wanted a biscuit.

He followed her through into the living room, flopping down on the sofa next to her. After a minute, he shifted over to lean on her shoulder.

"You sure you're alright?" she checked, as she turned on the television.

"Yeah. Just want a hug," he said. Mum hugs were comforting, even when she didn't know why she was giving them.

"You're not a normal seventeen-year-old," she teased. He tried not to sigh, and to work up the nerve to say that no, he wasn't. Except that wasn't how he wanted to do it either. He didn't want to label himself as "abnormal."

"And you've got the biscuits." He reached over to take a bourbon from the open tin.

"That's more like it." She laughed and gave his shoulder a squeeze.

He watched the quiz with her until he'd got through two biscuits. He carefully dissected each one by biting off the top layer (both times, it came away clean and complete, one of life's satisfying little victories) before nibbling away around the cream filling, removing the plain part so that only a cream-covered single layer of biscuit remained, which he dunked in his tea. This little ritual made him feel more settled, but he still wanted to be upstairs.

"Think I've seen this one. I'm gonna go read." Niall peeled himself off the sofa.

"I can find a different episode if you want," his mum offered.

"No, s'alright. Got new books while I was out."

He trailed back through the hall, picking up his backpack and heading upstairs.

He closed his door, flicking the small hook and eye lock into place. The privacy was more symbolic than anything. His parents were pretty good at remembering to knock. His brothers had learnt early on how to slip a postcard through the crack in the door and flick the lock out of place. There had been a fairly steady stream of them all winding each other up until Dan and, later, Steve had gone off to uni.

He tipped his backpack out onto his bed, running his hands over his treasures. Jamie would think the sweater was stupid. That steadied Niall's belief that liking it was the right thing to do, whilst simultaneously reducing the chances that he would ever wear it outside of this room.

He pulled the sweater on, not daring to confront his reflection. In his head, it transformed him into someone who was bright and colourful and didn't care what anyone else thought. He wasn't ready to catch a glimpse of himself and realise that it had no such magic powers, and he still looked like himself, but more ridiculous. It was all those same old clichés that were so easy to spout but difficult to enact. Be yourself. Don't let other people bother you. He ran a hand over the necklace, his fingers exploring the grooves of the strange carved symbols, wondering what it would take for this version of him to be able to step out of the door.

Something good. Some little piece of good to come his way. That was all he asked.

Chapter Nine

Subterfuge, it turned out, was an addictive habit. A few weeks later, Draven was applying those same skills at work. Though this time it was more because the contents of his research were private, rather than forbidden.

During the never-ending filing jobs on low amber days, he'd been able to take peeks at some of his own graphs. They were bothering him because, for the last two weeks, he'd been dropping lower and lower—further than he'd ever gone before. He kept having the same recurring thought, *I'm an awful person.* He'd gone up and down in the past, but when he'd looked through his old data, he'd never done this badly before. He was getting close to contributing absolutely zero.

Except for the day at the library. The day where he'd ploughed through his tasks at record speed—where he'd felt excited by something. His graph spiked. It wasn't merely the fact that it had been so low before that made the line steep—where he'd dropped further down than ever before, he'd also sailed higher. So, was it still balancing out? He didn't feel balanced. His last two merit sessions had been small groups, working on park maintenance, and they had dragged. He knew it was him. The only thing that had given him life and hope was the Special Collections, but how was he ever going to get beyond the door?

He wondered how long he would have to perform below average before he got into trouble. They tracked individual data for a reason, after all. He needed to pull his weight. He wondered whether he should turn himself in—march into Mage Starkweather's office and point out that he was no longer helping the energy crisis, but was actively hindering it. He didn't want to be a member of the Energy Makers' Guild anymore but he was loath to burn that bridge, or to demonstrate what a terrible person he was, and have someone whom he still admired suddenly think very little of him.

The universe seemed determined to kick him while he was down because, as he pulled out the drawer he needed, Matthias came striding around the corner.

"What are you up to?" Matthias asked. Draven tried to keep his expression neutral. After all, he wasn't doing anything wrong. At least, he didn't think so. Surely, keeping an eye on his own data was useful. Not that he thought it would do much good but, well, not doing much good was actually his present problem.

"Looking for some records."

"What records?" Matthias asked.

"Exploring an idea. We're allowed to do that." Draven shrugged, meaning *"What's your problem?"* He felt a little edgy admitting he had a personal project to Matthias. Draven didn't want him sticking his nose in. On top of that was the attitude of the guild. For all they said original thoughts were encouraged, he had yet to see any evidence of that. For somewhere that was meant to be at the cutting edge, the place felt like it moved to a slow and sleepy rhythm, a shuffling, somnambulist's pace. He didn't move like that. The nail that stuck up from the bed got hammered down.

He snatched up the records he needed, so he could look at them once Matthias was no longer hovering, and returned to his desk, slipping the graphs under his other papers, trying to forget about them for the morning.

He managed it until tea break.

"This is your personal project?"

He turned to find Matthias holding the chart up.

"You went through my stuff?" Draven glared.

"Mislaid a piece of paper. Didn't mean to." The smirk on Matthias' face said that wasn't true, but what choice did Draven have but to believe him? People didn't go through each other's things, and they certainly didn't accuse another person of lying about that, or drive a fist into their smug face over it. "Are you okay?" Matthias asked. He held up the graph so it was clearly visible to everyone. "These numbers don't look healthy."

"That's private."

"Just concerned."

"He said it's private." Yvette reached to snatch the paper out of Matthias' hand but he moved it out of reach. "Give it back."

"I don't know." Matthias folded the paper between his fingers. "If Draven's tanking, maybe it's our duty to let someone know. We're after variables that affect the energy levels after all."

"You can't blame him for the whole energy crisis." Yvette crossed her arms over her chest.

"Of course not. But one little tweak here, a little tweak there, and we meet our five-year forecasts and all that. That's the grand plan to fix the energy crisis. Iron out the flaws." He looked directly at Draven as he emphasised the last word.

Without knowing what he was doing, Draven threw himself forward. He wanted his paper back, but more than that he wanted to grab hold of any part of Matthias' body and...and he didn't know. Hurt it. Make him hurt. He got as far as slamming into him, pushing him back, when Rowan's voice cut sharply across their fight.

"Hey! HEY! What is going on in here?" It was a marked contrast from her usual warmth.

"Matthias was winding him up." Yvette came to his rescue.

"All I said was that these are concerning." Matthias threw the sheet onto the table in front of Rowan. "You can't have a harmonious society with an unstable element."

"Don't...name call?" It was clearly a rebuke Rowan wasn't used to delivering. Or maybe she was unsure whether it counted because Matthias was quoting a popular saying. It certainly felt different when it was directed at him, but Draven was more concerned with watching Rowan's face as she looked over his graphs. Her eyes traced the lines, then returned to do it all over again like she hadn't trusted what they'd told her the first time.

"Let's go have a word about these?" she said.

Draven followed her. He didn't think Yvette or Melvin would gossip about him but he felt like he could already hear whispers as he stepped away from their table.

"What's going on?" she asked him, once they were sitting in a small side room used for private meetings.

"I don't know. I think I might be a terrible person," he admitted.

"I'm sure you're not," she said. Draven wondered why she was looking at him like that if that wasn't the case. "Leave it with me?"

"Are you going to show Mage Starkweather?"

"I feel like I ought to. I'm sure you won't be in trouble, but I don't know what this means."

"No. That's fine. I want to know." He would have taken them himself but he wasn't sure he could waltz into her office whenever anything upset him, for all that Matthias thought he was some sort of special favourite.

He returned to his desk, although he couldn't concentrate, and the morning of number crunching went slower than usual. At eleven fifteen, Rowan passed through, handing him a note.

Could you come to my office at 12? Sorry to cut into your lunch break but I have no other time today, and it sounds like you're rather worried.

He fidgeted through the rest of the morning, trying to work out what the note implied. It was urgent enough to need immediate action, and to schedule a meeting over lunchtime. That made it sound serious. But on the other hand, she was talking about how *he* was worried. Was it that nothing was wrong but she wanted to put his mind at ease? Was he making a fuss over nothing if that was the case? Still, he couldn't reply to the note. And for all that it was phrased as a question, it was a command. He would have to go and find out.

* * *

"Our chat the other week didn't change your mind, did it?" asked Mage Starkweather, her eyes wandering down the line that documented Draven's severe lack of recent contributions. Her voice was not judgemental, she was just searching for facts.

"Not really," he admitted. "I mean, I appreciate what you're doing. I'm sure it's a good plan. But I don't fit into it."

"That has you feeling rather low? You don't want to be here, but you don't like that you don't want to be here?"

"Something like that," Draven agreed.

"I don't think we need to worry that you're not contributing at all." She tapped the high point on his graph, raising her eyebrows. "What were you doing here?"

"Library."

"I'll make sure that's where you're stationed for your next few sessions. Repeat what's working and work on the rest."

"Sounds good." It was easy enough to agree to that, when it lined up with the one place in this world he still wanted to be—the one that sounded like it had a way out of it.

"In the meantime, try not to worry?" Her smile was sympathetic, like she knew that was easier said than done.

"I'll try," he promised, getting up to leave.

"Oh, Draven?" She stopped him as he reached for the door. He turned, finding her pulling several books from her desk with a sheepish smile.

"Would you mind dreadfully if I asked you to return some things to the library for me? I know strictly speaking it's not part of your job here or there to run my books back, but as you're going anyway..."

"Of course," Draven said, amazed that she sounded so genuinely apologetic about asking him to do such a simple favour.

"Thank you. I trust that you'll see each and every one of these ends up back in its proper place." She handed him half a dozen books.

"Absolutely," he promised. "I'll see to it personally."

Chapter Ten

After Assembly on Saturday, Draven headed to the library. Mage Renaud had no particular jobs for him, just general returns, tidying, and so on. Draven stamped Mage Starkweather's books back in, his eyes curiously roving over their titles as he did so. Most were history books, though there was a mystery novel in there too. The title of the fifth book caught his eye, causing him to do a double take. It appeared to be a book all about generator maintenance. It made sense for her to be reading that; however little she liked them, they came under her department's remit. But he had never seen anything like it in the library. He wielded the date stamp, ready to slam it down in the "return" column but when he opened the book there was a column of signatures instead. The paper was headed "Galdorsfarne Library—Special Collections: all books to be signed out and in." Mage Starkweather's signature was in the "out" column next to that of one of the head volunteers. Draven flicked through a few of the pages, but they were a blur of technical words and diagrams. He was about to slip the book back into his bag, hoping for a chance to read it later, when Mage Renaud reappeared.

"What've you got there?" he asked.

"Mage Starkweather gave me her books to return," he said, doing his best to sound innocent.

"Unless I'm much mistaken, I need to sign that one back in," Mage Renaud held out his hands, and Draven had no choice but to hand it over. "I'll put it back for you," Mage Renaud added.

"I can shelve them. It's no problem," Draven tried, hoping his desperation to hold onto the book wasn't as obvious as it felt.

"This one you can't." Mage Renaud tapped the "Special Collections" header. Draven felt horrible about the complete lack of mistrust in Mage Renaud's voice. As if Draven had simply not noticed the sheet in the front of the book.

Because, after all, he would never knowingly read something he wasn't entitled to, or try to hang onto it.

"Oh. Yes. Enter only with permission," Draven quoted the door. "Whose permission does it need?"

"A guild head's," Mage Renaud replied. "Otherwise, the warding spell will keep you out."

"Is that full of dangerous and dark magic?" Draven joked, nodding at the volume in Mage Renaud's hands.

"No. Nothing like that. Most of the books are rare. There's a lot of valuable information there, but...well, it makes sense to have a solid reason to study it, to make sure the resources get well taken care of."

"Right. Thanks." Draven tried to console himself that he'd at least got something useful out of the conversation. He knew how the door worked, though apparently getting access hinged on him having an idea worthy of studying whatever was behind it and convincing someone else of that. It wasn't hopeful.

He wheeled the trolley out, starting with the history books which would at least let him stare at the door. They also meant he could assure Mage Starkweather that he'd done something right. It was a small act of kindness, putting the books away, but as she'd pointed out, that still counted for something. He'd promised her—

He'd promised her.

He froze with the book halfway to the shelf, trying to remember what exactly he had promised. The door needed permission from a guild head, and she had asked him—asked him *exactly* what? Magic listened to your words, not your intentions. What words had she used? Had she said he had to put them back? If he'd kept the book in his hands, would it have been his key to opening the door? His hand clenched tighter around the one he was holding.

"You'll see each and every one of these ends up back in its proper place."

Those had been her words, hadn't they? Not that he would put them back but that he would see they had been put. He held his breath. He was going to have to be patient. If that worked, he couldn't go in when anyone was expecting him to be available elsewhere. Tempting as it was to try the handle, he wasn't sure whether it would work only once, if it worked at all. He would have to wait.

He attacked his shift with a distracted, haphazard air. He was trying to get it done. He was trying to care. He was trying to look totally normal and not at all distracted.

It was the longest a merit session had ever felt, even though by the objective measure of the hands ticking round the face of his watch, it had definitely been shorter than some of his recent efforts. But at last, the green light flickered, and he wheeled his trolley back to the desk.

"See you," he said to Mage Renaud. It was a perfectly natural thing to say at the end of the shift, regardless of whether he was heading out or back into the library to enjoy it as a patron. Just because he fiddled with his shoe long enough that Mage Renaud departed for the break room and didn't see which of those Draven had done didn't mean he was sneaking.

Okay, he was totally sneaking, and it was sort of thrilling.

He returned to the history aisle, waiting until it looked like no one else was nearby. He got his break, and walked towards the door as purposefully as he could. He thought he needed to be purposeful for the door to believe him, and he had made sure that no one else was looking, so he didn't need to combine that with seeming casual, because those two things didn't go together. He wondered whether he ought to say something—to state that he had permission to be here— but he hadn't seen the mages who entered doing so. Instead, he focussed as clearly as he could on the memory of Mage Starkweather asking him to personally see to it that her book was back in place and pressed down against the cool metal of the handle. This time, it yielded.

Draven was not sure what he had expected to find behind the door, but the scene that greeted him was almost eerily normal. There was no radical shift as he stepped through, closing the door behind him. There were simply rows and rows of books, with every detail—from the shelf style to the floor tiles—a continuation of the room he had left behind. If he had seen a photograph of this room, he would have known in an instant that it was part of the library. The only difference was that there was a slight curve to the shelves. The intrigue, he supposed, was in the details—what was in the books, and what else was in this room?

He walked slowly up and down each aisle, his eyes skimming over the titles, wondering where he would start if he found himself with time to read. *Mages in the Field: Case Studies of Hands-On Work with Disadvantaged Populations* sounded fascinating. What populations? Where? Did it mean outside of Galdorsfarne? And there was history here! Books with dates he had never read about stamped onto their spines. He lingered, tempted for a moment, but he had noticed something—the curve which had barely been apparent as he entered the room was becoming more pronounced as he worked his way along, and there was a sense that he was getting towards the centre of something. There was something odd about the quality of the light in this part of the room. It hadn't been noticeable when he had been keeping his nose pressed to the spines of the books, but as his eyes travelled up, trying to determine how far back those dates went, he could see a kind of tinge to the space above the shelves.

He rounded the corner, and there it was. He had clearly reached the centre of this room, the curves being included in the shelves so that they could be arranged around the glowing green pool in the middle.

Draven stood over it. He had never seen anything quite so beautiful. It appeared to be made of light and it was rippling gently. He could practically feel the power radiating from it. He could have stared at it, basking in its energy all day.

But the voices had said "through."

Whatever this was, it was a thing you could go through. If he dared. It was strange to feel that much raw power, and to think about throwing himself at it, notwithstanding the comments about what lurked on the other side.

What did lurk on the other side?

The fact was, that question thrilled more than terrified him. He would jump. In the back of his mind, he knew that he would. He had no idea whether the invitation he had to be in this room would last (technically, he had not yet found that book and verified its position). He knew he couldn't walk away. Right now, he didn't feel like he could go the remaining two steps forward either. He was wondering what it would take to make him move when he heard the door to the room opening and closing again. He was no longer here alone. There was every chance the person was just here for a book and would not cross paths with him. There was every possibility that this idea was completely unsafe. But the footsteps moving through the Special Collections made him more anxious than the pool did. If he didn't screw his non-existent courage to the sticking spot, he might get caught and lose his opportunity forever; whatever the door thought about his business in being here, he was sure a human being would evaluate the situation differently.

He took a deep breath, and jumped in.

Chapter Eleven

Niall sat on the floor of the historical fiction aisle in Bedewell Public Library with his back against the shelves, wishing his weekend away. The library was busy. It was blowing a hoolie outside, and no one wanted to be outdoors. He couldn't blame them. January was tailing off but the weather wasn't. The holiday lights had all been taken down, the weather was still shite, and his New Year's Resolutions weren't going to change his life just by virtue of existing.

He had chosen to sit at the end of the historical fiction aisle because he did not feel like being out in the world with people—especially not happy, chirpy weekend library people who were not outcasts and due to die miserable and lonely deaths. One of the appeals of coming to the library was the chance to get away from people, so he might as well do it properly. Also, there was more natural light by the window, and sunshine—if the grey, watered down daylight struggling in could be called that—was meant to make you happy or something. It had not. This had just made his butt go numb from sitting on the hard floor, and his shoulder cold from leaning up against the metal shelf.

He dropped his book into his lap. It was a vintage sci-fi that he was struggling to get into. He counted the pages until the end of the chapter. There were more than he wanted there to be. He wanted a comfort book. Something he had read cover to cover so many times he knew it inside out. Something that was guaranteed to entertain him, and to make him feel quietly content, like pulling on a favourite sweater. He marked his place in the sci-fi—not quite ready to believe that he would give up on it because he did not give up on books as a rule—and got up to stretch out his cramped limbs. He stumbled slightly as he stood, partly because his foot had gone to sleep but also because he was no longer alone. There was now a boy about his own age rounding the corner of the aisle.

The first word that sprung to mind about him was "strange." Mostly because... Niall's initial reaction was that the boy looked like he had raided a charity shop in order to dress himself, but given that they were Niall's main source of clothes, that would have been a tad hypocritical. It wasn't even that the boy looked like he had raided the worst items of a charity shop. Again, that was an area where Niall had some expertise. This boy's clothes were nowhere near those levels of atrocious. They were just... Niall wasn't sure he had ever seen anyone wearing flares, outside of a costume party. Nor a velvet blazer. Let alone together. None of it was bad, per se (actually, the blazer was pretty cool. Niall coveted it, or at least, wanted to stroke it) it was just...odd. Niall's own outfit was rather more pared back in comparison—skinny black jeans, black t-shirt, skinny fit red flannel shirt. A hoodie and a bundle of winter clothes had formed a (fairly ineffective) pillow between him and the shelf. He'd also dared to wear a little plastic daisy chain choker, easily visible at present due to his shirt being unbuttoned but easily hidden if necessary. If he felt threatened or uncomfortable. The boy in the middle of the aisle didn't make him feel that though. It was hard to feel threatened by someone in velvet, and especially someone who looked a little lost, dazed and confused.

"Hi," Niall ventured. "Are you okay?"

"I believe so."

Niall raised his eyebrows at this uncertain response. "Are you—" he began, but the boy cut him off.

"What are you reading?"

"I was getting up to get something new actually. Maybe reread the *Redbloom* trilogy." It wasn't the most intellectual answer, but anyone who didn't love those books with all their soul couldn't be—not that he was thinking in those terms anyway.

"I'm not familiar with it." The boy swallowed hard, looking like he was struggling not to address those remarks to his shoes instead of Niall.

"Oh." *Damn.* But also *what?* He knew that he was biased but he was pretty sure you had to have been living under a rock not to have noticed the series. "Not much of a reader, or not into fantasy?" Niall asked. The former seemed unlikely, given where they were meeting, but both were disappointing prospects.

"No. I um...never had the chance? What's it about?"

"Same broad idea as the films," Niall tried, not ready to believe that someone could be unfamiliar with even the basic concept. But seeing as the boy still looked lost, he expanded. "There's this group of teenagers, and they know the apocalypse is coming, but if they can find these certain mystical items, they might be able to prevent it. The items give them different magical powers. But there's this sinister group, the Redbloom, who want the apocalypse to happen, so they keep trying to stop them. I mean, it sounds like fairly standard fantasy stuff when you say it like that, but I find the characters relatable. It's a lot about them working out their priorities, or at least in the books it is, a lot of that gets cut out, or it's harder to show in the films which is why I don't like them so much— Sorry, I'm rambling," he added. Normally someone would have cut him off with "whatever, nerd" before he got that far, and in the absence of that happening, he found he'd been rather chattier than usual.

"Why are you apologising?"

"I...I dunno," Niall managed, finding himself on the receiving end of a penetrating stare that clearly expected an answer. He wondered whether said stare had ever prompted anyone to provide such a thing, as it made him want to cease ever having to speak again. "I...um...people don't always like..." he trailed off.

"Well, I did. Thank you for sharing. It sounds like an interesting story, if a tad unrealistic in its expectations of magic."

"Well, yeah. It's a fantasy novel." Niall shrugged.

"Right." The boy ran a hand through his hair, squirming under Niall's gaze. Which was weird, because Niall was pretty sure he was the least intimidating person imaginable. "I mean— I meant— Erm, maybe I should—"

"I could show you," Niall offered, because the boy had taken a step back, and Niall recognised the look of someone trying to extract themselves from an awkward situation— he'd worn it often enough. He felt bad, trying to prevent a fellow nerd from bolting for cover, but he also didn't want to be thought of as an awkward situation. He didn't bite. And this was easily the longest and most productive conversation he'd ever had with someone cute. He was aware that spoke to how low a bar that was, but he didn't want the boy to go. "If you're interested, I could find the first volume for you," Niall said, acutely aware of the desperation in his voice.

"Really? Yes. Please. That sounds great."

Nerves played on the edges of the boy's voice, but the enthusiasm seemed real. There was a smile that went all the way to his eyes.

"Okay. Let's go." Niall was pretty sure his own smile was as big (but more goofy and less attractive, so he did his best to hide it), as he scooped up his pillow of winter clothes.

"Are we going out?" the boy asked.

"Oh. Um, no. Just safer not to leave it lying around."

The boy frowned at him in confusion for a second but stopped short of asking whatever question had been forming.

Niall led him over to the sci-fi and fantasy section. He knew exactly where to find what he was looking for, though he needed to shuffle through the copies for a few moments. Partly because he needed to find the right one, and partly because he couldn't help but notice that a good-looking boy was being enthusiastic about fantasy novels with him. He was surprised that he had managed as many coherent sentences as he had so far. He was sure all of human language was going to fall out of his brain at the least convenient moment.

"Here." He handed a book over. "The original cover art. All the other copies are film tie-in editions." He disliked the bright, glossy pictures of the actors and the slogan *"As seen in cinemas!*" like that was a good reason to want to read a book. "I think it's more fun to imagine it for yourself," he added. Niall picked out volume two for himself, torn between the annoyance of not starting again at the beginning versus reading a film tie in edition, with the latter horror winning out. "Um, I'm Niall, by the way," he added, realising they hadn't exchanged names yet, and it was getting to the point where it was going to be awkward to bring it up. Possibly they were past that. Probably. He was probably being awkward. He was good at that.

"I'm Draven."

"Cool name," Niall acknowledged, and he meant it, though he imagined that secondary school must have been absolute hell.

They made their way back to the window. Niall was drifting on autopilot, and Draven followed him. It was only when he prepared to sit back down against the unforgiving library shelf that he realised it probably wasn't the best move in terms of trying to keep Draven around.

"Cushion?" he offered, holding out his hoodie, pretending his heart didn't skip when Draven took it.

Niall sat cross-legged, making sure he didn't intrude on Draven's personal space, even though his limbs were inclined to take up most of any available area. He bent his head over his book, trying to concentrate. The familiar words washed over him, his eyes feeling entirely disconnected from his brain. Except for the moments when they looked up and saw Draven sitting with him, reading his favourite book and...well, not exactly *wearing* his hoodie, but leaning on it. Close enough.

Niall let him read, trying to keep his focus on his own book.

"Let me know when you reach the end of a chapter?" Niall asked. "I want to know what you think but I don't want to interrupt."

"I'm halfway through chapter two." Draven looked up, smiling. "I'll be with you in"—he paused to count—"three pages."

Niall bent his head again, but found it kept bobbing up, wanting to make sure he was available when Draven paused.

"Mira's the cutest." Draven broke the silence.

"Yes!" Niall agreed, enthusiasm bubbling and then flattening out as he found himself hoping Draven didn't mean that too literally. Mira was easily Niall's favourite because he related hard to her. If Draven was talking in terms of personality, that was a good sign. "What do you like about her?"

Draven thumbed the edge of the book, biting his lip for a moment.

"She doesn't feel like she fits in. I guess I can relate."

"Yeah." Niall's agreement was a little more subdued, even as his heart clenched with the joyful and painful realisation that he and Draven were on the same wavelength. "Me too."

This was met with silence, Draven still thumbing the edge of the book.

"Do you want to be reading?" Niall asked.

"I want to talk to you," he said. "But I think I might not be very good at it."

"I know the feeling," Niall sympathised.

"How come?" Draven looked up, brows furrowed.

"I...I just...I'm not always good at finding what I want to say to someone." The tips of his ears burned at putting one of his flaws out on display. He'd thought he'd found a kindred spirit, but Draven seemed to be getting at something different. He was also pretty sure that admitting you were bad at conversation was a surefire route to no-one knowing what to say. It was like announcing, *I hope an awkward silence doesn't develop right now."*

"I'm normally okay at it." Draven sighed. "Maybe I should read. It'll give me more things to say." He raised his eyebrows, waiting, Niall realised, for permission. He nodded, returning to his own book.

Should he ask what Draven had meant about not fitting in? He didn't want to pressure him. He tried to read. But he wanted to talk to him. He wanted him to stay, and talking might scare him off. He glued his eyes to the page. But not talking might make it worse. But so might talking. He should read.

After what felt like forever (but in which Niall had only managed to drag himself through a chapter and a half), Draven spoke up again.

"I like it. And I see what you mean. The magic—" He cut himself off, taking a moment to gather his thoughts. "The magic isn't important. I'm already really curious about all the characters. I..."

"Go on," Niall encouraged, because Draven talking had been the best thing, and not only because it stopped Niall being responsible for keeping things going, but because he was animated and his eyes were shining with excitement over one of Niall's favourite things, which made him even cuter.

"I have some theories. But you've read it all. You have to promise not to laugh if I'm miles off?"

"I promise."

"Don't tell me whether I'm right or wrong. I want to guess but I don't want to know."

"Poker face at the ready." Niall did his best to keep a neutral expression as Draven chatted away, sharing his theories of who would get together with who, who was secretly a traitor, where the hidden clues were coming from. He kept his face impassive until Draven ran out of steam even though there was one thing he was dying to say.

"I'm not telling. But something interesting, about what you've said, I think I had all the same theories." He couldn't help but smile. Was this what it felt like to flirt with someone you liked? Or was this just making friends? How were you supposed to tell the difference? There were some forms of flirting that were fairly overt. Like, telling someone they were hot, or giving them That Look, or grinding up against them at a party. Not that he had ever done any of those things. But he didn't want someone who was going to casually pull him at a party because they'd drunk enough to stop him being ugly. He wanted someone who would discuss his favourite books with him, and who wanted the same. How did he decide whether a book discussion was just a book discussion or something more?

"Sounds like I've got lots to look forward to," Draven said. Except he was tucking his finger in between the pages, closing the book and shifting his shoulders. Niall's own were protesting too.

"Um. So... Um." That was a good eloquent start. But at least it forced him into making a follow up. "Do you like tea?" he asked. There wasn't much point getting attached if the answer to that was "no."

"Yes."

Right. Okay. Good. That was step one.

"Me too. If you like tea... I mean, I like it even if— But um do you...um, want tea? With me? Now? Or later. Any time." And there it was. English had broken. He raked a hand through his hair, then immediately regretted it because now he had no idea whether it looked even stupider than usual. He suspected that what had started as a minute possibility was rapidly dwindling to zero. The boy looked decidedly like he would have backed away if he wasn't already sitting against a shelf.

"Does getting tea involve going outside?" he asked.

"No. Uh, I mean, there is tea outside. But here too." Niall blinked, wondering whether the weather, and not his own entire lack of suave, could really be the problem. "Is that all you came in?"

"It's warmer than it looks." Draven tugged his blazer around himself, looking up at Niall like he expected to be challenged.

"Fair enough." Niall wanted to keep it friendly. It wasn't unusual to see someone going hardcore, not bothering with a coat even in the depths of winter—there were photos whenever it snowed of girls still out on the town in their miniskirts and spaghetti strap tops. He hadn't exactly pegged the other boy as the type to worry about how tough he looked. He was wearing a *velvet blazer*. But whatever. "The library has a café but it's so-so. Town's not much better, but it's got one or two okay places." By which he meant they had distinctions beyond "*coffee or tea.*"

"I like it in the library. I'd prefer to stay here, if we can."

"Okay." Was that a yes? To him? He stood up, but Draven stayed rooted to the spot by the shelf.

"How much is tea?"

"I'll get them." The library café was not exactly bank-breaking, but the other boy seemed worried about it. Niall wanted to make it easy. Did that make it easy? Did offering to get them make it more like a date? It wasn't a date. Obviously. But did it create a date-like-atmosphere, and was Draven opposed to that?

"I don't wish to imposition you," Draven said.

Niall regarded him steadily for a moment, trying to decide whether he was taking the piss because who said "imposition" in general, but about a cup of tea from the library café, of all things? But he found no trace of irony on Draven's face—his brown eyes (deeper and richer than Niall's mid brownish wishy-washy shade) were a mix of earnestness and anxiety. Niall had the impression that he'd found someone who was more wordy and more frightened of the world than he was, which he hadn't been convinced was possible. It was strange, feeling like the brave one (again, over a flipping cup of tea) and the one that someone else needed.

"I want to get tea with you," he said, choking down the words *if you want but you don't have to forget I asked,* and hoping he was nowhere near as bright red as he felt.

Chapter Twelve

Draven held the strange, soggy bag by its string, letting it rotate a couple of times above his cup before he plonked it down on the saucer. Niall sat opposite, holding an opaque beverage the colour of dark caramel, which was apparently what happened if you answered *"yes"* to whether you wanted to put milk and sugar into tea.

Draven gripped the sides of the plastic chair he was sitting on. It was hard beneath his fingers. That was a common denominator with this world so far. The library was very unlibraryish. It had no wood and no warmth. It was made of nothing but sharp angles, even in the signs, which were all harsh edges and overly blunt white lettering. Whoever had designed the café seemed to think that painfully bright light glinting off scrubbed white surfaces was an ideal ambience. Even the smells wafting from the tea were wrong. Niall's smelt sour thanks to the milk, even if he'd tried to cover it up with sickly sweetness, and Draven's own smelt bitter. What was this place?

"You can read. If you want."

Niall's voice cut across his thoughts, and Draven realised that he'd been zoning out, and that his thumb had once again found itself working against the pages of the book—the only thing that felt right and soft. Besides Niall himself. Niall, who was kind and pretty, with his face dusted with freckles, magical brown eyes light enough to sparkle with hints of other colours, and cute curls which looked like they would be so nice to run his fingers through.

"No, I..." Draven began. He had wanted to fly away to another world, but he hadn't thought much beyond the actual act of going. He had never quite pegged himself as the hero in his own story. He was more the romantic lead—the one who got rescued by the hero. Stumbling into this strange place, which smelt odd and had unknown rules, was a tad overwhelming. "I want to talk to you," he said. Niall was the key to unlocking this place. Well, this specific place was a library. That much, he had been certain of upon arrival, however many things were wrong about it. It was hard to imagine a library, or its occupants, being mean or wanting to inflict harm. Libraries were fundamentally good, and any place that had them clearly had a modicum of civilisation. This one had also come with a pretty boy who wanted to show him the best books it had to offer. It was certainly nothing like the one and only Other place that had ever been described to him, and so he was tentatively drawing the conclusion that he was somewhere else. "What type of tea is this?" he asked. He hoped that was a normal question. Forcing Niall onto books had been a good distraction earlier, so long as Draven remembered not to make stupid comments about the realness of magic.

"I don't know. Probably bulk buy standard teabag tea." Niall shrugged.

This didn't answer Draven's question. He had never come across tea in bag form, and thus was not sure what was considered standard. He poked the teabag experimentally.

"May I open this?" he asked.

"I guess?" Niall said.

Draven pinched the fine paper of the bag, tugging it gently until it ripped, revealing the soggy black mush inside, which he dug through with his spoon.

"You have your tea leaves ground up very small," he observed. He was not convinced that was good for them but refrained from saying so because that sounded critical, and he didn't want to cast aspersions on the tea that Niall had so kindly bought him. He just wanted to know why it smelt so strange.

"I think that's what all tea bags are like. More or less," Niall said.

"Hmm." Clearly powdering tea and confining it to small paper sachets was a normal behaviour here. He was probably appearing odd by questioning this too deeply. "I'm leaving the teabag alone now," he promised, sitting back primly and attempting to drink the overly bitter substance in a manner which passed for enjoyment.

"You don't like it?" Niall asked.

"No. It's fine. Lovely." Draven had always been a terrible liar, and Niall looked far from convinced. "It's quite strong and bitter."

"Tea is bitter. That's why you add milk and sugar," Niall said. "What type of tea do you normally drink?"

"It depends on the time of day. We have smoked oolong for breakfast. I drink mostly green during the day—occasionally jasmine. We have a range of herbal tisanes for the evening, and at the weekends we tend to have Earl Grey. Tea comes in the form of leaves, not powder in bags," he explained, with a little trepidation. It was unreasonable not to answer, but for all he knew, he was talking a completely foreign language that was immediately going to mark him out as an outsider. Niall was sort of looking like he was having to swallow a lemon, and Draven was pretty sure he'd accidentally said something awful.

"Right. So you—I mean, it matters to—I know this place is kind of—I would have brought you somewhere nicer if I'd—I mean, not that I'm *bringing* you. This isn't— Sorry."

"You have nothing to apologise for. I chose to stay in the library," Draven pointed out. "The tea is fine, honestly. It's different. But it tastes better for being somewhere cosy and calm. You know that feeling, when the world outside is a mess and it's the nicest thing to be wrapped up warm and safe inside?" he ventured, relieved to see Niall soften a bit at that.

"Yeah. I like that feeling." Niall almost whispered it, like he was the one out of his depth here instead of Draven.

"Thanks for the safe-tea." He was glad that this got a grin out of Niall even though he tried to hide it inside his teacup.

"Here's the thing, about why I think I might not be much good at talking today. I don't feel like talking about me. Me is...complicated. I don't feel like I know how to explain myself. But I'd like to know about you. That's where we are. We're at the getting to know each other stage. Only right now, all the things that I want to ask you, I don't think I want you to ask me back, and that feels rude."

"What kind of things are you going to ask me?" Niall's eyes widened over the rim of his teacup.

"Normal, everyday stuff. What you do with your time when you're not in the library, for example," Draven said.

"Oh. I go to college."

"Tell me more." That felt like a much more natural turn of phrase to use than *"What does that mean?"*

"Okay. Um, I go to college in the city. I didn't fancy sticking around here. I study history, philosophy, physics and chemistry."

"What's wrong with here?" Draven asked.

"You're not from here then?" Niall raised his eyebrows. Draven's hands faltered on his teacup. "Right. No questions. Sorry. Here's... Do I get to veto anything I don't want to answer?"

"Of course."

"Okay. Well, here's... I just fancied a change. Not the same place and the same people I'd always been around." Niall pressed his finger into the grains of sugar on his saucer, then brushed them back off. He seemed occupied with choosing which things to tell Draven, and much as that was something Draven couldn't criticise right now, he wondered what Niall was holding back. "I have two older brothers. I wanted to pick somewhere that was mine, so I wouldn't just be 'their brother.' Not that there's a problem with that. I guess I wanted people's first impressions of me to be *me*, not them. Am I rambling?"

"No. I like it. I'm an only child," he volunteered, this seeming safe enough. He liked the way Niall opening up gave him little ways in, reminding him of small things that he could share in return. "The rest... I feel a lot like that too. Wanting to meet different people. Wanting to know that I'm choosing for myself."

Niall looked like he was about to probe for more information but checked himself. "You'll get me started on philosophy if you're not careful," he warned. "Free will, determinism and all that."

"I don't think I'd be sorry if I did." Draven wanted to be more flirtatious, but Niall's body language was kind of closed off. He couldn't blame him, given that Draven was hardly being forthcoming, but hopefully he could coax him out with a few well-placed smiles.

"Well... Um... Does it count as asking about you if I ask you whether you believe in fate?"

"I can probably answer that," Draven said. "Well, I'm willing to answer that. What I believe might be a wildly fluctuating bunch of incongruent nonsense. I sometimes feel my life is mapped out for me. I..." He stalled, thinking of the examples he couldn't give, about being put into a particular discipline that suited his talents. "Some things get chosen for me by other people in my life." He tried to gauge Niall's reaction. That got a sympathetic smile but no overt confusion or horror. "But it's hard to know where that comes from. From me? From other people's perception of me? From some big, predestined plan?"

"I get to choose most things," Niall said, "but I still wonder. I tend not to believe in destiny and all that. But, could I have made different choices? Or... It ends up relating to physics. Schrödinger's Cat?" he probed.

"Sort of. It's both alive and dead but magic's not involved, and I never got it," Draven said. This got a laugh. Cos that had been a joke. Cos magic was fictional. He swallowed a large mouthful of tea.

"People think is complicated but it's really not—maybe they get put off by it being physics, or maybe they don't get why it's useful. So, we have a cat in a box. Fictional, theoretical cat," he assured Draven. "There's a source of radiation and a thing that's going to happen and kill the cat if the radiation does a particular thing. Let me know if I lose you with all this technical language. How do you know whether the cat is alive or dead?"

"You look?" guessed Draven.

"Right. But there's this theory that says looking is what decides things. Until you look, the cat is both alive and dead—confirming it with your own eyes is what makes it a definite reality."

"That's weird."

"Right. Schrödinger actually wrote it as a critique of that theory, because he felt it was obvious that a cat couldn't be both alive and dead. But actually, it seems more and more like that might be true. When you take scales a lot smaller than cats, particle level stuff, things can exist in multiple states until you measure them, and then you force them to become only one version."

"How do you even test that?" Draven blinked.

"Um... With lots of science." Niall nodded sagely. He fiddled with the teaspoon for a minute. "You ever feel like you have a solid grip on something until you start trying to explain it, and then it just ends up being a mess?"

"Yes. But that wasn't."

"Thanks. Anyway, to bring us back to philosophy... That's kind of how I view my life. There are all these possibilities. They all exist until I do one of them, and then life collapses down into only being that—in that sense, it couldn't be any of the other options. Not because I wasn't free to choose, but because I can't live my life without also participating in and observing it—the only way for it to have multiple possibilities is to not actively experience it."

"I like that idea."

"Plus, you know, it lets you dream about cool parallel worlds and stuff where different mes made different choices. Like a me who did not take AS level physics, with all its headache-inducing properties, and isn't talking quite so much crap." Niall accidentally dropped the teaspoon with a clatter and winced.

"I don't think you're talking crap. And Different-Universe-You might have missed all the little steps that led to talking to me. To you being in the right place at the right time. I'm glad you were. I needed a friendly face."

There was a pause like a silencing spell had engulfed them, where the question "Why?" was clearly held back, the cogs whirring in Niall's brain, desperately trying to smush it into something else.

"Am I allowed to ask if you're feeling better now?" he tried instead.

"Yes and yes." Draven smiled. "I got a book recommendation and a cup of tea. Hard not to be happy."

"Yeah. Today is one of the days I'm glad to be this universe's version of me," Niall said. "You wanna go back to the sunbeam?" he asked, seeing as they'd finished their teas.

"Sure." Draven picked up his book, heart bouncing at the thought of resuming his imaginary adventures alongside his real one.

* * *

They passed the rest of the afternoon companionably. Mostly they read, although there were plenty of digressions. Draven would look up to read out a line he particularly liked, or to share how his theories were progressing. Almost every time they got drawn off on a tangent, if only for a couple of minutes. However, as the light began to fade outside, Draven knew he would have to go.

If his world existed via a portal attached to this library, did it exist within the library, or vice versa? He suspected that neither was true. A connection was not the same as containment. Therefore, it would be removing the book unlawfully from the library to take it back with him. Draven sighed and rummaged through his pockets, looking for something innocent and innocuous to leave behind. He pulled a scrap of parchment from his pocket. It read *I am pretending to take notes in order to appear diligent, but I might die of boredom.* He had scribbled it during a statistics lesson at work. He slipped it into the book, feeling power in leaving a mark that he had been in this place.

"I guess I'll have to finish this another time," he said. "I should get going."

"Yeah." Niall glanced down at his watch. "I guess this place is closing soon. We—" He cut himself off with a shake of his head. "You gonna check that out or come back for it another time?" he asked, nodding to the book.

"The latter."

"Cool. Me too. I mean, I come here a lot too. So…" He scuffed a shoe on the carpet and twirled a small black rectangle in his hand. Draven had noticed it buzzing and him occasionally fiddling with it throughout the afternoon. "Can I add you?"

There was a beat of awkward silence in which Draven wondered how best to deal with this most recent incarnation of not having a clue what was going on. Hesitation, however, was clearly not an acceptable response in this scenario, because the second a silence opened up, Niall rushed to fill it.

"Ornotwhateverit'sfineforgetIaskeditdoesn'tmatter."

"I'm not sure what you're asking me," Draven tried to stem the flow of words, deciding honesty was the best policy right now.

"Fine. Forget it. I just thought, maybe you'd want to hang out again." Niall was shoving his head hastily into his hoodie and grabbing his bag. But none of it was fast enough to stop Draven noticing that he was burning bright red as if Draven had deeply insulted or embarrassed him.

"I do," Draven insisted. Clearly, he was not reacting as anticipated in some kind of social ritual and it was causing Niall to get upset. "Please wait! I don't understand you, or what you're asking, but I do want to see you again and what is that?" He gestured at the black rectangle at the centre of this interaction.

"It's a mobile phone." Niall crossed his arms, and Draven shrank back against the glare he was receiving. That tempered it slightly. "You don't know what this is?" Niall still sounded hostile and suspicious, but his tone was more even.

"I'm sorry," Draven said. Clearly this was the wrong answer, he was getting it all wrong, and he was supposed to know about the mobile phone, and it was problematic that he didn't. "Is it to do with sounds?" He knew other words that ended -phone: "telephone," "gramophone," and so on.

"It lets you communicate with other people."

"Like a telephone?"

"Well, yeah. That's what 'phone' is short for."

Draven regarded the small black box suspiciously. He had some familiarity with telephones. They had been around in his grandma's generation and some of her friends still used theirs. They looked nothing like the small box Niall was holding. There was no dial, no receiver. It was just a box! A tiny box!

"Things are different where I'm from," he ventured.

"You wanna tell me how?" Niall asked.

He *wanted* to. But he wasn't sure what would happen if he did. Everything from the tea to the strange phone suggested he was out of his depth when it came to knowing the rules of this world. He wasn't sure how a curve ball as big as "*I fell through a hole from a magical land*" would go down.

"You don't have to though." Niall was quick to fill Draven's silence. "If you don't want to. But, how do I get in touch with you? If you really do want to see me again—"

"I do," Draven insisted. When Niall had brought up the subject of home, he had wanted to back away. But Niall seemed gentle enough not to push for answers that Draven couldn't give. He had generally taken gentleness for granted—after all, everyone was more or less kind in how they treated each other—but he found he appreciated it here, where he was so far out of his comfort zone. He wanted Niall to believe that he wanted to see him again. "I don't know. We...we can make a plan, I suppose. We could meet here again next week. Maybe on Sunday?" Saturdays were a mess of Assembly, sometimes followed by merit, and he never knew how much of them he'd have to himself. Sunday was the one day that was totally his own. "Only, I don't know for sure if I can come again. Sorry. That's not much to go on. It's...complicated. I'm not sure whether I'm supposed to be here. I... It's hard to explain."

"You don't have to. Not if you can't. Or you're not ready. I'm here most weekends anyway. I mean, I can't promise that

I know what I'll be doing every Sunday. Other stuff might come up. But, I can try to be here, and you can try to be here, and we'll have to hope it lines up?"

"I can leave you a note. If I come, and you're not here." Draven searched the immediate environment. Books could be borrowed, which made them less than ideal. He traced his fingers along the shelf, looking for a suitable hiding place. "Here," he decided, as he found the metal book end. It had a large flat plate that slid onto the shelf to keep it in place and make it moveable. The moving element was a bit of a risk, but it was the best thing in the vicinity. "Under here. You don't need to worry about leaving them for me. I mean, it's more likely that you'll be here. But I will try," he insisted, wanting Niall to understand how much he wanted to come back.

"I'll leave them if I know in advance that I won't be around. Or if I know that I'll only be around after a certain time," Niall said.

"Okay. Sounds good." Draven felt more like his usual, confident self now that they had something approaching a plan. Though his brightness faded a little as he added, "Guess I should get going."

"Yeah." Niall's shoulders slumped. "Um, hey. I don't mean to cross a line with the question thing, and you don't have to answer but are things...alright? For you? At home, I mean?"

"They're a little dull sometimes." Draven laughed, not reading anything more sinister into the question. "I've honestly been bored as heck with how my life was going."

"Oh. Okay. You're safe there?" he clarified.

"Oh. Absolutely. It's very, very safe there. So nice and so safe that no one could possibly want anything else." He sighed. "Here seems great, so far—lots of things I like anyway." He smiled at Niall.

"Thanks," Niall said, then added uncertainly, "You mean me, right? As well as the book?"

"Yes. I mean you especially, because without you I wouldn't have even found the book."

"Right. Well... You're welcome." He fiddled with the zip on his coat. "Hope to see you again."

"I'll have to find a way back," Draven said. "After all, I am indebted to you."

"How so?"

"I owe you a cup of tea. And a book recommendation."

"Serious stuff." Niall smirked, and Draven wasn't sure whether Niall was being silly, not taking this as a real promise.

"They are to me. Tea and books are serious business." This got a proper smile. Not an amused, half ironic one, but the one Draven had been looking for—a smile of shared understanding.

"Yeah, they are," Niall said. "Not that I don't trust an oath sworn on tea and books, but can I at least get...something. Your last name?"

Draven knew he had failed the phone question, and needed to offer something, but it was a powerful thing, to give someone your full name. Maybe a little risky. On the one hand, these people did not have magic, and perhaps that meant there was nothing Niall could do with this. On the other hand, maybe they had different knowledge and different powers—there could be dangers he didn't even know he was taking by offering up this information.

"Montrose. Draven Montrose. Use it well." It was a slight evocation, not even real magic. But it would have to do.

Chapter Thirteen

The portal on Niall's side was smaller, but still obvious. To Draven, at least. He was guessing people in Niall's world couldn't see it. He had left Niall several shelves away, not ready to ask *"Hey, can you see a gaping green-ish void at the end of that aisle?"* It didn't feel like a first meeting kind of question in a place that thought magic was made up. Maybe that was why they couldn't see it.

Draven stepped through the portal, and back into his own library, eyes adjusting and settling on the wooden shelves with their soft-bound books. In theory, this place had all the warmth. Now he was back here, the dark wood of the shelves and rich colours seemed to count for so little. It seemed cold in comparison to the place he'd left behind. He knew that out in his world, beyond these shelves, were the people he belonged with. The ones who would find the place he fitted. But none of that pulled him back towards his regular life. It felt empty here, and lonely.

He turned to the portal, reassured that it still glowed steadily. He had gone there and come back and nothing had exploded. That meant he could go again. It was strange how strong that pull was, to somewhere he had only known a few hours. He already missed it. Was that possible? He touched the shelf beside the portal, feeling the smooth wood against his fingers. His heart hurt at the thought of never going back. He thought about that world, going on without him. Of never finishing the book he'd started. Of never learning what all the strange machines were. Of never seeing that boy again. Niall. He played the name over and over in his head, feeling comforted by it. He stared at the emerald glow of the portal, pulsing as steadily and as brightly as it had before.

"Please don't disappear," he whispered.

He'd returned to the library before closing time, and after slipping carefully back around the door to the Special Collections, all there was to do was to wander through like he'd spent the rest of the day reading. It wasn't like that was out of character.

He stepped outside, his hand brushing the gryphon's beak from pure habit whilst his mind wandered off. The January air was chilly, and he drew his blazer around himself. It failed to shut out the cold entirely. Nonetheless, when he collected his bicycle, he cycled away from home. He needed time to process. To process, and to be ecstatic without having to explain to anyone why he was feeling that way, because he couldn't tell them. It was odd, having a secret. He'd always been an open person. But Niall was such an enjoyable secret to have. A person and a place that belonged entirely to him.

He left his bicycle at the bottom of the hill and climbed up the mound to the castle, his steps big and springy. He clambered over one of the gaps in the wall and made his way around the ruin, trailing his fingers along the stones and grinning.

"I met someone today," he told the walls or the ghosts, or whatever force it was that occupied the castle ruin and made it feel like more than a crumbling shell. "I met a boy. And I like him. His name is Niall and he's amazing, and no one here knows him."

He wanted to do something to commemorate the occasion, like writing their initials on the wall, but he knew that marking the place was wrong. Still, he had left a mark in Niall's world, and he felt like there ought to be one here too for balance. Niall deserved to exist here. He gathered a little assortment of stones, not quite sure at first what he was going to do with them. Make a pattern, maybe an N? Or he could build a little cairn with them. People did that sometimes, to show they'd been somewhere. He sorted his pebbles, picking two of the best. He took the bigger one and traced the shape on it with his finger, then held his palm flat over it focussing as hard as he could. A small "N" etched itself into the surface. It was only lightly scratched but it was legible. He knew that everyone else would regard this as a frivolous use of magic, but he didn't care. So long as Niall was real to him, it didn't matter. He repeated the procedure with the smaller pebble, adding a "D" to its surface. Part of him wanted to slip them into his pocket—to keep the token of the place and the person he'd discovered with him. But the point was to make a mark on the world, so he placed them carefully against the wall, and stacked the remainder of the stones around them protectively.

"I'm coming back," he whispered to the stones. "Next Sunday, I'm coming right back."

He sat back, contemplating. The only place he'd ever heard about was the Other World—a living hell, made up of incessant cruelty. It would definitely not have libraries, and sweet boys in daisy chain necklaces, and tea. It had been terrible tea, but it had been tea. Sometimes, he thought it might actually be good to find this Other World, so full of problems. At least then he wouldn't be bored. Wherever it was he'd stumbled across was pleasant but it needed better tea and maybe more softness in its library. He supposed that was something to be going on with. He pulled a notepad from his satchel, turned to a crisp, blank page and titled it "List of problems to solve in the world(s)," pausing to smile at the little bracketed "s" before adding:

1) Energy Crisis
2) Bad tea
3) Lack of library softness

At least he was up to three things to do now. That was, in fact, triple the number of problems he'd had to play with before, and the second one might be achievable without painful mathematics. At least, it was easy on the level of Niall. He could introduce Niall to proper tea, for which he would obviously be immediately grateful, and thus that world would be a better place. He wasn't sure how he would manage to overhaul their entire distribution and supply system. That sounded boring and logistical. Making cute boys happy sounded far more fun, so even if he only improved Niall's little corner of things, that was worthwhile. He sensed that, generally speaking, Niall was not happy.

Things were bothering him, although Draven didn't know what they were. That was a shame, and he wanted to do something to put a smile on the other boy's face. He had a few ideas about what might make Niall smile, and conveniently they were things he was interested in doing too.

He added "Solve Niall Silverstein's woes" as a fourth item on the list, smiling again at the simple magic of their full names crossing between the worlds, and wondering what Niall was doing with his.

* * *

Niall Silverstein: You HAVE to be online right now. And home
Ellen Sorn: Both. Why?
Niall Silverstein: Coming over.

Initially, Niall had thought he would want to keep Draven to himself, at least until Monday. He had visions of himself playing it all laid back, until someone got around to asking how his weekend was, at which point he could casually drop in how he'd met this guy. However, the power which Niall had exerted over the full name of Draven Montrose was the power of Google. There was nothing. No social media accounts either. He supposed that checked out with someone who claimed never to have seen a mobile phone. He'd needed to feel like he had verified that for himself. But he'd tried every platform, and every combination—initial and surname, any potential nicknames he could think of, dots and underscores. Nothing. Not even a hit on Google. No local paper report from a school sports day or GCSE results. According to the Internet, Draven didn't exist.

The Internet's unwillingness to conjure up Draven for him had him feeling restless. If he couldn't cyberstalk, then he needed to talk—to find a willing audience to recount his day to.

He headed out and grabbed a bus, jiggling his leg impatiently for the ten-minute journey to Ellen's place. She opened the door in lazy Saturday mode. Her short bubblegum pink hair was falling flat rather than gelled up and she was wearing fuzzy pyjama pants and a well-worn hoodie.

"Hey. What's with the cryptic drama texts?" She ushered Niall in with a wave of her hand. He stepped into the hallway which was crowded with fluffy boots and huge parka coats, designed to fend off the Northern cold. On the walls, lacquer work pictures and photos of Battambang did their best to evoke a warmer climate.

"Guy stuff. Good guy stuff. Maybe good guy stuff." He followed Ellen into her room, which was a stark departure from downstairs. It was no less cluttered but rather than the nick-nacks strewn around the rest of the house, it was covered in discarded t-shirts, and decorated with posters of threatening-looking bands. "I don't know. I met this guy, and I think he might be perfect for me and now I don't know if I'll ever see him again." He flopped face-down on her bed.

"How come?" Ellen lay down on her stomach beside him.

"There was this boy at the library. We got talking." He slowed down. *There was a boy, and we got talking* was pretty much the whole story, but he wanted to relive it properly—to make Ellen understand how great the afternoon had been. But there was the crux of the problem to deal with too, the thing that had made him fidgety enough to seek out company, like she was magically going to be able to fix this. He tried to think how to phrase it. He knew how it sounded on the surface of it. It was going to sound like this guy hadn't wanted to see him again, and like he was gullible for believing the line he'd been fed. But it hadn't felt that way. Okay, that was what he'd thought too, at first, but he was convinced by Draven's sincerity, and by his lack of presence on social media. "He's cute, and he's a dork and we talked all afternoon about books."

"So, has Library Boy read all your favourites?"

"Nope." Niall grinned.

"Okay. I'm surprised that's not the end of the conversation as far as you're concerned." She raised her eyebrows. "You have vetoed people over lesser crimes."

"But he wants to. I started him on them today. So, it's even better. I get to watch him discovering them. We talked through what he'd read so far, and it was like getting to read them again for the first time—having all that excitement about what might happen." That was the launchpad from which he got to burble on happily about the way he and Draven had spent the afternoon together. How great a time they'd had. How they'd shared ideas on books and history and life itself. He was sure that all she was hearing was *"nerd, nerd, nerd,"* but she was a good enough friend to let him sit and fizz with happiness even if it wasn't what floated her boat. She looked genuinely happy, and it was because his own smile was so infectious, and he had never had that effect before. He had never been so happy that he lit up a room.

"Then he had to go home." Niall's shoulders slumped, and the light went out.

"So, let me guess, You didn't ask for his contact info and now you're kicking yourself?" Ellen asked.

"No. I did."

"He didn't say no? Jerk!" She pushed herself up, looking like she was ready to go kick the universe solidly in the nuts for betraying him. He appreciated the loyalty. It had taken a lot to take the plunge. He was much more of a watch-from-a-distance guy, or even a construct-an-elaborate-fantasy-life-instead-of-face-reality one. His stomach twisted as he recalled the utter silence his remark had been met with, and that moment where he thought he was about to be brutally shot down by the only guy he'd ever admitted to...well, wanting to text. He was probably still several million steps from admitting he liked him to his face.

"No," Niall corrected her. "Well, not exactly."

"What's that mean?" she asked, raising an eyebrow.

"He doesn't have any— He's not online." Niall tried to make it sound as credible as possible.

"What? Niall, everyone has something. Even if it's just a school email address." She sounded like she was trying to work out how to let him down gently.

"No, I really think... He's unGoogleable." He led with his most convincing fact.

"No way. What's his full name?"

"I'm telling you—" Niall began. Draven's full name was the only thing he had, and he was reluctant to share, but Ellen was clearly only going to believe the evidence of her own eyes. "Montrose. Draven Montrose."

She pulled out her phone and spent a concentrated few minutes tapping away. Niall waited impatiently, sure he had already tried everything she was trying (and anxiously, in case she was able to turn up something he hadn't). But, even if she didn't want to admit that he was right, Ellen had to drop her phone and concede defeat.

"Weird," she said. "I mean, he could have fake named you. It's a pretty ridiculous name."

"I believe him."

"Seen his ID?"

"No. But, I believe him, okay? I get the impression his parents are kind of strict with what he reads too. Makes sense that he doesn't have a phone or any accounts."

"That bodes well. Parents who restrict their kids' books are usually super fine with them being queer."

"Yeah... No... I dunno... I mean, he might not even be into guys, knowing my stupid luck. I was kind of worried, but when I tried to push a bit about his homelife it sounded fine. It didn't seem fake."

"You've known him for a few hours."

"Yeah. I know but..." He weighed up his next remark, pretty sure Ellen was not going to agree with him, but the more he thought about it, the more it made sense. "I think he might be part of a cult."

Predictably, she laughed.

"No, I mean it," Niall insisted.

"Yeah, I believe that you mean it. That's what makes it funny. Sorry," she added, and Niall suspected he looked a little wounded. "But, seriously? A cult? You don't meet people from cults down the library. Certainly not round here."

"He's unGoogleable," Niall repeated. "And..." He hesitated. He wanted to say there was something off about Draven, but he didn't want Ellen's first impression to be that Draven was kind of weird. Admittedly, he was. But in a cute way. In a way that made him seem kind of vulnerable, and like he needed looking after. And only a teeny bit like his parents might be in a weird cult. There were so many good things about him. Ellen needed to understand that and understand how well they had been getting on for her to not write this whole thing off as some guy who hadn't wanted to give him his number, and Niall being gullible enough to believe it. "Maybe that's too strong a word but like, off-grid hippy types. That's the only explanation I could come up with for a lot of stuff," he added defensively. Ellen was smirking at him.

"Like what?" she asked.

Niall tried to piece it together, tried to find something more solid than *"I just get this vibe."* There was definitely *something* there—the way everything seemed so alien to Draven. The look of wonder and curiosity in his eyes hadn't only been there when he'd been reading—it had constantly roved around, checking out the smallest details of the world around him. The most concrete evidence was the phone thing, but clearly she didn't buy that.

"He hadn't even heard of the *Redbloom* trilogy," Niall said, aware that this probably wasn't going to be the argument that won Ellen away from the *"we're in special Niall land"* standpoint but unwilling to explain that his crush was fascinated by teabags.

"Not everyone's life revolves around those books, Niall," she predictably pointed out.

"I didn't say he hadn't read them. I said he's never heard of them. Like, you would have to be living under a rock not to recognise the title."

"I guess." Her eyes were still narrowed in suspicion, but at least she had let go of the idea that Niall had been brushed off. "So, got a picture?" she asked.

"No. Can't cyberstalk him, remember?"

"Next time, ask for one," she said.

"You think there's going to be a next time then?" He straightened his shoulders a little.

"Here's hoping." She shrugged.

"Yeah."

He had told one slight lie, which was that the hippy commune was the only explanation he'd been able to come up with. It was the only explanation he'd been able to come up with that she might have believed, and even that had been laughed off. His mind had gone into ultimate overdrive, thinking of fantastical explanations. Draven could be a time-traveller, for example. But this was reality. He was supposed to be sticking to it, not getting caught up in his own head.

Still, it couldn't hurt to pay attention to the details if they met again. Whether Draven was something mysterious or some confused mess of homeschooling gone wrong, Niall would get to the bottom of it—and keep him safe from the rougher edges of the world.

Chapter Fourteen

Draven had promised to see that Mage Starkweather's book was back in its place. Although his eyes had wandered over many titles in the Special Collections, they hadn't landed on that particular volume. Given that this by-a-thread technicality had been good enough once, he was fairly sure it would be again.

"Fairly sure" was not "totally sure" though. The following Sunday, he was back outside the door. His palm was sweating as he gripped the handle, his breath catching as he pushed.

He let out a sigh of relief as the door opened, and he was able to slip inside.

He didn't waste time browsing the books, but made a run straight for the portal, throwing himself in without breaking his stride.

He tumbled out the other end, finding no one in sight of his sudden, surprising entrance. More disappointingly, when he rounded the corner, Niall wasn't there. There was also no note, which was a good sign. Niall would come. Draven just happened to be here first, which was lucky because it would save Niall worrying about whether or not he'd show up. He would round the corner, and find Draven here already, reading.

Except... He bounced on the balls of his feet. Draven had come here expecting company. He was feeling chatty and cheerful.

He made his way towards the front desk, which had a grey-haired lady scanning books with a strange beeping claw. This had the added advantage that Niall would see him as soon as he walked in, and he would be reunited with him at least thirty seconds earlier. "You have a lovely library here." He smiled at the lady, whose name tag declared her to be called Pat Stephens.

"Do we?" She arched her eyebrows, eyes flicking around the building, and he wondered if she saw what he had—the boxiness, the dull grey metal of the shelves. He had assumed that people here were used to the way the library looked, and how it smelt.

"Yes." As he'd stepped out of the portal and found it unchanged, he'd felt a rush of relief. It had struck him as far less cold this time, as he was so happy to be there. "I mean, all libraries are sort of inherently nice places, aren't they? There's something pleasant and trustworthy about a library."

"I suppose so." She offered him a shadow of a smile. "Though I'm not sure this one has much to recommend it beyond that."

"Your library makes Niall happy. I hope it makes you happy too," he added because she seemed sad about the library which, coming from a librarian, he found confusing.

"Sometimes."

"Like when?"

"Pardon me?" Her smile disappeared.

"What are some times that the library makes you happy?" Draven persisted.

"That's quite a personal question, isn't it?" she asked.

"Sorry," Draven said. Talking about the good in the world was a popular subject back home—after all, it was what kept the lights on. But maybe here was different. Maybe in a world without magic, they didn't find it so important to think about goodness. He banished that thought quickly, because that sounded too like a particular story he'd heard growing up, and this place wasn't *that* place. He was sure of it. "I think it's a nice thing to talk about. Or to think about, if you don't want to tell me. I didn't mean to do something wrong."

"You're alright, pet. It's just been a bad morning." She stopped, and Draven wondered whether he was supposed to ask about that, or whether it would be rude. Or result in her telling him things he didn't want to hear. But the advantage to him keeping quiet, was that she found more to say.

"The library helps people," she answered eventually. "It helps them, and it doesn't expect much in return, except that you try to be polite—bring your books back on time, that sort of thing. It feels like that doesn't happen much, and it's worth being part of."

"That's a lovely reason," Draven said, although his brightness dimmed. Her description of the library had been a description, as far as he was concerned, of how the whole world worked. His world, anyway. He glanced towards the doors of the library, wondering what sort of place lay beyond that made the library so unusual in its regard for other humans. Though as he looked up, he found a reason to be distracted from that line of thought.

"Hello!" He offered Niall an enthusiastic hug as he reached the desk. Niall, like the shelves around him, was cold and unyielding. Draven felt a hand tentatively touching his back just as he pulled away.

"We were talking about how wonderful the library is," Draven added.

"Your friend certainly has a unique way of looking at things." Pat arched her eyebrows, nodding at a boarded-up window.

"I've always been fond of it, warts and all," Niall said.

"Aye. It'll do." She gave the desk a little pat. "Enjoy your day."

"Let's go read?" Niall suggested to Draven, and they headed into the library, back towards the section they'd occupied last time.

"You're here." Niall smiled.

"I seem to be able to get back here pretty reliably. For now." If it had worked twice, it would keep working. So long as he didn't get caught. He looked around him, once again tingling with the sheer thrill of being in an unknown world. It was strange and bright and harsh in everything, from how it was lit to how the tea tasted. But he would sort that out, and then what reasons would there be to give up coming here? He already knew he wanted to keep seeing the boy in front of him, even if he ran out of problems to solve. "I don't know if it's always going to be like that though," he admitted. "Do you still want to hang out?"

"Yes!" Niall answered, without missing a beat. "I mean, yeah," he said, running a hand through his hair. Draven weighed up the two responses, which conveyed the same message, although with Niall being far less emotive about it the second time.

"I think I liked your first answer better." He raised his eyebrows, trying to tease the enthusiastic, warm Niall back out, but he only blushed and looked at the floor. Maybe feelings were meant to be more closely guarded here?

"Am I allowed to ask how your week was?" Niall said.

"It was boring. I missed you. How was yours?"

"Classes were interesting enough. I missed you too," he said quietly. Draven noticed that Niall had needed to swallow and take a deep breath before saying that. "On which note," Niall added, hurriedly. "Can I get a picture of us together?"

"I don't know. Can you?" Draven asked, with genuine curiosity.

"May I?" Niall asked, fishing his black box out of his pocket.

"You said that was a phone."

"It is. Mostly. But it does a lot of things," Niall explained. "You can access the Intern— It has a calendar. And you can play games and stuff."

"I see." Draven tried not to regard the box with suspicion. He believed Niall, even if it was incredible that such a tiny box could do all that. He couldn't even see any part you could write on like a calendar. "Shall we ask Pat Stephens to take the photo? She seemed helpful."

"Nah, come here. Let me introduce you to selfies."

Draven shuffled over to sit beside Niall (which felt like someone had cast a warming charm all over him). Niall held the phone up in front of his face, and Draven blinked in surprise. So did the little Draven on the screen.

"So, now it's a mirror?" he asked. "How does it make pictures?"

"Like this. Smile." Niall grinned, then carefully closed his mouth, positioning his face a few different ways before sighing and clicking one of the buttons. A tiny copy of their faces went whizzing into the corner, and Niall tapped it, opening it and showing Draven.

"We're in the mobile phone!" He whispered because he was aware both that they were in the library, and thus shouting would be frowned upon, but also because he was pretty sure that most people around would find this fact utterly unremarkable.

"We are, and I look horrible. Can I take it again? Or maybe take one just of you?"

"You don't look horrible. But we can take more?" he asked, eyes shining. "How many can we take?"

"A lot." Niall shrugged.

They clicked their way along happily, and Niall let Draven control the phone, pointing out which buttons to use. Draven giggled his way through pressing them, capturing himself and Niall again and again and again. He only paused when he wondered how much energy this was taking. Nothing at home that was this much fun was free.

"It's okay to use it so much?" he checked.

"Yeah, the battery life's pretty good." Niall indicated the icon, which read 79%.

"What happens when it runs out?" Draven asked. He felt reassured by the fact that Niall took his lack of knowledge at face value.

"I recharge it."

"With?"

"Electricity."

"Oh." Draven's eyes skimmed the room, looking at the strangely bright lights, hearing the hum in the walls again. "Is that how you do things? You must have an awful lot. We have a couple of generators where I live, but they're ancient and basically falling apart. Does that make sense?"

"Yeah," Niall said.

"So, how do we get the photos out?" he asked, handing the phone back to Niall.

"Oh. Um." He hesitated. "You can get them printed. But you'd have to go somewhere to do it. If it stops raining, we could walk into town later and do it. And see what other tea we can find."

"Maybe." Draven liked the sound of photographs he could hold, and of fancy tea shops, but he was mindful of what Niall had said last week—the implication that it should be inherently obvious that someone wouldn't want to be here. There was also what Pat Stephens had said that morning, suggesting that, outside of the library, people were not kind or respectful. Both of these things bothered him. This world was sweet. It was his fun little adventure place, and it had Niall and libraries and, beyond the tea, bad things were not supposed to exist. Niall seemed to have accepted his total ignorance of things here, which helped open up the possibility of asking questions. He could ask if it was safe. He considered the question, and all the possible things Niall might say in response. "If you think it's a good idea," he said instead. He trusted Niall. Niall understood the world they were in and understood that Draven didn't. Niall was not the kind of person who would lead him somewhere dangerous. And, if he avoided asking questions that he might not like the answers to, he wouldn't have to hear anything unpleasant.

* * *

Niall watched Draven as they walked through town, gaining evidence for the theory he had started to form last time. It would have been hard not to notice, even if he hadn't been looking for it. On the one hand, Draven was clearly wary. He was more tense than he had been in the library. He also looked around him with a certain degree of intensity— his eyes didn't skim over things the way Niall's did, dismissing them as everyday and mundane. He paused to read adverts. His behaviour stood out too. He kept his excitement close to his chest as they printed out photos in Boots, but it was evident the machine fascinated him. Outside, he stooped to pick up litter, carrying it to the next available bin, perplexed by its presence on the street.

Niall was used to striding along, due to long legs and no need to loiter between the little boltholes he'd developed around town. He found himself having to slow down for Draven. Nothing about his hometown had ever particularly struck him as worthy of special attention. It served to confirm his idea that something beyond ordinary levels of odd was going on, and he was curious what was going through Draven's head.

The café he'd chosen was small and cosy. It smelt of the warm leather that made up most of the seats, with a mingled air of tea and coffee. Niall usually opted for a table in the back corner, and automatically went to sit there, though once he had, he noticed Draven's eyes were drawn to, or rather through, the large glass window. The café undeniably made for good people-watching, and the tables in the window might have suited Draven better. Still, Niall felt more comfortable in the back. The trouble with looking out was people could also look in. He wasn't sure about being seen with a strange boy who no one else knew. He wasn't embarrassed by Draven or his strangeness—or at least, he didn't want to think he was—but it already felt a good deal more exposed being out here in town than it had done in the library, and he needed to retreat to his corner.

They ordered (English Breakfast with milk and sugar for Niall, Earl Grey, black for Draven) and Draven went to wash his hands from litter picking.

"So, what were you thinking?" Niall asked, as they settled in with their mugs of tea. "I can't imagine town looks great today," he added, nodding at the gloomy grey sky that still swirled overhead. *Or any other.*

"Studying the language, mostly. We don't quite tally, you and I."

Niall nodded. It was more than accent that marked Draven out as...as what? Again, "different" was the word that sprung to mind. Niall's own Northeast accent was more of a slight suggestion—he thought most people would tell he was from here, but people would only fail to understand him if they'd already decided not to listen. He couldn't pin down where Draven was from. His vocabulary was on the posh side, but he accented a lot of his vowels the way that Niall did. He couldn't work out if he'd started out as broad Geordie but had it half pulled out of him by some secluded boarding school somewhere, or…or what? He almost sounded like an old recording, sometimes, not only the vocabulary but the way his accent lilted, still definitely Northern but somehow clipped and different. Or was Niall willing the data to fit his own theory?

"You seem more formal than I am," Niall said.

"Do I?" Draven smirked. "My mother always tells me off for dropping too much slang into conversation."

"Like what? What's a popular word where you're from right now."

"Hmm. There's cuppa."

"As in…?" Niall gestured at their teas.

"As in someone who is your cup of tea. Someone you'd like to get to know better, if you get my drift." He raised his eyebrows playfully.

"Right. Um. Do you have one of those? Back home?" Niall asked. He was surprised by his own directness, but he knew he'd kick himself all week if he let slip the opportunity to find out if Draven was attached.

"Not back home, no." Draven smiled, and Niall felt the other boy's foot sliding up against his. "You?" he asked.

"P-pardon?" Niall stammered, concerned by the turn a perfectly interesting conversation about slang had taken. Out here. In semi-public.

"What do you call that, and do you have one?" Draven asked.

What if the guys from his old high school saw? Rationally, he knew that he and Draven were well away from the window. Someone would have to be at an impossible angle, perhaps under the table, to get a glimpse of the fact that Draven was almost definitely playing footsie with him right now. But he was sure, as he always was whenever he dared to peek out from behind his carefully constructed parapet walls, that anyone looking at him was going to somehow *know*. He suspected there was some truth to that, in that he was capable of turning particularly spectacular shades of scarlet, and he could already feel his cheeks glowing. What if it was witnessed by someone who was a jerk? Or what if his mum came in? What if she saw him with this strange boy that she'd never met, leaning across the table making eyes at him, and that was how she found out? It wasn't like his mum was going to have a problem with it. He knew that really. But still...

"I dunno. How's your tea?" he asked, instead of answering the question, abruptly shifting his foot away. He regretted both actions almost at once. Both had been done clumsily, and it showed in the look of confusion that passed across Draven's face. Niall wanted to apologise, but what was he supposed to say? *Sorry, I'm not used to guys hitting on me? Sorry, you don't have to stop—that was nice? Sorry, I like you?* The remarks running through his head all sounded like they were going to dig him into a bigger hole than he'd just made, varying from sounding like he was kind of homophobic to outing himself. It didn't seem like that was a secret. Whilst some of the other are-we-just-making-friends-or-is-there-something-more-here stuff was pretty subtle, sliding your foot up someone's calf was solidly not just friends territory. It suggested Draven liked him. He wanted that. But talking, having a real conversation about the possibility of Them was also a lot scarier once it was really on the table. Especially when that table was in public.

"My tea is lovely." Draven's voice was calm, but the look he gave Niall over the rim of the teacup was calculating, trying to understand what was going on. He looked like he was going to say something else, but lifted his mug, swallowing down whatever it was with a gulp of tea.

"Do you know what I mean if I tell you you're being a worky ticket?" Draven asked. "Not that you are," he added hastily. "But, back to slang?"

"I do." Niall did his best to relax back into the conversation. "Our old chemistry teacher was proper fond of saying that. So..." He hesitated, assuming that the question embargo was still on. *"You're not from too far away then?"* sounded too personal. "Someone calls you that? Often?" he teased.

"Yes," Draven admitted.

"What for?" Niall asked, deciding to push his luck a little.

"I ask too many questions. I want to understand too many things."

"That doesn't sound like a bad thing."

"That's why I like it here. Or at any rate, with you. You understand. You answer things. You think. At home, it's not like I mean to get in trouble. I don't think I'm a bad person. I try hard not to be. But I don't see things the same way as everyone else. Am I a terrible person, for not seeing it how they do?"

"No. Of course not. Why would you be?"

"Disagreement is like, a big deal. I'd be disrupting everyone's calm."

"Sometimes things need shaking up. Society never moves forward if people keep thinking the same things they always have done."

"I've often thought so too." Draven got a faraway look in his eyes. But it was the kind of faraway that took Niall, at least his words, with him. Niall wondered whether Draven was satisfied with being close in thought—whether this counted a bridging back over the gap he'd created with his clumsiness. But it wasn't as if he could ask.

* * *

As the library windows darkened, Niall noticed Draven fidgeting and glancing at his watch. He wondered whether he should ask if he needed to get going. Clearly, he needed to. But Niall was not keen to hurry him. Since they had returned to the library, things had felt, in some ways, much more comfortable. Except that Niall was still beating himself up in his head over what had happened earlier.

"Hey, you know what time it is?" Draven sighed, closing his book.

"Still really, really early?" Niall placed a hand over Draven's watch.

"Sadly not," Draven said, eyes tracing the hand on his wrist.

"You are going to come back again, aren't you?" Niall checked.

"Of course. Soon as I can. The debt's up to two cups of tea now," Draven pointed out.

"Right. But I didn't... Upset you? Put you off?" For all they had returned to something like normality this afternoon, Niall still felt he couldn't be sure. It felt fake. They had crept into new territory, and he had forced them to beat a hasty retreat, like it had never happened.

"I want to see you again. And I want to hug you goodbye. Is that allowed?"

"Yes," Niall said, relieved that he hadn't managed to push the door closed completely on physical contact. He stood, pulling Draven to his feet. Draven's arms slid under his, around his back, and Niall found himself resting his head on top of Draven's. He could smell a faint herbal aroma, more delicate and pleasant than the "Cool Ice" and "Game On" sold to boys (and which, now Niall considered it, he had no idea how to describe, other than artificial mass market teen boy). It wasn't how you hugged a friend. He felt that twist of anxiety in his stomach again, at being so intimate with another boy in public, but he also didn't want to let go. He kind of wanted to pull back enough to be looking Draven in the eyes. To be face to face, so they could... But hadn't he put the brakes on that? Wouldn't it be confusing to unbrake it right now?

"Bye then," Niall murmured into Draven's hair, making no move to break away from him.

"Yeah, bye," Draven echoed, pressing his head against Niall's chest.

"K... Bye," Niall said again. It would definitely be confusing. Right? They didn't have time to talk about what it meant. He didn't know how to kiss someone, and he might make a mess of it, and if that happened, he'd like to at least have time to try again, and what if he had horrible tea breath and...and he wasn't ready. He was making all these excuses to himself, but the bottom line was he was coming up with those because he plain didn't have the nerve to do it.

"Bye," Niall repeated, with something close to resolution this time, pulling away. He hesitated, his hands on Draven's arms, then stepped back. "See you next week?" he confirmed again, because as Draven stepped away, Niall thought he looked disappointed.

"Yeah." Draven gave him a last, longing look. "Next week."

He left. Niall slumped against the bookcase, wondering whether banging his own head against it repeatedly would be a good course of action, because he had definitely made the wrong move. Again.

Chapter Fifteen

Monday morning rolled around again. The most painful point of the week. The high of seeing Niall was wearing off, and it was the point at which there were the most hours in the Energy Makers' Guild still ahead of him.

The morning crawled by, with time moving like pouring treacle. There was not enough tea in the universe to make him feel like his soul wasn't steadily choking on the stagnant atmosphere.

He was pretty sure he wasn't even doing a good job of faking any kind of attention today. Instead of the tedious sheet of numbers in front of him, he was occupying himself with the much more pressing problem of what was going on with him and Niall. Why had Niall pushed him away when he'd tried to flirt with him? Why hadn't Niall kissed him? The obvious answer to both of these would be that Niall didn't feel that way about him. If it had just been the flirting thing, maybe he would have convinced himself that that was the case. But Niall had gradually drawn him back in over the course of the afternoon, until they had ended with That Hug. Standing, with his face buried in Niall's shirt, finding out that he smelt sharp and strange, like everything else in that world, but not being able to pull himself away. It had been perfect. Maddeningly so. It had been the "if you don't end this by kissing me, I think I'm going to die of frustration" kind of good-bad-amazing.

Longing like that could not be one-sided. Niall hadn't wanted him to leave, and everything about that moment had sent shivers running down his spine. Draven had replayed it over and over in his head since Sunday, most of the time giving it a different ending, one that involved him getting pushed against a bookshelf in the most unambiguous of terms. Fun as such mental indulgences were, they didn't answer his question as to why that hadn't happened. Given that they were not particularly suitable work thoughts, he was pursuing the question instead of the fantasy.

It sucked that he couldn't talk to anyone about this. He couldn't fudge the details and say "some guy" because everyone would then be watching who he was hanging out with and might realise that he wasn't hanging out with anyone in particular. Niall's world seemed to have no such problem. They had slipped through the streets with apparent anonymity, not needing to smile at or make small talk with everyone they met. But here, people might notice Draven was spending most of his Sundays simply disappearing into a shelf of books. He actively needed to not draw attention, and keeping everything he was thinking and feeling inside his own head was hard enough. There was scarcely storage space, let alone room to start shuffling it about to make sense of it.

What would stop him, if he liked someone? He couldn't think of anything. His eyes landed on Melvin, working across the table from him. It was considerably harder to imagine him asking someone out. So, maybe Niall was shy? Except he wasn't, not with Draven. They talked for hours. Even if he was too shy to ask someone out, that wasn't the same as pushing them away when they tried to flirt with you. He thought about things that had held him back. He'd certainly put the brakes on with a fair few guys, where he'd not been feeling it. But that was just a wordier way of thinking what he'd already thought—he was sure Niall was feeling it and—

"What?" Draven mouthed, when he felt Yvette kick him under the table. He managed to at least be somewhat covert because that was usually meant to be a subtle attention getter. Even though he'd been a million miles away, he could, apparently, still return to the world with a degree of subtlety. "Oh," he muttered as he caught sight of Rowan coming out of her office. He bent his head over his page, scribbling numbers into the column whilst she went to get her files. "Thanks," he added to Yvette.

He was pretty sure it was not the first time he had completely zoned out that morning. Realising he didn't give a flying piece of sage, combined with falling head over heels in love was the most lethal combination imaginable for his productivity. He tried telling himself he needed to maintain some air of being on this plane of existence, and meeting his deadlines, because if he didn't, if his cover got blown, he might not be able to go back and see Niall again. He thought that might be the one and only way to motivate himself. Still, even with the incentive that he was scanning mindless columns of numbers in the pursuit of true love, it was far too easy to let himself think about Niall instead and assume he'd be productive later. He felt that a huge portion of his energy was going on bullying his brain into not being distracted, so that he was working painfully slowly. But he was still working. He made a point of ploughing diligently through his numbers until tea break, at which point Yvette caught up with him.

"What's got you so distracted?" she asked.

"Like you don't think staring off into blank space is more appealing than this," he countered. Yvette was the hardest person to hide this from, both because he wanted so badly to tell her, but also because she knew him well enough to read him.

"So, what were you dreaming about instead?" she asked, and he knew she wasn't going to let it go without a good answer.

"A cute boy." The basic shape of the truth could be conveyed easily and safely enough, so long as he avoided specifics.

"Ooh, who?" she asked, her eyes lighting up.

"That would be telling," Draven said primly. That would only pique her curiosity, but at least it gave him time to think.

"Yeah, it would, and that'd be interesting." She raised her eyebrows. "Since when are you the type who doesn't kiss and tell?"

"There isn't any kissing to tell about." Those few words contained all the misery of his current predicament. Even if he couldn't tell her more than that, it was a relief to share part of it.

"How come? You're not shy. Oh no, don't tell me he isn't into guys. Don't do that to yourself," she said.

"No, I'm pretty sure he is. I think he might even be into me. I don't know—I guess that's why I don't want to name names. It feels like it's jinxing it given that nothing's happening right now," he added.

"Okay…" He could tell she was a little disappointed, possibly even suspicious given that he usually gushed about the people he liked. But it usually didn't work out, so perhaps there was some logic to the line he was feeding her.

"He's kind of quiet. No, that's not it," he added hastily, because the first person that came to mind when he said that was Melvin, and the last thing he wanted was Yvette thinking their cohort buddy was his cuppa, or worse still, trying to nudge them together. "I mean, we talk lots. We can have a great conversation about what we're reading, or what we think of the world. But he gets shy about relationship stuff. I feel like if I go in there like 'Hey you're hot as hell and I'm dying to press you up against a bookshelf,' he's going to die of embarrassment. I prefer my boyfriends alive."

"Shame there's no Guild of Necromancy. Cos then you could try that strategy and if it went badly wrong, no harm done."

Draven laughed into his tea, feeling very grateful for Yvette. "Thanks."

"No problem. If you want to come over after work, we can always try asking the candles or the cards," she said.

"Is that your answer to everything?" He tried not to sound too sceptical but it was hard not to.

"It's fun to try." She shrugged. "Turning your problem over a few times with someone else usually gives you insight. I'm guessing most of that's not magic, otherwise it wouldn't be free to use, but what's the harm?"

Draven imagined himself floating his problems past Yvette and having her and the arts of divination reply. There was no way to ask all the what-do-I-tell-him, how-do-I-make-this-work questions without it sounding suspect, little as he believed that any supernatural force would intervene to help her provide the answers. People didn't meet tall, handsome strangers, or go to unknown places. There was no need to hide or explain magic when mages were the only people in the world. And even if Draven made it vague, the idea of hiding one's true nature was incomprehensible, when the merit and apprenticeships were designed to uncover exactly who everyone was and where they fitted. Still, as she'd said, it was more about hanging out.

"Sure," he said. "That sounds fun. Thanks."

"No problem. You'll tell me as soon as there's something to tell, right?"

"Of course." He swallowed down a ball of guilt. "You're my best friend." There was already plenty to tell, but he couldn't. That wasn't going to change, even if things between him and Niall did.

He redirected his focus to more immediate issues. "Any advice on how I survive that?" He gestured at their worktable. "Or at least pass for someone whose head is in the game?"

"Stare at the paper instead of off into space even if you're not thinking about it," she advised. "That's what I do."

"It physically hurts," he mumbled, leaning back against the tea table.

"Your brain from processing the data, or your poor heart?" she asked, and he knew she was being tongue in cheek, but he sighed and answered honestly.

"Both."

* * *

"Hey." Ellen dropped into the seat next to Niall on the bus. Their transport times didn't always overlap but on Monday mornings they both had a class first thing, and mostly ended up on the same bus, if Ellen got up on time. Niall usually looked for her out of the window, ready to call to the driver to hold up if he saw her running, but today he had been bent intently over his phone. He hastily pushed the power button, switching his phone to its lockscreen (updated to be a silver rose, as of the weekend).

"Before I forget, I was at yours Saturday night if my parents ask," she said. Niall was sure he would hear about whatever date, vodka-fuelled debauchery or combination thereof he was covering for in due course. "Good weeken—" Ellen cut herself off as Niall struggled to contain his smile. "Library boy came back, didn't he?" she asked.

"Yes!"

"Aaand?"

"And he's awesome. We talked about books, and he's interested in everything I'm doing in my classes. And..." He hesitated. He sort of felt the need to confess his failure and have someone make it alright. Ellen was the easiest person to tell, but he knew her advice would be to grow a pair and do it.

"Aaand?" she pressed. "You lectured him on sci-fi and physics and I'm sure that's super-hot on your planet. Did you kiss him?"

"No. And keep your voice down, please?"

"Sorry. Tell me more about your date?" she whispered coaxingly, and Niall didn't need much persuasion to return to a subject he was enjoying.

"I got pictures." He held up his phone and opened it, sliding through a few of the photos he'd been looking at. Ellen was quick to seize the phone.

"These aren't going to get X-rated if I go too far are they? Wait, how many did you take?"

"A lot. I told you, his parents won't let him have a phone, so he was sort of fascinated by it."

"Ok, but half of these are blurry as hell, you could delete this one for starters."

"Don't!" He grabbed his phone back. "What if he doesn't come back? What if these are the only pictures we ever get to take together?"

"You will move on, date a boy from this universe and will not want shite, blurry selfies of some guy you met twice and never even kissed," Ellen said.

Niall traced a finger over the picture. That was how Ellen worked, not how he did. If he never saw— He couldn't even finish the thought.

"He said he'll keep coming, if he can, and he was more optimistic than last time." He jutted his chin out, defying her doubt, even if—or especially because—she was saying the exact thing he kept trying not to think. For a second, Ellen looked like she was going to argue the point, but then she backed down.

"He is cute. I'll give you that," she said. "You look good together. Look at you snuggling in for selfies." She nodded at the phone still clutched in Niall's hand. "How come you didn't kiss him? Look how close you are."

"I dunno." That technically wasn't true. He knew exactly why he hadn't, but he also knew it wasn't a valid reason to keep holding himself back. "Just...stuff."

"But you want to?" Ellen prompted, sounding excited.

Niall twisted a finger through his bracelet. He had often talked in the abstract about how he wanted a boyfriend, but he'd never latched on to any specific person before, in spite of all Ellen's prompting. It wasn't like college was swimming with choices, but even when they were people watching, she'd try to draw him out and he'd shut down.

"Yeah. I do," Niall admitted, with a wistful smile. Wanting to and getting to felt like very different things.

"He wants to kiss you too."

"Do you think so?"

"Yes! Look at how he's looking at you."

Niall looked. It was an especially cute picture, with Draven's eyes turned away from the camera, looking at Niall instead. It was easy to make up a story to go with that image. It was easy to think it could be the moment before a kiss. But was he seeing that because he wanted to? "How do I know? What if he doesn't?"

"Niall, I swear a guy could walk into Oxfam books waving a rainbow flag and declaring that he wants a knowledgeable young man to appraise his Phillip K. Dick, and your response would be to dive behind a bookshelf. Read the signals. Act on them."

"Yeah, I think he does. Or did. He was being kind of touchy with me."

"And?"

"I freaked and got him to back off."

"Niall!" Ellen punched him lightly on the arm. "Is this about your mum?"

"Okay, that makes it sound way more Freudian nightmare than it actually is."

"Give me your goddamn phone and I'll text her right now. 'Dear Mum, I'm gay.' Job done. Your mum's cool. She's not going to care."

"I know. I..." He folded in on himself, not sure how to handle it. In some senses, he felt like there was nothing to announce. He knew his parents would be fine with it, so why make a big deal out of it? Except, they obviously didn't know. There was also the plain teenage embarrassment about talking to them about anything to do with his love life. It had made it easy to put it off, especially when he didn't have one. Now though, now there was something to tell. He didn't like feeling like Draven was a secret, not when he made him so happy. He also wanted to make sure he told his parents, rather than someone spotting him swapping saliva with Draven against the library wall and it getting back to them that way. He supposed one way to stop that happening was to avoid doing that with Draven, but that was not a particularly appealing option. "I'll tell them. Or my mum, at least. She's usually in when I get home."

"It's gonna be fine. Next time you see Library Boy, go for it. Preferably before—"

"—the world ends, yeah I know," he said. He was never sure if Ellen was joking when she said things like that. It was depressingly plausible, and he tended to agree with her, but he preferred not to believe it. "What if that isn't the right thing to do?" he asked. The memories of Draven playing footsie and sliding his arms around Niall's waist replayed, but they seemed like something that had happened to someone else. They were drowned out by the loud mental siren that told him he was clumsy and bad at this, and that even if Draven had liked him, he'd blown it.

"Better to know. I am now your relationship adviser. I told you to get pictures, you did it. I am telling you to make a move, or don't come back to me."

* * *

"I've always loved your room." Draven followed Yvette in, staring up at the whole of the galaxy, which was produced incredibly realistically on her ceiling. The Mirror of Venus was directly above her bed, giving strength to her divinations, which he forgave even if it pushed his favourite constellation, Antinous, off to the side. Other people's houses always fascinated him. His parents were relentlessly practical, and it was the best way of blending in. Not that there was any disapproval to go around. Not that it mattered to stand out. But it was the sensible option, in line with what most people chose. Yvette's house was artsy, and her room was easily the best bit.

"Thanks. Remember those stories my mums used to make up about all those completely crazy buildings? Like, places where the bed floated in the middle of the room, or windows that would show you a different view every day," she said.

"Or huge old castles with secret passageways concealed by spells and you'd have to do a dance to open them," Draven finished the list. "I remember." He had lived for those stories.

"So, carro or carto?" she asked, returning to the business of the day.

"No tea leaves?" Draven asked.

"You always pick that. It's so slow. You have to wait until you're done drinking to get your questions answered."

"I thought the point was hanging out?" he teased. He had never been the most patient person either, but the idea that life's answers were at the bottom of a teacup sounded about right. Besides, it would give him some extra thinking time on how to handle any awkward questions. "We can play interior design while we wait."

"Alright," she agreed, pulling a tattered magazine from the shelf and dropping it on the bed. "Have a look through that while I make some tea."

Draven lifted the artefact, turning it over carefully in his hands. It was in colour and out of fashion, and had always been one of his and Yvette's favourite things to look through. The cover had been ripped off, and thus the date wasn't visible. A number of the pages inside were missing or damaged. But the ones there gave a glimpse into a world he'd only barely been able to imagine. It wasn't as outlandish as the buildings Yvette's mums had described for them, but it still overflowed with magic. Wallpapers with moving patterns had been in vogue whenever this had been made. Whilst there were some practical ideas—curtains which drew themselves back so you could be woken by sunshine instead of an alarm clock—most of it was frivolous. It used magic for the fun of it.

"Can you imagine living like this?" he asked when Yvette returned with their tea.

"I know." Her eyes traced over the faded magazine. "So, if we had a green day would you go for the moving wallpaper or the singing kettle?"

"Oh, if we had a green day, why not both?" He laughed. "You?"

"My mums always said they wished they could make my stars shine for real." She gestured at the ceiling. "I'd have them shimmer and move like the actual constellations. There'd be a whole guild dedicated to doing things like that. Or no guilds at all—I'd be a painter and make all these fun things."

"You could do all the spells from my grandma's book," he added, referencing the old book of beauty spells they'd spent half their childhood poring over. It was crammed full of wild hairdos, and suggestions of a morning routine that would cost a lifetime of merit, even if it was legal.

"I wish we could read more stuff like that. Stuff from when magic was more powerful. It's really hard to find."

"Guess they don't want us to be jealous," Draven said. "Wouldn't be good for productivity."

"I suppose. But, is having something to dream about so destructive?"

"Not sure." Draven had always needed something big to believe in—the idea of turning the whole world upside down. Getting that back had kicked him out of his slump. But he was aware he was marching down a different road than the one he was supposed to be on.

They perused the magazine, decorating imaginary houses to their hearts' content until their tea had cooled sufficiently to drink.

"Right, tip out your tea leaves and speak your question," Yvette demanded.

"Why aren't things going anywhere?" he asked, holding out his saucer.

"Y'know, the mystical forces would probably be guided better if you were a tad more specific," she informed him, raising her eyebrows. "A name might help."

"And magic works best when you have pure intentions," Draven reminded her. "If this was a ruse to get me to tell—"

"It's not. But you might want to avoid words like 'thing.' You wanna ask the cosmos why you can't get laid, tell it that. You're not going to make it blush."

"I don't just want to get laid. I want something real. With the boy I like. I want to know whether that's possible, and what's holding him back."

"Better. So, I see an arch... A circle... This could be something with a tail. I'm going to look those up." She fished out her symbol dictionary. "Anything you see?"

"Blobs." Draven rolled his eyes, but with a fond smile. "You still need a dictionary?"

"Course I do, there's bloody loads of these things. Tarot's way easier to memorise."

Draven watched, as Yvette flipped through the book and made notes. It was always hard to gauge how seriously she took this.

"Okay," she concluded, after a few minutes of consulting the dictionary and his saucer, "you've got an arch which usually means success—the bridge to a good thing, or even something life-changing. So, I'm guessing you're on the right track—he's good for you, and he's interested. A lot of the things I looked up lead to the idea of change or adventure. Being a bit of a restless soul. I can't tell if that's something that's happening, or something that's standing in your way. You said he's quiet. Maybe you're kinda scaring him with your energy."

"But he likes me anyway?" Draven asked. Because even if he knew that most of this had to be coming from Yvette knowing him, it wasn't a million miles wide of the mark. The library lady had accused him of getting too personal too quickly. Maybe he was too much for people over there.

"Seems likely. But... Hmm, that's weird." Yvette traced a thin wiggle that had formed on the edge of the saucer. "How can he be good for you and dishonest?"

"It says *he's* being dishonest?" Draven asked.

"Well, no. There's dishonesty. But it wouldn't be you."

Draven tried not to squirm with guilt. "It might be." He was keeping a huge secret from Niall. It felt like they'd got to know each other but that was kind of one-sided. Without knowing the truth, Niall wasn't going to be able to understand whether he could trust Draven to keep showing up. Draven didn't know if he could trust himself on that front either. But he couldn't ask Niall to take the gamble on him unless it was all out on the table.

"How come? That's not like you." Yvette scrutinised him.

"I got all in my head about something, but you're right. I should just be myself. What tipped you off?" he asked. It all looked like crumpled tea leaves to him.

"Snakes can mean deceit. Or at least, the need to shed something off before you start again."

"Sounds like a plan," Draven agreed.

* * *

Niall let himself in, preparing himself. He had played the scene out a few times in his head but still wasn't sure what he wanted to say. It sort of depended on what his mum said first. But as he opened the door, and called a tentative "hello" into the house, nothing but silence came back to him. He was home first. He'd spent the bus ride back playing this over and over in his head, getting more and more nervous. Now she wasn't in. She wasn't in for him to come out. He found himself giggling at that, but also his brain kept hashing and rehashing ways to phrase it. *I like this boy… I like boys… I'm gay.* The last one was the most factually unambiguous, but it was a weird response if she led with *"How was your day?"* This wasn't specific to today. It was a sort of ongoing thing.

He needed tea. He wandered into the kitchen, putting the kettle on and clutching a large striped mug to his chest whilst he waited for it to boil, already deriving comfort from the thought of having the mug warm and full in his hands. His mind half drifted back as he waited. Maybe he could dwell on the best things about Sunday instead of worrying. He'd found someone he actually liked. Draven seemed to like him back. He smiled to himself. Before the kettle had boiled, however, he heard the key in the latch and felt his heart in his throat.

"Aha." His mum poked her head around the door, hearing the soft hiss of the rapidly heating kettle. "Your summoning spell worked. Got enough water to make a pot?" she asked.

Niall nodded, well aware that any of his thought through responses were not going to segue well off that and waited for the next question.

"Had a good day?" she asked breezily.

"Yeah." Niall managed to add a word to the second nod, but felt like the rest had dried up.

"What have you been up to?"

"College," was all he managed, and obviously she knew that. His voice was trembling. It was practically squeaking.

Why was it fucking trembling and squeaking, like this wasn't embarrassing enough, and like he was about to go to pieces when this didn't have to be a big fucking deal? It was just a conversation that he knew was going to be fine and—and now his mum was obviously alert to the fact that he was not fine and had paused in fetching the biscuit tin and was turning back towards him.

"Are you okay?"

"Yes." That was true. He was—or at least he was supposed to be. "I... It's just...um... Mum, I'm gay."

"Oh. Okay."

There was a beat of silence in which he waited for any further response, wondering whether that was okay fine, or okay bad, or okay neutral. It was the least indicative word possible, or at least it felt like it in that moment.

"Is that all you're going to say?" he asked.

"What would you like me to say?" she asked calmly.

"I...I don't know. Isn't this a big deal?"

"Well..." She paused, and Niall was sure she was picking her words carefully, which was supposed to be a considerate thing to do, but right now he wished she'd say something— anything. "I guess maybe this moment is, and I'm glad you told me." She reached out to offer him a hug. Niall, who had long since overtaken her in height, collapsed in on himself in order to fall into her arms and be squeezed. "But in any other way, of course not, love. Did you think it would be?"

"No. I...not really. I just...I wasn't sure how to say it."

"Well. That worked," she teased him. "Kettle's boiled. Let's make that tea and talk about it."

"Talk about it?"

"You can tell me whatever you want to tell me," she rephrased. "Do you want to talk about this or go back to chatting about nothing?"

"Yes." He was aware that his response was not helpful. He sort of wanted to say a million things, now that he could, now that it didn't have to be a secret, but he also desperately wanted to not be the focus of intense attention. It didn't feel like they could go back to chatting about the weather (though there was a lot to say about that, it had been quite ridiculous that day, up and down like a yo-yo) but it was sort of comforting to know they could end up back there, once he'd vented out all his feelings.

They carried their tea into the living room, and he tapped his fingers against the cup, trying to work out how or where to begin.

"Any particular reason today was the day?" she asked.

"Yeah. Kind of. I mean, I wanted to. For a while. But now, there's this boy." He fidgeted, looking more at his tea than at her. "I like him. I think he likes me but I got sort of freaked out about it, I guess."

"Well, if you think he likes you back, that's a good start. Someone at college?" she asked.

"No." He closed his hands tighter around the tea. He didn't want to have to explain Draven because he knew he couldn't.

"Why did you freak out?"

"I think he was flirting with me. And, I guess that's good. But then I thought about other people seeing. I thought about if you saw, and if that was how you found out. It also feels like a big difference to know I like boys and to actually try having a boyfriend." Little as he liked to admit it, Ellen had sort of hit the nail on the head. He liked the idea of having someone, but whilst it had still been a fantasy it had been safe. It could be fluffy and perfect and never go wrong. Doing it in real life was a lot more complicated.

"Well, I'm glad you told me. But I wouldn't want to be the reason why you don't do things. It's your life. So long as what you're doing doesn't hurt anyone, and isn't bad for you— You said it's not someone at college, where did you meet this...boy? Man? How old?"

"My age. At the library."

"Ok. Good. It's scary to take the plunge. It always is. And I know there are different kinds of scary out there for you." She sighed. "Are you being bullied?"

"No." Not at college. But he didn't say that part. Because it would be obvious what was being left out of that sentence, and it wouldn't do to worry about things that were in the past.

"Is there anything I can do about things right now?" she asked.

"Hugs?" He leant in. It felt good to have his mum on his side again. Not that she ever hadn't been, she just hadn't known that she needed to be. Now she did, and she was being the best. "It's probably going to be okay," he assured her, and himself. "Like you said, at least he might like me back. And I've got you, and Ellen and people."

And, he thought, taking a steadying sip of tea, *no more excuses to avoid acting on my feelings.*

Chapter Sixteen

Choose a book and leave, Draven thought, managing not to glare at the mage casually browsing the history aisle. He knew full well the door to the Special Collections was in easy sight of where she was standing, because it was almost exactly where he kept watch from, checking whether or not anyone else had gone in.

He had things to do. He needed to jump through a portal and confess to being a mage. Was that really what he was planning on? It sounded so far beyond his wildest imaginings. Then, hopefully, he was going to drag Niall to some quiet corner of the library and not put him down until it was time to come home. Assuming Niall didn't...do what exactly? He had heard of people burning magic-users alive, but he wasn't sure if that was real or a myth, and anyway, Niall wasn't the sort, however badly he took the revelation. He shouldn't take it badly though. He liked magic. He liked Draven.

Finally, the other mage made her choice and moved on. Draven gave a quick glance around and bolted through the door.

He ran so hard and fast, straight for the portal, that he rounded the end of the aisle in Niall's world slightly out of breath.

Niall was there. That was step one, although Draven hadn't really doubted that he would be. Draven had just enough time to grin at him, before he noticed the tension that was radiating off Niall.

"Hi. It's good to see you?" Draven tried, finding it squeaked out like a question.

"You too."

Okay, that was a good start.

"Don't we hug?" he asked. He was aware that he might have pushed a bit far last time, that he had perhaps rushed Niall and been too forward, as the library lady had said. But he hadn't expected that to put them further back than they'd ended last time.

"Yeah. Um. If you want," Niall offered.

"I always want hugs. So long as you want them too," he added, because Niall wasn't looking any less uncomfortable. Still, Niall moved forward, long limbs jerking mechanically, until he was near enough for Draven to wrap him in a hug. This wasn't his world, but it felt like he was in exactly the right place because he finally had what he'd been missing all week. He was relieved that, when they parted, Niall was smiling to himself.

"That's better. You look more like yourself now," Draven said as they separated.

"I...I'm pretty sure the awkward mess is me, actually. I'm not sure what you do to make that go away."

"You don't give yourself enough credit."

"I'm glad you came back," Niall said.

Did you think I wouldn't? Draven held the question back, because it was an entirely fair thing for Niall to think. One he needed to find a way to explain.

"Do you want to read outside?" Niall asked. "The library has a little bit of a garden."

"I can't take my book," he pointed out.

"Sure you can. I'll check it out for you."

"What if I run off with it and sully your good name with the library forever?" Draven teased.

"I trust you not to. You seem like too much of a gentleman."

"Thanks. It's nice to be trusted." Draven smiled. *Hey, speaking of trusting me not to be a jerk who runs away...* Except he wasn't going to promise that. He was going to tell the truth and let Niall judge for himself whether he was worth the risk. Niall, who bought him cups of tea, and checked out books for him, and was always waiting right where Draven had left him. For the first time in his life, Draven found himself thinking someone might deserve better than what he could offer.

"It's nice to have someone to trust," Niall replied. There was that pause, that beat again that so often passed between them. They were great at creating those little moments that would have been perfect to fill with something—with taking his hand, with leaning in to kiss him. But it still wasn't fair for Draven to do that.

"Shall we go?" Draven asked, nudging him.

"Yeah, sure." Niall nudged him back.

They made their way outside. It was one of those freak spring-like days that broke through early in the year, confusing all the plants and risking that they stuck their heads above ground too soon. But it was hard to be unhappy with it as they made their way through the small scrap of green. They found a spot towards the far end of it. Even with the weather, the garden had few visitors—those who wanted to make use of the library were inside, and those who wanted to be outdoors had gone in search of better greenery. They sat, and Draven ran his hands through the grass. Niall was picking at it, some of his usual tension resurfacing in the repetitive gesture. It wasn't exactly a terrible eco-crime, but the idea that Niall was feeling prickly and destructive didn't set Draven's mind at ease.

"I might read for a while. Be rude not to, when you went to the effort." Draven took his book and lay back on the grass.

"I might join you," Niall said.

Maybe he just meant reading. Even if he didn't, Draven shouldn't push. He shouldn't flirt. But it was difficult, when Niall was so easy to flirt with.

"Do," he invited. "It's ever so comfy."

They had been sitting toe to toe like usual, but now Draven was stretched out away from Niall. Niall could lie back from his own current position. He could stretch or sprawl out on any given piece of the grass.

"Does that mean over there?" he asked.

"If you like." Draven smiled, enjoying the fact that Niall was a little more brave today, responding better to the idea of them getting closer.

Niall lay down on his front next to Draven, glancing across at him. Their eyes met, and Draven found his stomach full of butterflies. He should not have done this. They had now entered what he thought of as the gravitational field of a kiss—they had been caught, and short of the absolute and abrupt end of the world, there was no way out. They were going to keep sinking closer and closer to that moment, both dancing around it a little, but always going forward, closer and closer until... But Draven hadn't told Niall the truth yet. The closer Niall was, the more distracting he was, making Draven's brain go all fuzzy, which did not help with working out what he wanted to say. It made him want to take the plunge and leave the details to work themselves out later. But that wasn't fair. Because this wasn't going to be a quick spring day thing in the library garden. This meant something to both of them.

"What's all the tiny grass for?" he asked, nodding to where Niall was still shredding. He wasn't sure he could go back to his book. It went against gravity. But nor was he ready to hurtle the final few metres to impact. He knew he had to have The Conversation with Niall first, and The Conversation was scary enough that it put the brakes on his flirtations. More or less. Gravity meant that maintaining a conversation with eye contact was still dangerous territory.

"Dunno." Niall glanced across at Draven. His fingers traced circles in the shredded pile of grass dust. "I guess there's something on my mind. Kind of."

"Hmm. Mine too." Draven peered at Niall, trying to work out what his secret might be. "Do you want to go first?"

"Not really. Maybe. I don't know. Do you?" he asked.

"Yes and no," Draven said. What if the thing on Niall's mind was something awful? Like he'd met someone, or the library was shutting down, or he had a Sunday job? Though the way Niall was looking at him, Draven thought the most likely words out of Niall's mouth were going to be a confession of feelings for him.

"Is it a good thing or a bad thing?" Niall asked nervously.

"Neither. I... It's just a thing. I feel there's something I have to tell you. If we're going to keep hanging out. There's something you should know about me."

"Same." Niall raised his eyebrows. "Maybe it's the same thing."

"I doubt it." Draven shook his head. "I mean, it has to do with... It's kind of...how I'm not like other people."

Niall paused, tilting his head at him.

"Same," he said again though more cautiously. "There's nothing wrong with not being like other people," he offered. "I like you being you. I like being me when I'm around you." Their hands were lying side by side, and he touched the lightest tip of his little finger to Draven's. "Something to do with this?" he asked, winding his fingers one by one between Draven's.

"Yes." It related to that, or to how comfortable they should get doing that. And while it was fantastic that Niall had suddenly learnt to flirt and was being more open, it would have been convenient if he could have picked a less distracting time to do it. "Something I feel I should tell you. Because, maybe it'll change your mind about how friendly you want to be. With someone like me."

"It won't," Niall assured him. "I'm pretty sure we're on the same page here. But I get it, if you need to say it out loud."

"It's..." Draven swallowed hard. It was definitely not the same thing. The more Niall became convinced it was, the harder it was to throw something out there that was going to come as a surprise—one that was potentially going to derail everything. "It's... There's a thing, and the thing is... Well, it's..." he stumbled.

He swallowed hard, wondering where his voice had gone. Niall was not going to react badly. This wasn't a bad world, where people were cruel and disbelieving.

He found himself turning his eyes away, not able to meet Niall's, who was looking at him with concern. Because, Draven knew, he was being weird, and awkward. He could practically feel the heat of his own anxiety radiating off himself, which wasn't at all like him.

Of course Niall, sweet, sympathetic Niall, wanted to make that go away.

Which was why Niall filled in the silence—why Niall said, "I want to kiss you," right as Draven found his voice and managed to say, "I'm a mage."

Chapter Seventeen

There was a beat, as they both processed what the other had said. Niall abruptly let go of Draven's hand. He sat bolt upright, pulling away from all the intimacy that had been there a second ago.

Stupid. Stupid, stupid, stupid. Why had he said that? Of course, putting himself out there, admitting he liked someone was never going to work out in his favour. He pushed himself even further back from Draven, locking down hard on the part of himself that had come creeping out of its shell over the past few weeks. The part that had learnt to bump shoes or twist his fingers in between another boy's.

"What did you say?" were the first words out of Niall's mouth, even though he'd heard. Thought he'd heard.

"I'm a mage. I live in a place that I don't know how to explain. It's sort of related to here but—"

"Are you taking the piss?" Niall asked. He searched Draven's face for some sign that he'd been meaning to say the same thing as Niall had and had bottled it. Had Draven come out to anyone? If his family back home was super strict and weird about everything, maybe he'd never actually said it out loud before to anyone except his own reflection. Niall knew that feeling. He had practised those words himself, quietly under his breath, getting used to them. With Ellen, it had always been a fact, it hadn't had to be an announcement. Now he'd told his parents, and he could see how saying it out loud would feel necessary and validating. And scary.

But Draven was staring at him, eyes as earnest as ever, though now slightly wounded. Niall looked away, not wanting to have to see that and feel responsible.

"I am fairly confident that I am not," Draven concluded.

"That isn't real," Niall said, hearing a hint of doubt in his voice. Hadn't he been thinking for weeks that there was something more going on than met the eye? He had considered the possibility that Draven was a cultist or a time traveller. Was this a million miles away from those? But he wasn't sure how fully he'd believed himself. It also didn't make it stop hurting that the one time he'd put his feelings on the line, it turned out not to be what the other person was thinking at all. There was an added sting in the tail, because wasn't this every childhood daydream he'd ever had? He had always wanted magic to be real, and now someone was telling him it was. He was a long way from believing that could be true, but worse still, he wasn't even sure he wanted it to be—he thought he'd give it up in a heartbeat if he could have Draven wanting to be his boyfriend instead.

"I see." Draven's voice was flat. "Perhaps I should go."

"No!" Niall's head snapped up. "But..."

"Either you don't believe me, or you do, and this information makes you dislike me." Draven folded his arms over his chest, but Niall could see, beneath the frown, a mirror of himself; someone who was trying to hold themselves together because the person in front of them was breaking them apart.

"No." This was all wrong. He didn't want to hurt Draven or push him away. "It's not that. But... I thought... It doesn't matter."

"I believe you said something about wanting to kiss me. Now you're acting as if you don't want to talk to me."

"Yeah...well...I did. I said...but it doesn't matter."

"The only thing I can see that's changed is that I've told you I'm a mage. If that doesn't make you dislike me, why are you acting this way?"

"Because it's not the only thing. I thought— Forget it."

Draven paused. Niall could feel his eyes on him, but he kept his own down. Now that Draven wasn't about to run away, he didn't want to look at him—didn't want to see Draven analysing his remarks.

"There's what I said. And there's what you said. Which of those do you now have a problem with?" Draven asked.

Niall felt his tongue sticking in his mouth as Draven edged closer to what was bothering him. If this wasn't what was happening here, he wished they could move on and forget it. Maybe they could read and talk about books. Or about the magic thing. Why did both of those have to sound so unappealing? Any other day, those would have been beyond awesome ways to spend the afternoon.

"Are you mad at me for being what I am? Or for telling you?" Draven tried.

"I'm not. I'm not, at all— I'm sorry." He was being kind of a butt right now, and he knew it, but those particular words hit a chord with him. How could someone hate someone, just for who they were? That sounded like a familiar, pained refrain. "So long as you don't hate me for what I said."

"Why would I hate you?" Draven sounded genuinely shocked.

"I...I dunno. You might feel weird. If you don't feel the same way and—"

"But I do. Wasn't that obvious? I was practically pulling you towards me."

"Well, yeah...I thought so. I thought that was what was going on, but I thought it was what you were talking about as well, and then it really, *really* wasn't." He swallowed hard. "I've never told anyone that I like them before," Niall admitted.

"How come?" Draven asked.

"I guess I never met anyone who I thought would like me back." It had never been worth the risk. It was obvious, in most cases, that he was barking up the wrong tree, and why open himself up to heartache and humiliation? He'd denied plenty of crushes. When he'd hung around a bit too much, and people had started to tease, he would insist it wasn't like that—they had a project together, or he was just trying to be friendly. It usually freaked him out, the thought of people knowing what was going on inside his head. "I...you do? Like me?" he checked.

"Yes," Draven insisted. "I didn't want to kiss you without you knowing who I really am. Please, come here?" He reached tentatively for Niall's hand. Niall let some of the tension in his shoulders go. "That doesn't mean I don't want to kiss you," Draven clarified. "So long as knowing doesn't put you off?"

Draven wanted him. Draven wanted him. He should have been punching the sky and singing. But his head was still spinning. Draven was a mage, from a different world.

"What does that mean for us?" Niall asked.

"I don't know," Draven admitted. "I'm sort of not meant to be here."

"Maybe begin at the beginning?" Niall suggested, feeling like he was coming in halfway through. He sort of wanted to ignore it all and pull Draven in and kiss him and be happy. But it seemed like it was going to be more complicated than that. He was still processing, and it didn't feel like they could immediately pick up where they'd left off. Also, magic was real. "If I'm going to know who you are, maybe you'd finally better tell me." Now he was over the initial shock, excitement welled inside him. He was finally going to get to ask all the things he'd wanted to know about Draven and hear about his life. What was more, it was going to involve magic! "You are allowed to tell me stuff right?" he asked, the hope flickering for a second. "About the magical world? Can I go there?"

Draven hesitated a beat too long, and Niall knew something not good was coming.

"You can't," Draven said. "Everyone knows everyone. It's a very small place, compared to here. There'd be no way of explaining who you were or what you were doing there. I can tell you about it, though it's not that exciting, not like it is in your books."

At least it was only a partial shooting down. Magic was still real. And Draven liked him back. A visit would have been the icing on the cake, but he wasn't sure anything could bring him down right now.

"You can do magic." Niall beamed. "That's so cool. Like, what kind of magic? What's the most powerful spell you know?"

"It's not that impressive. There are limits, you see." He began to explain about the ambient magic levels, the restrictions, and having to do merit to contribute back to the system. "All of which is the equivalent of having to pay a utility bill for the gas—only magic. So, as you can see, it's not all that—"

"It's still freaking cool!" Niall bounced where he was sitting. "I thought maybe you were a time traveller. Or in a cult."

"Ooh. Which would you rather—be able to do magic or time travel?"

"Magic. Every time. Time travel's messy. You?"

"Time travel could be fun. Guess you always want what you haven't got."

"But would you give up magic and be whatever I am to have it?"

"Maybe not," Draven said. "No offence. It's not like I think there's anything wrong with you. But I've always been able to do magic. I can't imagine not having it, even though there's so many limits. How do you keep warm? Do you *always* cook on gas? What are all the things a mobile phone can do?" he asked.

Just like that, they were off again—back to the relative merits of magic versus time travel, coming up with wild theories, and Niall found himself having to explain what a microwave was.

"So..." Niall took a deep breath, almost as scared of this next question as he had been of confessing his feelings. He had started to realise he was gay somewhere in his teenage years. He'd believed in magic for so much longer. Draven wanting to go out with him was the most exciting thing ever, and what he wanted more than anything. But Draven had also dangled the possibility that Niall could have everything he'd ever dreamt of. Niall still half believed that Draven was about to laugh and tell him it had been a joke, or in some way crush a dream he'd had since childhood. Which would also rather crush the boyfriend thing. "Can I see some magic?" he asked.

"You don't believe me?" Draven said.

"I do." Niall twined his fingers between Draven's and squeezed (it felt amazing to be able to do that). "I promise I'll believe you even if you can't show me. But I'd like to see."

"I don't know. I don't know whether it works here. Or whether I should." He paused, weighing it up, and Niall tried not to look too eager. "One teeny, tiny spell. If I can." He bit his lip. "Is your nose cold?"

"Yeah, a bit," Niall said.

Draven took a deep breath. He worked his fingers in a complicated pattern, then touched a finger gently to Niall's nose. Niall felt a glow of warmth, far more than could be accounted for by Draven's finger. The feeling spread, in a way that wasn't normal from just being touched.

"Better?" Draven asked.

"Judge for yourself." Niall leant in, touching his now warm nose to Draven's still cold one. "How does that feel?"

Draven's attempt at an answer came out more like a tangle of consonants. He held for a second, nose nuzzling against Niall's, before leaning in, just as Niall moved too, their lips coming together. Draven's hands slid over Niall's shoulders, around his neck, up into his hair. Niall wasn't sure if it was the charm—if Draven's hands were now enchanted to leave little trails of warmth wherever they touched—or whether that was just how he felt. Draven's lips were soft, and where their mouths met was even warmer than where the magic had touched him. He felt Draven's mouth pushing more firmly against his, and that was good, he liked it. This was rapidly turning from a sweet, gentle kiss into more, and he wanted that, except he was pretty sure that meant tongue and, well, he was familiar with the theory, but he'd not exactly done the practical. He had never been able to imagine how sliding your tongue into someone else's mouth was going to feel anything except weird. He could feel Draven's mouth opening and he tried to do the same and lean into the kiss—and bumped front teeth with him.

"Sorry," Niall muttered, pulling back.

"S'okay. It happens."

Niall bit back a question of how many people Draven had kissed and bumped teeth with, deciding that he didn't want to know that right now.

"I dunno what I'm doing, and I'm probably horrible at this," he admitted. It came out as more or less one long word.

"No, you're not," Draven reassured him. "Just relax. Don't overthink it."

"I am the captain of overthinking things. I cannot not overthink."

"Challenge accepted." Draven grinned, leaning in and grazing Niall's neck with gentle kisses, which had the effect of immediately shutting him up. "Better?" Draven worked his way slowly up Niall's neck.

"Um... I... Hang on," Niall managed, and Draven pulled back. It had been wonderful. On the one hand, he could feel his brain going fuzzy around the edges and was actually convinced there might be a place he could sink into where it felt like that almost all the way through. But stabbing at the edge of that was the need to be alert. The feeling of open air on all sides. Of exposure. He picked up their books, pulling Draven's wrist, and taking them over to the back wall of the library. It was scarcely enclosed or private, but someone would have to come right round the building to see them, and there was little reason for anyone to do that. He sat back down, worried that their height difference was going to lead to weird and confusing neck angles if they stayed standing.

"Sorry," he mumbled, not quite sure why he was apologising, but it being the thing he defaulted to when he felt uncertain. "I...just..."

Draven waited, giving Niall space to get his words out, but they dried up.

"Permission to resume kissing you?" Draven checked.

"Yes." Niall smiled, relieved not to be the one who had to work out how to reinitiate. Draven picked up where he left off, and Niall tried to let his brain relax. The kisses that landed on his neck were distracting but so was the loud voice in his head that screamed he was a hopeless loser. Except, Draven's kisses were getting firmer, and Niall's hands stroked around Draven's waist. He had thought that brushing his hands across him would satisfy this sudden feeling in his fingers, this itch to touch, but now that he had it, he wanted more. His hands wanted to explore, and he wanted his lips to be against Draven's again—except Draven's were currently busy toying with his earlobe. He wanted to connect at as many points as possible. Draven's mouth was moving down towards his cheek. Niall turned to meet it, his mouth already half open, and—and he was still thinking about the mechanics of what they were doing, and of how tongues were really weird things, but that it was also weird how not weird it was. It felt natural for them to slide together like this, and just...good. All very...good. And...and...he... For the first time in his life, he gave up having a train of thought and just let himself be kissed.

Chapter Eighteen

Draven stepped out of the portal and into his own library, leaning back against a shelf with a huge smile on his face. He wasn't sure how he was going to keep this kind of happiness to himself. The portal swam in his eyes, and he wished he could dive back in, to be with the person he could share this with. The afternoon had been far too short. Time always played with him in that world—it always ran out when he was getting to the good bit of his book. He hadn't spent a lot of time reading that afternoon, but it had been equally cruel. Although there wasn't a point at which he was likely to want to put a good book down, and he strongly suspected the same applied to Niall.

He stepped away from the portal. It felt like Niall was within reach whilst he was here, but now he had to step outside the Special Collections, then outside the building, and Niall would really be gone, closed away from him for another week.

As he left and began ambling towards home, his euphoria started fading. If anything he had a slight headache, and the air around him seemed determined not to help. It was heavy. He glanced up, trying to think about himself and Niall looking at the same stars, but it was more likely they would be looking at the same weird clouds. He thought it would've been fully dark by now, but the clouds had that backlit look they sometimes got as they gathered greyly in the early evening.

Back home, he made his way to the kitchen, glad to find it unoccupied. He didn't feel like chatting, although he supposed he would have to force his way through dinner. What was he supposed to say? He'd had a brilliant day, the best day, but now it was over, and he was stuck back here. He gulped down a large glass of water and put the kettle on. He definitely had a headache. He made himself tea and went upstairs. Setting the tea on his bedside table, he flopped face down into his pillows, telling himself he would lie down and rest his eyes until his tea had cooled.

* * *

"Good morning, Galdorsfarne!"
Draven blinked his eyes open to daylight and a cup of cold tea on his nightstand.

The morning presenters were always chirpy but this time it was almost offensively so. What was there to look forward to about a whole week away from Niall? What did this world have that could make anyone that enthusiastic at seven AM? A whole five minutes of hot water? More if it was high amber? Who cared?!

They were practically bubbling over with joy. Was it just his own bad mood, or had they cranked it up a notch?

He didn't have to wait long to find out because they were passing over to Sandy for the weather.

"I can't believe I'm about to say this but... The ambient magic level is...green."

"I think Sandy's been waiting her whole life to say that, so we didn't want to take it away from her!" the presenters chimed in. *"We have a prepared statement here from the head of the Energy Makers' Guild herself. She's going to be coming in later to help us analyse this situation and work out what it might mean."*

"'Citizens of Galdorsfarne. We are thrilled beyond belief that the ambient magic has shifted so substantially in our favour. We want to celebrate this unusual occasion, whilst being mindful of the needs of the community. Our banking technology has been improving, and we should be able to store up to fifteen percent of today's energy to feed back into the system over the coming months. The city is fully operational, and there are no restrictions on the types of magic you may use. Each citizen of age is granted three additional spells beyond their usual allowance.

'We want this day to be a memorable occasion for all citizens, and thus today is declared a half day holiday, and

a small festival will be held this evening. In the meantime, there is much to do, especially for those of us at the Energy Makers' Guild. We will be looking into possible causes for this shift, as well as working to preserve as much of the energy as we can."'

The presenters were off, speculating on the causes and talking about what spells they'd be trying. Draven swung himself out of bed. A green day. That holiest of grails. He wandered into the shower, idly wondering how long he could let the water slide over him. But he'd got used to short showers, and although it continued to be warm, pleasant and available, he shut it off before it cut itself off. He was supposed to be excited. He supposed he was. The news had broken through his haze. For a whole two minutes, he had been actively interested in something the world had to offer. He wasn't sure it was worth losing his head over though, the way he'd always assumed it would feel. It was hard to imagine that this was it, crisis solved. They didn't know why this was happening, and until they did, they couldn't be sure of how often it would happen, or how to make it keep happening. Having a green day was not going to revolutionise the way the Energy Makers' Guild did things. It just gave them an unusual data point to analyse. And analyse, and analyse.

He got dressed. By the time he'd had breakfast with his family and headed out to catch the tram, he felt more into it. It was hard not to enjoy the atmosphere. Everyone was smiling. If they'd ever needed proof that the ambient magical level was not linked to the weather, today was it. It was drizzling steadily, and he'd rarely seen the sky looking more moody, but it wasn't denting anyone's spirits. The tram stop was a hive of activity, the map on the wall a sprawling, brightly lit web. All lines operational, all citizens permitted to travel, long trams snaking into view.

At work, the data lab was overflowing with people. Suddenly data was interesting. A number of the scientists who usually worked upstairs had come down voluntarily, and it was all hands to the pump. This day was important, and thus the data surrounding it was vital. The answer had to be somewhere down here.

Draven suspected that all the data likely to yield interesting results was being snapped up by senior mages, if any such data existed. He was beginning to believe there was no real pattern to it. Or, much like the weather, even if there was a pattern it would move in its own way, without them being able to control it. They could predict it, like the weather, he supposed, but would that help much? You could take an umbrella if you suspected it was going to rain. On a personal level, everyone already kept stocked for low amber days, and he couldn't see that changing. On the community level, it wasn't like they could store up more or balance the books any better than they were already doing. He was more interested in checking a particular piece of information—had there been anything anomalous in the warming charm he'd cast the day before. Had it taken masses more energy? Was he going to get busted over it?

"Ah. Draven. There you are."

He froze as Rowan called out to him, wondering whether she'd already found out somehow.

"I've got a list for you." She passed him one of the familiar file lists. "Sorry, not the most glamorous task, but everyone wants extra files pulled today. I think that's what you and most of us juniors will be doing for the next couple of hours. Everyone also needs to fill out a detailed account of their activities yesterday, especially anything unusual that happened."

"No problem." He took the list and the form. He would be lying through his teeth on that. Jumping through a portal to another world definitely counted as unusual, but he'd done that twice before without triggering any kind of magical super event. It had been a noteworthy day for him on a personal level, but unless the universe super approved of boys making out in libraries, it wasn't relevant. He was sure they were looking for merit, things you'd done that were exceptionally good, and he hadn't done anything of the kind. "Anyone got any idea about what's caused this?"

"Oh, only everyone you ask. Any of them actually going to pan out? Well, we'll have to see. Have you got any ideas?"

"If I did, I'd be running a lab. But for now…" He gestured at her list, making his way towards the files. He spent the first fifteen minutes dutifully pulling the data he'd been asked to or noting when it was missing—a lot of people were making simultaneous demands on the same resources. Once he was sure everyone had settled into their own lists and stopped paying attention, it was easy enough to slip over to the usage files. He pulled his out, wondering with a sudden stab of anxiety whether using the portal itself counted as doing magic, and what it would show up as if it did. How often were these records checked? They autogenerated, and clearly his hadn't set off an alert system, if that was even a thing. Would it only be found if someone got around to pulling this record for data? Or was Mage Starkweather getting statistics reports, where he'd show as an anomaly? He held his breath. Would he rather not know than know that he should stop? But he was going to eat himself inside out worrying about this. He pulled his record.

Nothing.

The portal trips didn't register but the warming charm wasn't on there either. That had been magic. Actual, concrete magic. It hadn't shown up as anything odd, which was good, but it was odd that it hadn't shown up as anything. He glanced at his watch. It had been less than twenty-four hours, so maybe he should check back later. In the meantime, he would keep holding his breath. And pulling files.

The morning was busy enough to blur past, even if it wasn't noticeably different or more thrilling than usual, and at lunchtime, he was free to head out and make the most of the holiday.

* * *

"Do you still have that book?" Draven asked his grandma.

"Narrow it down?" She raised her eyebrows, nodding to the rows and rows of shelves that lined almost every inch of her house.

"You know the one. *The* Book. The one I liked looking at when I was little."

"Ah. You mean this one?" She pulled the beauty book from a shelf full of recipe books, where he knew full well it did not live on a day-to-day basis. She'd been expecting this.

He was never sure why the book had disappeared from his childhood. It had lived in his grandma's room with a few others. He was allowed, if he asked politely and showed that he had clean hands, to go up and spread himself out on the rug up there, reading them to his heart's content. The beauty book had been his favourite. Then one day, when he'd asked about seeing them, his grandma had got a strange look on her face, and said she'd had to do some rearranging. He had asked why, and she had said they didn't get read much anymore—looking back, that wasn't really true because he read them almost every week, but to his small self a week's gap did seem like a long time. He'd asked if the books could be got out, and the answer was always the same—not today, honey, too much stuff to move around—until he'd got tired of asking and invented new ways to amuse himself.

It had that practical air of books from bygone days where readers expected substance over style. It had crammed as much information into every given space as possible. How to set, to curl, to cast glamours, how to make your eyes sparkle. He remembered looking through the spells when he was little, the black and white drawings so entrancing. It was so simple and so casual on the surface of it, and these little line drawing people had no idea that they had magic he might never be allowed to try.

"Where did the book go?" Maybe there had been more to it than he'd realised at the time.

"It really did get put into the back of a cupboard. What's the question you're always asking that gets on people's nerves?"

"Why?" asked Draven, with a grin.

"On the one hand, it got more controversial to own such things. I decided I'd rather put them away and keep them quiet than have them taken away. On a more personal level, I think your mother thought it might give you ideas. Fill your head with nonsense that you weren't ever going to see, and that would make you unhappy. Did it?" she asked.

"I don't think so. Well, I suppose you could argue my head's full of nonsense. But I think I've been growing out of that," he said. Or rather, the things he'd thought were nonsense and fantasy were turning out to be real. He thought about the conversation he'd had with Yvette. His grandma had always encouraged his dreaming, more than any other adult he'd met. "Is there anything wrong with wanting the world to be more bright and colourful?"

"No, so long as it's not all there is. Some things are more important than a shiny hairdo."

"The things we have," Draven recited obediently. "Kindness, tolerance, taking care of each other."

"Something like that."

"I'm not saying I'd swap. But, can't I have both? People used to."

She paused a long time before answering. "Yes and no." She looked down at the book, away from his eyes. "Think of it more like a life with ribbons and bows on it, but what it was wrapping up was a lot more complex. So, that's whether or not your head's full of nonsense. What about the other half? Did you end up unhappy?"

"I don't think so."

"That's not a very reassuring answer."

"I'm sixteen," he pointed out. "I'm supposed to be miserable, aren't I? Angry and rebellious or broken-hearted or plain misunderstood." He was being flippant, and he knew it, hoping to get away from something that he was finding an increasingly difficult question. He had moaned a lot about not having a boyfriend, but apart from that he had always been happy. He had thought the best about everything and everyone, and been all set to save the world. Now, he wasn't sure. The Energy Makers' Guild had sapped some of his strength. It had made him question what was going on here, and what could possibly give his life meaning. But now he'd found Niall, and things were great. Except that was rocky as hell, and had been born of his dissatisfaction with being here. "I feel like I'm figuring out where I belong," he answered the question more honestly. "That's complicated, and when it seems like there might not be a clear answer to that, it feels scary. But I don't think a book of hairstyles is responsible."

"Well, you're allowed to feel that way when you're sixteen. And I don't know if it makes it better or worse, but also a good deal of the time afterwards. Anything I can help you figure out?"

"Have fun while we're allowed." He turned the book around to her. "Help me decide which of these to use. The rest... Not right now, thanks. It helps to be able to say I'm clueless out loud and I want to know what happens, in the end. But the only way to do that is to have the patience to get there." The only way to determine what was happening in your life was to exist in it. "I know that. Thanks." He smiled, because even if he hadn't told her exactly what was wrong, it helped to admit that things were on his mind. Plus, it had brought his thoughts back round to Niall, to how their brains worked similarly, and their lives ticked along on constant interconnecting lines in spite of the distance.

He turned to the book and spent a long time looking through the pictures. He suspected that pulling off unfamiliar beauty charms was not as simple as it looked.

"Are you going to do any?" he asked his grandma.

"I thought I might." She flicked through the book. "I always liked this one. Never could quite get it right without magic though." She read over it a couple of times, and Draven watched her fingers working, practising the shapes. She began for real, and her hair twisted itself, the long silvery strands curling into all manner of waves and rolls.

"Wow," he breathed.

"How about you?" she asked.

"Nothing that complicated." He ran a hand through his hair, streaking it with sparkling powder blue, just for the heck of it. The spell was pure vanity, of the like he'd never been allowed to try before. "What does it say about casting a basic glamour?" he asked.

She turned directly to the appropriate section.

"'The trick to a good glamour is all about deciding what exactly it is you want to radiate. There's no such thing as blanket attractiveness—that "sparkle" that some people have is always a part of their personality shining through. Maybe their confidence in themselves. Maybe their kindness. Most people will notice there's something about you, but you'll only be more attractive to the ones who like that trait.' You can make yourself mysterious, or enticing. Are you trying to entice tonight?" she asked.

"No," Draven said, and realised he'd said it far too quickly. Because wasn't he always talking about how he wished he could meet someone? Now his grandma was telling him he could magic himself up to draw in the right kind of person, and he was shutting her down. "I just thought it might be fun to have a bit of a spark. It's a little bit insincere, isn't it? Luring someone in this way."

"Nothing wrong with making yourself look good to catch someone's eye. Where's the difference between that and putting on a sharp suit, or doing your makeup? It's only insincere if you're always pretending. Not letting on who you really are, wouldn't you say?"

"I agree." He could meet her eye because that was the honest truth. He had hoodwinked no-one. "Now are we glamourising me or not?"

"Sure. How about this one? Radiating confidence. I mean, you do anyway, but it's best to play to your natural strengths."

Draven studied the spell, practising the unfamiliar hand movements. When it was cast, he turned, admiring its effects in the mirror. In his head, having a glamour on had been akin to some kind of allover sparkle. Which, he supposed, was not necessarily rational because he wasn't sure that being literally shiny was a trait most people valued (he totally would find it both attractive and a talking point, but he had long since accepted that he was not most people). It was as his grandma had said—he was like himself but somehow better. Moreso. He just had something about him. He still thought he might have preferred to gently glow or sparkle, but he did have some powder in his make-up bag that would achieve that, and one more spell. He'd keep that in case he saw something fun to do whilst he was out.

* * *

The city centre was packed. For such a small community, it was amazing how busy it could feel when they all gathered together. Lights hung in the air. Draven thought about low amber days, when some streets weren't lit at all. Now the city was not only fully illuminated but additional lights were hanging, suspended in midair. They swirled around, dancing in the sky, their colours gradually shifting as they made formations.

There were different areas of interest, to keep people moving around, the whole thing having the atmosphere of a street festival. Some things were familiar, like the string quartet which was playing itself in a booth near the river. It was unusual to see it outside of a major holiday, especially side by side with so many other rare treats. Some things were new, like the vendors selling candyfloss that would make you levitate. And the people... He suspected he was not the only one rocking a glamour. Everyone was a better version of themselves. Better dressed. Brighter. Sometimes it was obvious, in a garment which changed colour or moved as if it was caught in a breeze. But it came in smaller ways too; every little twist that was giving oneself a treat or was downright forbidden—suddenly they were the norm.

He crossed paths with Yvette and did a double take. The streaks in her hair were gradually cycling through all the colours in the rainbow, but there was more to it than that. There was movement, each colour sliding down as if the new one was growing in from the roots in that moment to replace it. He was pretty sure she was also rocking a glamour. A strong one at that. He couldn't stop staring. It wasn't like it changed anything—he wasn't attracted to her. But it was like if he took his eyes off her he might miss something, something important.

"Wow, works on you then, does it?" she asked, catching him staring. "Am I the most impressive thing you've seen tonight?" She gave him a little twirl.

"Quite possibly. You're powerful."

"Yeah, I think it comes with the artsy side. Shame it's illegal most days. I finally found my niche, and I won't be allowed to do it again."

"You think this won't happen again?" he asked.

"I think I can't rely on it. But my mums animated my ceiling! And I enchanted some of my make up, so hopefully it will last a while."

"Smart thinking. Your lipstick is..." Draven wasn't sure he had an adequate word for the way its colours gently pulsed and shifted.

"Thanks. Want some?"

He only realised what she meant when she puckered her lips and blew a kiss at him.

"What? No! It's not like that. You're...very...something right now. I want to follow you and stare at you and maybe touch the shiny bits in your hair, but girl kisses are still yucky." *Anyway, I have a boyfriend.* Draven found himself feeling cut off again, not able to share the day with the person he wanted to be with, and not able to share that fact with anyone around him. It was a pretty big secret to be keeping from his best friend.

"Fine." She gave a friendly roll of her eyes. "You're not too bad yourself," she added, with the air of a craftsperson evaluating a piece of work.

"Confidence is sexy." He ran a hand through his hair, trying to get his focus back. "So are blue sparkles."

"What did you use your other one for?"

"Still got it, just in case. Want to look around?"

* * *

Hours later and utterly exhausted, Draven flopped into bed. The evening had undoubtedly been fun. In a lot of ways, it had been what he always wanted green days to be, and what he had thought they would never deliver, even if they ever got one. But with everything he looked at, he found himself wondering what Niall would think. He would tell him all about it, and he was already looking forward to that because Niall clearly loved magic and was bound to be excited. Draven had got his grandma to take some pictures, and eventually he could show those to Niall too. It wasn't as great as Niall's little box where they could see themselves while they took it. It wasn't as good as being able to show him now. For all the fun there was in playing with those spells, he wasn't sure he cared as much for green days as he'd thought he would. Or rather, it had been half the fun it ought to have been because he'd been missing the person he wanted to share it with. The spells were frivolous. He'd always known that. It was why they'd appealed, because why couldn't life be a bit more fun? But the joy in such silly things was sharing them with other people. He'd appreciated the quality time with his grandma, and they were her spellbooks after all. But even though it had been practical and basic, he had enjoyed making nose warming charms for Niall more than he'd enjoyed getting to be all fancy. He pulled his pillow to him. He had one remaining spell. Just because he could use it for something extravagant didn't mean he had to. He traced the familiar outline of the warming charm over the pillow, and buried his nose into it, wishing it smelt like harsh, strange scents that he didn't have a name for.

Chapter Nineteen

"Tell me you have hot gossip, or I will be forced to throw this flapjack in your face, and that would be a criminal waste." Ellen dropped into one of the blue plastic chairs of the college snack shop.

"For someone who's so desperate to hear it, you weren't able to make the early bus?" Niall smirked.

"Mornings are hard. Now spill."

"I have a boyfriend!" He'd said it several times already—as he walked home from the library, as he brushed his teeth in the evening, as he lay down to sleep with memories of Draven playing through his head. It still sounded wonderful every time he made it real. It was even better saying it to other people. He'd told his parents already, and they had been happy, but Ellen was squealing and throwing herself in for a hug.

"Did you make out? Is he a good kisser?" She bounced up and down as she quizzed him.

"Yes, and yes." Niall could feel himself blushing a little, but he was still grinning broadly underneath it. He couldn't help it.

"Did you do more than make out?"

"What? No! We were round the back of the library. Don't you dare set that as homework for next week. I like where things are at. I like kissing him. A lot. Oh my god." He melted into a happy, pathetic puddle on the table as his mind wandered back to the weekend.

"So long as you're happy. Go on." Ellen poked his arm. "What happened?"

"What do you mean?"

"I mean, tell me the story. Who initiated?"

"Both of us?" Niall sat up a little, pulling his mind back to the present.

"Yeah?" Ellen motioned in a way that clearly indicated "go on."

"Yeah," Niall confirmed, rapidly trying to edit down the scene from Sunday. "We went outside. It was sunny, so we were lying in the grass outside the back of the library reading. And it just sort of happened." Those were the main points anyway. Whilst he'd never had any kissing to kiss and tell about before, he thought Ellen probably wouldn't be surprised by him being a bit closed mouth about it. Hopefully it wasn't too obvious that half the story was missing.

"So, when are you seeing him again?"

"Next weekend, probably." Niall deflated.

"What?!"

"What? I told you, he can only come over on the weekends. He lives kinda far away."

"Where?"

Niall took a sip of tea to cover his thinking time. "Just far."

"Where though?"

"Does it matter?" he asked. "He can't come over during the week."

"Just asking. Alright. So, he's our age, yeah? What's he studying?"

He's doing an apprenticeship. The words would pass, there were apprenticeships in their world, but it wasn't an accurate picture of what Draven did. And not that it was fair to be snobby, but people sometimes were about people who were doing apprenticeships. He didn't want Ellen to be able to find fault with his boyfriend. "He's not in college right now. He had some stuff going on."

"Weird family cult stuff?" The words were teasing, but Ellen was looking at him with real concern. He knew she didn't believe in the cult theory, but the phrase "stuff going on" was obviously serious. It was serious enough that she'd back off without making him tell, but also it was going to make everyone worry. It clearly wasn't the perfect lie to tell.

"Yeah," he said it with enough of a grin that he hoped he could reassure her. Though he wasn't sure how many times he was going to be able to dodge questions like that.

* * *

"You want to wash or dry?" Niall's mum asked, once his dad had cleared the table.

"I'll dry." He followed her through into the kitchen, where she ran a steaming bowl of water and pulled on her rubber gloves. Niall pulled a tea towel with small colour pictures of Northumberland castles from the handle of the oven door.

"So, this boyfriend of yours," She dunked some barely used cups and glasses through the hot soapy water and passed them to Niall, who snapped out of his frozen state to take them, "when do we get to meet him?"

"I dunno." He wiped the dishes and returned them to their cupboard.

"What's going on—this whole phone business, him not being around?"

"He's a mage from another dimension," Niall stated flatly.

"You are a funny boy." His mum looked up from the plate she was scrubbing to fix him with a puzzled stare. "You don't get out of introducing us that easily. How about next time you see him, you ask him over for lunch the weekend after?"

"Okay." Niall wiped the plates. What else was he supposed to say? It was very much not okay. How was he supposed to put Draven in a room with his parents? With anyone? He'd gone over the phone thing, and had sort of steered his mum towards the idea that Draven lived in an alternative community. That had sounded more mum-friendly than "cult." Besides, it wasn't a cult. It was a weird magical dimension. He had at least tried telling the truth, even if he knew he was going to be written off as being facetious.

"You'll invite him?"

"Yes! I'll invite him! He'll come! If his parents let him out or whatever."

"Mm." She pursed her lips. "Found out any more about that?"

"No. I'm not in the habit of interrogating him. Please don't, when he comes to lunch."

"I won't. But this community, its mindset is concerning."

"You can't judge him by where he comes from. That's not fair." Niall realised he was standing there holding a dripping plate, and he set it down on the rack, not bothering to wipe it.

"I'm not judging him. But I worry. It's not going to make your life any easier, dating someone whose family doesn't want you to be part of his life."

"But that could happen here." Should he have said "*here?*"

"Anywhere. I mean, with someone whose parents are homophobic."

"I wouldn't want you dating someone whose family thought that way." She dropped a saucepan into the sink and let it sit, turning to stare at him.

"So, people with horrible parents don't deserve to get boyfriends?"

"No—I'm not saying that. But I want good things for you. Not complicated messy ones."

"I know. I mean, yeah if I could wish for it not to be complicated and messy, I would. But it is."

"And you want to keep seeing him anyway?" She gave him a smile that was a mixture of happy and sad, and which said she already knew the answer to that question.

"Yeah, I do."

"Okay." She shook her gloves over the sink, reaching out to give him a hug which didn't include her hands. "Bring him over, and we'll figure out how to make it work."

"Thanks." Niall returned her hug. Everyone around him seemed to have accepted the one fact he thought was frankly impossible—namely, that someone was willingly dating him. He thought they would find it more of a stretch than he had to believe in magic.

Chapter Twenty

What was Draven doing right now? It was a game Niall had taken to playing with himself to get through the week. By all Draven's own accounts, the weeks slid by slowly, and he spent most of his time sorting data. Still, every time the wind nipped at Niall's nose, he thought about the warming charm. Every time he flicked a light switch, or turned up the heating, he thought about Draven doing the same by magic.

Sunday morning meant he was waiting to find out the details of that week for real. When Draven had left last week, he'd shown Niall the place where the portal was—plain as day to Draven and invisible to him. He stood, staring at the spot until his eyes burned, and he wasn't sure if the shimmery haze he'd started to pick out was real or just the product of needing to blink.

"Geez, you scared me! I thought I'd been caught!"

Draven's voice cut across his thoughts, and he realised he'd zoned out at precisely the wrong second. There had been no dramatic flash. No flicker or shimmer. One second there was nothing, the next Draven was there. He suspected the portal was deflecting his attention.

"You have been." Niall pulled him into a hug. "Gotcha."

They exchanged a long, non-verbal hello up against one of the bookcases. Niall was worried he might have forgotten how kissing worked in the intervening week, especially as he wasn't that confident to begin with, but with Draven there, everything made sense again. When he was around, it was fine—it was easy. Even though Niall had to slouch or stoop to kiss him, it felt like they fitted flawlessly together.

Eventually, he pulled back. His mind was bubbling with all the ways he wanted to tell Draven that he was amazing, and he wanted to look at him—just look at him and see that he was real and looking back at Niall as mushily—and he couldn't do those things whilst kissing him.

"Do you wanna go out somewhere today?" Niall asked.

"Like, into town?"

"Somewhere else," Niall said. All week long, the thought of introducing Draven to his family had played on his mind. He had a stay of execution on that for one week though. Which meant he and Draven could have some fun; go on a real date. He still couldn't quite imagine Draven sitting at the dining table with his parents, but there were other places that mattered to him, ones that he was sure Draven could fit into. "Somewhere magical." He raised his eyebrows.

"Magic doesn't exist here." Draven frowned.

"Well..." Niall was reluctant to say that it absolutely didn't. "One of the places that always made me believe in it. You can give me your expert opinion."

Draven scanned the window. Niall followed his eyes, though all they would be landing on from here would be a sky dotted over with grey clouds. He wasn't sure it was the weather Draven was worrying about though.

"It'd be an actual adventure. Out into your world," Draven said.

"Into one of the nicest bits of it," Niall promised him. The flicker of alarm across Draven's face suggested that hadn't been as reassuring as he'd intended. Still, Draven shook off whatever he'd been thinking.

"If you say it's fine, it must be," he said. "Alright. Let's go."

Niall leant in to give Draven one more quick (not so quick) kiss on the lips before carefully tucking that part of himself away, like straightening out the collar of a shirt before you left the privacy of your room.

As they walked towards the library doors, he could feel his anxiety mounting. There was still the bus through town to get, with a weirdly dressed outsider. However, the thought was driven from his head by Draven.

"You'll never guess what happened this week!"

You met someone else. You got caught. You got permission to come back forever and ever?

"What?" Niall asked.

"We had a green day!"

"Holy shit! Did you get to do all kinds of crazy, forbidden magics?"

"I gave myself a blue streak in my hair and cast a glamour. It doesn't sound wild like that, but it really was something else seeing everyone all fancied up. We took pictures—I'll show you when they're developed. Not that the glamour will show up in them. It's more like an air you give off that makes you more compelling. It draws people to you."

"Who did you use it on?" Niall looked round sharply.

"Myself. Oh, you mean—no, honey. I mean, it made people notice me more, but I didn't use that. I was just playing around. Obviously, I wasn't trying to attract anyone." He reached out and gave Niall's hand a squeeze.

"Good." Niall tucked his hands inside his pockets as soon as Draven let go. "You and me it's serious right? And it is just you and me?"

"It is for me." Draven raised his eyebrows. "You?" he prompted when Niall didn't answer.

"What? Yeah. Obviously. I had enough trouble asking one guy out."

"Well, you might have developed a taste for it," Draven teased.

"Nah. Just for you."

"Sounds good."

"Um. Speaking of you and me and serious..." Niall took a breath. "My parents want to meet you. Next weekend. For lunch."

"People know about me?" Draven glowed as he said it. "How much do they know about me?"

"They know you exist and you're my boyfriend." Niall smiled as he said it.

"But?"

"They don't know about the magic thing. They'd think I was joking or losing the plot. Sorry."

"If they meet me, are they going to think I am?"

"Depends how many teabags you dissect at the table or how many questions you ask about the microwave. They know you're a bit..."

"Odd?"

"Different."

"I don't mind being odd." Draven shrugged. "I probably am. But whether it's to a degree that will cause problems?"

"I guess it's going to cause different problems if you refuse to ever meet my family and friends. My mum will think you're nefarious and Ellen will think you're imaginary, in spite of photographic evidence to the contrary. So, lunch next week?"

"Lunch next week."

So. That was settled. It would be fine. Draven was getting the hang of things here, and Niall could brief his parents and tell them what not to ask about. Today he would get a test run. He would see what happened when he put Draven out into the wider world. He swallowed down a ball of nerves. It would be fine.

* * *

They stood on the bridge between the platforms. Half of the walkway was sectioned off behind glass windows and given over to art—currently, papier-mâché local landmarks made by primary school children. The wrought iron rafters of the station arched overhead, echoed again and again in every direction. Below them was a spread of treasures. Everything from cupcakes with a stiff peak of icing as high as the cake itself, to old bric-a-brac, to quirky jewellery and locally made art. Whilst shoppers browsed on either platform, vivid yellow metros hurried in. It was early in the day and, in spite of the grey skies outside, the proportions getting off for a day out far outweighed those shuffling back on to be taken away.

After his promise of magic, Niall was worried that he'd oversold this. But Draven had looked excited as soon as they'd got here, and Niall had pulled him up onto the bridge, promising he could look at everything soon enough, but first to just look at it *all*. Draven was, and was looking as enchanted as Niall had hoped he would.

"Let's explore?" Niall suggested. They made their way down, meandering between the stalls.

"I like your pictures," Draven said to a lady with wavy, fair hair. "I can't buy them, but I like them," he stated bluntly.

"That's fine. Take your time," she said. Niall found this curious. Not that the five-foot-two blond lady with her jaunty scarf and cheerful round red earrings was threatening. But she seemed like a grown-up. She was standing on the other side of a trestle table and had business cards and confidence. She clearly had her shit together in a way that Niall could only aspire to in the vaguest possible terms. He was in that fuzzy space where he was regarded as a legal adult in some ways but not others. He was clearly a lot more mature than when he'd been in school, but there was a difference between him and what he thought of as "real grown-ups." The stall lady looked like she went to cool indie nights he saw flyers for and regretted being too young to go to. He wouldn't have ever tried talking to her like an actual human equal. Draven had no such qualms.

"That rabbit looks angry though." Draven pointed to a particular picture.

"That's because it's a vampire rabbit," Niall supplied with a grin. "It's a carving on one of the buildings behind the cathedral," he added hastily, before Draven could ask something embarrassing like whether they were real. Maybe the lady would assume he was joking if so.

"Is there a story that goes with it?" Draven asked, keeping his voice low. "Or does everyone know what they are?"

"It's mostly a mystery. I read one account that it was put up to frighten grave robbers—like centuries ago, when that sort of thing happened." He hoped his tone, intended to convey to Draven that it didn't anymore, wasn't too pointed. He thought that was a reasonable thing to say, under most circumstances. He'd also heard the more mundane account that it was a reference to someone called Hare, but that was such a let-down that he didn't mention it.

They moved on, browsing the stalls in a leisurely way. Niall forced himself to trail, letting Draven set the pace, giving him time to be fascinated by the things Niall usually skipped over, like the bread stall. He enjoyed the paintings a lot. All the people being local artists, there were a lot of local scenes.

"Where's that?" he would ask Niall quietly—one thing Draven was shy of was displaying ignorance about this world. He barrelled into conversations without thinking for a second someone would take a dislike to being chatted to, but he dropped his voice whenever he asked for Niall's help to understand things. When Niall was able to tell him, he would always follow this up with "Do you have a story about being there?"

Draven lingered, he peered at everything with interest. Some of the stallholders eyed him up, wondering whether he was worth bringing out their sales patter for. Niall kept expecting people to laugh at him, or to get annoyed with him for being a timewaster, but they didn't. Some were friendlier than others, more in the mood for a casual chat. Draven went around complimenting things, pointing out what he liked or what they were good at. Niall had never imagined anyone cared what he thought, but he watched (at first, warily, checking Draven was not about to land himself in hot water) and people lightened up a bit after Draven talked to them. Would it be so hard to tell people the positive things you saw in them and the world? It was having a higher success rate than he might have imagined—enough so that Niall could believe the world and his boyfriend might not be so wildly incompatible after all.

"I think this one's my favourite," Draven said, as they browsed the old photo stall, stuffed with boxes and boxes of loose photos, or whole albums, who had lost their families. Niall and Draven flicked through the pictures, making up histories for them. The salt air tickled Niall's nose, laced with occasional wafts of mint chocolate or butterscotch from the cake stalls. "Definitely magic," Draven whispered, running his hands over the edges of curled and faded photographs. "Someone loved these once. They aren't left to be forgotten. They get another chance to be cared about."

"Ellen likes this stall too." Niall smiled as they browsed the photos. Admittedly, her take on it was that these people were almost all definitely the dead relatives of other dead people and they made the perfect props for horror aesthetics, but common ground was common ground. In fact, she'd been talking about picking something up for a photography project here. There was an album with a faded paisley cover that he thought she might appreciate. He bought it, handing it to Draven to slip into one of his cavernous pockets when no one was looking too closely.

"By the way," Draven said, as he stowed the album. "You're not the only one with surprises to offer today. Is there somewhere we can sit?"

"There is. In fact, I was going to ask you to take in a special view." Niall felt giddy. His favourite person was in his favourite place, and there was one more magical element he wanted Draven's opinion on.

He led them out of the station, down the road, past the church-turned-market, and the shop across the street that had rainbow everything. It was the kind of place he browsed for ages, wishing his own room looked that strange and funky. Perhaps he'd take Draven in on the way back, but for now he wanted to be outside.

At the end of the street, the world dropped away, down to the beach and the swirling sea below. On the head of the cliff were the remains of the priory, one mostly solid wall evoking the sense of what the building would have been; the high arched windows took up almost the whole height of it, topped by a formation of smaller arches and circles.

"We'll go in sometime." Niall's stomach fizzed at planning a future outing like the world was theirs, made of nothing but casual Sundays in which they could make lazy day trips to the beach. "But when I'm just looking, I like to sit here." He perched on a low stone wall that formed the barrier between the pavement and the substantial drop down to sea level on its other side. "So that I can look at the priory or the beach, depending which way I feel like facing," he added, nodding to the sweep of sand below. The sea was chopping about a bit, but not bad for the time of year. Niall loved it when it was calm, and when it was hurling itself so hard against the pier that you could watch for hours, placing silent bets on whether it would come crashing over the top. There was always something deeply hypnotic about the sea.

"I heard a voice there." Niall gestured to the priory. Draven was probably the only person in any world he could tell about that. He wouldn't think Niall was strange, he might even be able to explain it. "On New Year, I was standing there and I heard—"

"Me!" Draven exclaimed. "You heard me. One of my favourite places back home is the ruins of this old castle. I was there on New Year's too, and just after midnight I heard—"

"—someone saying 'Happy New Year!'"

"But sounding rather sad about it." Draven peered at Niall.

"I wasn't having fun. But hearing that made it better. You?"

"I wanted the world to be bigger than it is. That's why I love the castle. There's something so evocative about ruined buildings, isn't there? It's part of the past that's still standing, here in the present, but it feels like it comes from somewhere completely out of reach."

It echoed Niall's thoughts from New Year—all he had wanted was someone who saw the world the way he did. With the crisp sea air stinging their noses and perfectly overlapping thoughts about the beauty of ruined buildings, it seemed silly to worry about lunch with his parents. In the places that mattered—in the library, out here taking in his favourite view—Draven fitted perfectly.

"I'm glad you like it." He cautiously, subtly, reached into the space between them on the wall, letting his fingers bump up against Draven's, planning how they were going to have picnics here in the summer. "I love you," he said softly.

This time, Draven didn't come out with any shock revelations. He did the thing you were supposed to do, and matched what Niall was thinking, feeling and saying.

"I love you too."

Chapter Twenty-One

In Draven's mind, there was only one logical conclusion to a statement like that, which was to throw your arms around the other person and kiss them. He leant forward, but he was the only one who did. Niall sat, looking at him, with that magnetic force in his eyes like he *wanted* to pull him in, but the rest of him was shuttered off. The way it had been all day. Draven had pretended not to notice that every time he had reached for Niall's hand, it hadn't been there. That every attempt he had made to coax one of them out of Niall's pockets with a hand on his arm or a tug on his elbow had been met with stiff resistance.

"Are public displays of affection frowned upon?" he asked.

"No. Not entirely. Not really. I... It's just better if we don't."

Draven glanced around, feeling that they were the exception rather than the rule. People other than Niall were being perfectly warm with each other.

"It's a you thing, not a here thing?"

"Somewhere in between." Niall traced circles in the thin dusting of sand on the rock. "Some people do." Niall avoided Draven's eye. "I... It's not... It's easier for some people. It's more allowed."

"Which one?" Draven asked. "Cos those are different things."

"Are they?"

"'Allowed' implies that there's rules about it. 'Easier' is more how you feel about doing it, or how many things are in the way. So, it's awkward, or it's not allowed?" he clarified.

"Awkward," Niall said. "Here, anyway. Some places are stricter. Sorry."

"You didn't make the rules." There were more questions spinning through his mind, but he'd always been told that asking them would lead him into trouble. Niall had never subscribed to that philosophy. But Draven was getting the horrible feeling that everyone else might be proven right if he asked too much more, and that he might not like what he heard.

"So," he said, hiding his disappointment behind a smile, "your surprise." He dug into a pocket, pulling out a flask. "I brought tea."

"Oh. Thank you." Niall was smiling, but he didn't sound amazed, and Draven wasn't sure whether it was the conversation they'd just half had or something else. But a magic surprise should surely perk things back up.

"It's still hot," Draven said.

"Uh-huh."

"That's magic," Draven pointed out, wondering why Niall was failing to be impressed by this.

"Oh. Right. Um. That's nice. Only, we uh, have something quite similar," Niall explained.

"Oh." Draven's face fell.

"Sorry. I don't want to mix you up more by pretending things aren't what they are. It's still a lovely surprise—I get to taste this famous tea of yours," Niall said.

"Well, I'm not making any promises of how it's going to taste after you dump milk and sugar in it."

"You brought milk and sugar?" Niall asked.

"Of course." Draven fished a small bottle of milk and a bowl of sugar from his pockets along with two cups and saucers. "You look surprised."

"Well, for one, *that* was the impressive magical part." He nodded to the assembled tea things. "And two, I thought you thought it was a moral crime to add milk and sugar to tea."

"It is. You're dreadfully unsavoury." Draven pulled out a teaspoon and tapped Niall on the nose playfully. "But it's how you take it." Much as he was appalled by Niall's habits, it would be more appalling to serve someone tea in a fashion they found unappealing.

"You're sweet." Niall smiled.

"I also have a book for you, and a lot of stories to tell you about it." Draven pulled The Book from his pocket and handed it over. "Good surprise?"

"Yes. Very good surprise."

In spite of his words and his tone, Niall was still closed off. He was curling both hands around his teacup, like he needed something solid to hold onto.

"There are all these spells." Draven flicked the book open. "I could do your hair too. Or use the perfume spells on the library."

"Why?" Niall tilted his head.

"Oh, the library smells kind of weird. I could fix it for you."

"The library does not smell weird!" Niall protested.

"Okay. Sorry."

"Anyway, these are forbidden, right?"

"The spell I did here never showed up on my account. It doesn't seem to count when I do it here." He could do anything. He finally had the power to do whatever he wanted—to make the world a better place!

He'd brought tea. He'd made Niall happy. Apparently, he didn't think the library needed fixing. So that meant pretty. Shiny. More fun. What else was there to do? Because bad things didn't exist, not truly bad ones.

"I want to make your life better," he said, his voice coming out very small. The wind rippled the pages of the book, and he had to place a hand on it to stop it blowing away—it was too flimsy, too insubstantial.

"You do," Niall assured him.

The air was crackling again, sparking with the kisses that weren't happening. They should have been punctuating every sentence. The rock was rough under his fingertips where Niall's hand should have been holding his.

"This isn't fair," Draven pointed out the obvious. "I want to take your hand, and take you down to the beach, and get lost in you until the waves start running into our shoes." He kept his voice low, out of deference to Niall, even though he also wanted to leap up and stand on the rock, shouting all of that out to the world.

"I know. Me too. But..." Niall shook his head.

"Is it...is it to do with us both being boys?" Draven asked.

Niall looked down, looking like he was wrestling with himself over what to say to that.

"Yeah." His voice was only a whisper, but Draven could still hear the crack in it.

"It's a big deal here, isn't it?" Draven asked, reviewing the past few weeks—how Niall had freaked out when he'd tried to flirt with him in the café, and how he'd been so scared when he'd thought that Draven didn't like him back. It had been more than the mere disappointed sting of unrequited love, more like he'd put himself in the firing line by admitting his feelings. The fact that some people could hold hands and others couldn't.

"Sort of. Sometimes—not to everyone."

"What's the worst that can happen?" he asked.

"You really want to know?" Niall asked.

"You said we were serious." He sighed. Even when they had said that, he hadn't expected it to include so much actual seriousness.

"People can be hateful," Niall admitted. "Because of this."

"Why?" asked Draven. "That doesn't make sense."

"I don't know."

"Can you ask the mobile phone?" Whenever something baffled him about this world, Niall typed words into the little box and explained it.

"I think this is more complicated than the microwave thing. Sorry." Niall shook his head. "Do you...do you want to go home?"

"No." Draven shook his head. "It's Sunday. It's our day."

"Yeah. I know. But this is a lot. I figured you might need some time. Or you might not want to—"

"I'm staying! Sod the world for how crappy it's made you feel. You deserve every bit of that making up to you."

He needed to find more old magic. Something better than hairstyles and glamours. Words he never thought he'd find himself thinking. He'd seen so few examples but—but he had seen one!

"I can do it!" He began tracing in the sand on the rock, trying to recall the runes. "I know a spell. An old one. To make good things happen. At least, I saw it once." He scrubbed out the runes, they weren't quite right. He tried again but the more he tried to grab hold of it, the more it slipped through his fingers.

"Wait. Is it this?" Niall reached out a finger, tracing a series of familiar shapes into the sand. Draven sucked in a breath.

"How did you know how to draw those?"

"I found a necklace with them on, in a charity shop. I bought it because I thought it might be magic. It feels so weird to be able to say that out loud and not be laughed at." Something like real excitement crept back onto his face. "And to be right?"

"Yes. I saw that necklace in the storage room at work. They were going to scrap it, so I pushed it to the back of the shelf."

"Your world and mine, they keep finding all these little ways to get through to each other. Did I do magic with it? Or is it magic by itself?"

"Probably the latter. You never know though," he added, wanting to give Niall reasons to hope. "Magically imbued objects are different to spells."

"What did you say it does?"

"Brings a little goodness into your life."

"Well, I'd say it overachieved." Niall smiled at him.

Draven tried to smile back. He liked being a piece of goodness, but it seemed like it was going to take more than a tiny drop of that to fix everything that was wrong with this world.

"I'm going to find a whole bunch more like it," he promised Niall. "I'm going to fix everything."

Chapter Twenty-Two

It had been a long day. In literal terms, no longer than any of his other visits, but between straying further into the world than he'd ever been, and finding out more about it than he'd wanted to, Draven's mind was spinning. His image of the pleasant world he'd known felt tarnished. What kind of place hated people for falling in love? A cruel place. A place he'd been telling himself for the past few weeks that he wasn't in.

He was loved too. There was a warm feeling in his belly that was at war with the storm in his head. When he put them together, they made a fire. Mages had fixed things in other places before. They'd only left because they ran out of magic, and if his magic didn't count there—he could find old spells. He could fix it. He'd told Niall he would make it all better, and he'd meant that.

Stepping out of the portal, he stared around the Special Collections. All the knowledge they kept from him. Things it wasn't relevant to teach them anymore. He had already seen the dates he knew nothing about, stamped onto the spines of some of the books. This was where things went when people didn't want to talk about them.

He checked the index numbers on the spines nearest to him. He was in the history and geography section, and yes, the numbers were the same as the ones used in the main library. There were maps at his fingertips. All of them labelled with places he wouldn't have known a few short weeks ago, but which were becoming increasingly familiar. He pulled something called an *A-Z of Tyne and Wear* off the shelf, and flipped to the index, skimming past Bamburgh Terrace, and Bedeburn Road and...Bedewell. Bedewell Public Library. With a page, and a grid reference. He flicked to it. A tiny, dark red square, labelled with neat black letters stared back him. They knew about it.

Shaking, he shoved the map back on the shelf. He needed spellbooks. He knew the library filing system inside out, he just had to follow the numbers. He traced them back, through a literature section of unfamiliar titles, past technologies he'd never heard of. In the main library, the spellbook section wasn't one he visited often. It was small, with a handful of spare copies of the household spellbooks, and a few resources on the guild magics, though most kept their own copies to supply to apprentices.

He rounded a corner, finding the numbers on the end of the shelf lined up with the reference he was looking for. So did the shelf above. And below. And the ones above and below that, and each shelf ran on, out of sight. There had to be a mistake. But as he checked numbers against titles, it only confirmed it. These were *all* spellbooks.

Where was he supposed to begin?

Subsections. There had to be subsections. He skimmed the titles, mentally dividing up the shelves. Beauty, household, illusions. He brushed past them all, with an aching heart. All of his dreams were at his fingertips, and what did he need instead? Protection magic. Healing spells. How to mend breakages he didn't even understand. He pulled a book from the shelves, opening it with trembling fingers. "How to contain greed." "How to grow kindness in a cold heart." "How to combat hopelessness." But these weren't single spells. These were chapter titles. Paging through them, it seemed like the answer again and again was that no one knew.

He grabbed several spellbooks which followed more familiar formats. They sparked some hope of doing good in the world, before he remembered there was nothing he could do with them right now. He couldn't take them home to study.

He placed them in a pile at the end of the aisle, working out how many more trips he could make during the week. He would add to the pile, and study what he found, so that he had a ready stack of resources to take to Niall's world.

He stood, staring down the endless shelf, trying to find the energy to search for more. But a glance at his watch exonerated him. The library would be closing in five minutes. He ignored the relief flooding through him at putting his quest on hold for now. He was supposed to be a hero, not a scared and overwhelmed teenager.

His feet carried him without conscious thought back through the shelves. He bit his lip, unable to taste the salt of the sea air on his skin anymore. He tried to shuffle the feeling of the breeze, and the smell of cupcakes to the front of his mind. He wanted to hold onto something pleasant. But it slipped away, like a hand being tucked into a pocket, out of reach. He turned the handle of the door to the Special Collections and stepped out into the main part of the library.

"What were you doing in there?"

He looked up, startled, realising too late that he hadn't even checked whether the coast was clear. Now he was face to face with an infuriated-looking Matthias.

"Nothing." Draven knew it wasn't polite to sound so sullen, but he was too tired to think up a lie or try to defend his actions.

"It's not exactly like it's open for casual browsing. What were you doing?"

"Mind your own business." Draven glared. "If I didn't have permission, I wouldn't be able to get in. Try for yourself."

Matthias narrowed his eyes and reached over to the door handle, which remained unrelenting under his grip.

"Fine." He glared, in a way that left Draven under no illusion that this was going to be the end of things.

* * *

Draven did not have to spend much of Monday morning sweating it out. At least, not over wondering what Matthias would do with the information he'd gleaned. The other boy dropped into his seat fifteen minutes late, flicking a note and a smug look across the table. Draven opened it. A summons to see Mage Starkweather. The only surprise was that she had given Matthias the time of day. Draven pulled himself promptly from his chair, trying not to give Matthias the satisfaction of seeing this affect him. He only gave in and allowed the heavy, leaden feeling in his stomach to slow his steps once he reached the corridor.

Still, however slowly he crept, he soon found himself sitting in a now familiar office. Except the chair he was in no longer felt comfortable, and he could not meet the eyes of the person across the desk from him.

"I just had an interesting conversation with Mr. Bourne," Mage Starkweather informed him. Draven felt his shoulders tense but did not reply. "He was very keen to prove himself, to get included on whatever special project it is you've been assigned."

Draven, for once in his life, kept silent. Of course Matthias had made it sound like some worthy endeavour. When, in fact, Draven suspected he was a jealous, petty piece of shit. There was a beat of silence while each weighed up what the other knew. Only guild heads could give permission. That was a wide enough range of people that she didn't automatically know he'd been abusing her request, but it was probably narrow enough to make her suspicious.

"I've been wracking my brains," she continued when he wasn't drawn out, "trying to work out which guild head would give one of my apprentices access to Special Collections. Then I realised, I did, didn't I?"

There didn't seem much point in pretending, and so he nodded, wondering how angry she was going to be.

"And you, being as curious as you are, have no doubt been taking full advantage of that. How is the Other World treating you?" she asked.

Ice clenched in the pit of his stomach. Not at the fact that she knew. It was hard not to notice a great gaping portal in the middle of the room. He suspected you were meant to be in on that before you were allowed to access the reading material that was kept there. Her knowing he'd been in that room had been akin to her knowing exactly where he'd been. But she had called it the Other World. Disappointment settled over him the same way a creeping pain that had been plaguing your temples did, when you finally had to acknowledge it had spread to become a full-on headache. He had been kicking back against that idea whilst every piece of evidence confronted him that it couldn't be anything else. He thought back to the list of simple problems in his journal, and the promise he'd just made Niall.

"You think it's the Other World?" he asked, desperate for there to be some alternative.

"What makes you so sure it isn't?"

"Because there are wonderful things there. Everything I've been told about the Other World, it doesn't fit at all." There was a library, and there were tea shops, and there was Niall. There were people who hated people like Niall too, though. There were reasons to be careful.

"That sounds plausible. It wasn't all fire and brimstone there, you know. It was what lurked under the surface that you had to watch out for."

Draven felt the knots in his stomach tighten. The Other World had always been described to him as so lacking in redeeming features that he couldn't imagine it passing for such a charming place. On the other hand, he rarely doubted what his mentor told him. There could be room for both, he supposed. She could be right, that the Other World had had its moments, but that didn't mean it was irredeemable. It had Niall. No one could meet Niall and believe there was anything dark lurking inside him. If the Other World was still as riddled with problems as they both thought, then Draven had to help him.

"I think a lot might have changed," he said, trying not to feel like his whole life hinged on how true that proved to be. Or how willing she was to listen to his evidence. "Since however long it's been."

"Really?" This was uttered with something approaching genuine interest, and her face was open and curious. "Tell me more," she invited.

"I—" he hesitated. He wasn't sure whether to reveal he had met someone. It had always felt perilous and forbidden that he was dating an outsider, but that was because going there seemed frowned upon. If that in itself wasn't going to get him in trouble, perhaps it was safe. But perhaps not. Once he told, he couldn't untell her. "I found a library. The people there are kind. I haven't had any trouble there." He remembered Niall drawing away from him in the tearoom and wondered how much of his "good luck" was down to someone else's sense of self-preservation. If he had been more openly himself, what would have happened?

"It's going to take more than a library to convince me that you're safe, Draven."

He was disarmed by the concern in her tone. It was less like he was being told off and more like there was a fretful parent looking at him.

"Please don't say you're stopping me from going back," he begged.

"I need to think about this. I'm the reason you're there, and I'm responsible if anything happens to you. What makes you so determined to go back?"

Draven looked down at his hands. It hurt, keeping Niall a secret.

"Draven, if you want me to take this seriously, you have to tell me what's going on there. I don't want to be blindsided later on by something I should have known about."

"There's a boy," he admitted. "There's this boy, and I love him."

"I see." Her tone was impossible to read. Draven tried to take comfort from the fact she wasn't immediately recoiling in horror or telling him "no." She leant back, thinking it over for what felt like five eternities. "Bring me proof," she said.

"Proof?" Draven asked.

"Bring me proof that the Other World is kind and safe. Then you can keep going back there."

* * *

Niall flicked through the pictures on his phone, whilst "Sight for Sore Eyes" thrummed in his ears. Every song about being happy in love and every song about the miserable agony of separation was about him and Draven. Given that his boyfriend was a mage from a different dimension, he was getting pretty good mileage out of no one understanding what he was going through. He started with the first photos they'd ever taken, with Draven laughing with glee as he learnt to operate the phone, along to ones of their most recent Sunday. Maybe he was imagining the difference between those two smiles. But Draven had been subdued for the rest of the day. He still hadn't been himself when Niall had been forced to let him go. He guessed he'd invited realness into this, and maybe that meant taking the rough with the smooth. But this was a bitter pill to swallow because it wasn't like he was letting Draven in on all his issues, or they were seeing the bad bits of each other and having to decide whether the good outweighed it. He was having to teach Draven that the world might want to hurt him, and that didn't feel fair. Probably because it wasn't. Niall had promised to introduce him to his family, and he wanted all the horrible things not to be true or frightening. But they were.

The clock ticking down to next Sunday was already moving at a weird pace. In some ways, six days was nowhere near a big enough buffer zone between Draven and Niall's parents, especially when he had no more chances to coach him on what to say and not say. On the other hand, it was far too long to leave Draven alone with the thoughts that Niall had put into his head, and to not be able to comfort him.

He pulled out his headphones as Ellen joined him on the bus.

"Mondays suck." He rested his head on Ellen's shoulder.

"I see you've come round to my way of thinking," she said. "Is everything okay?"

"I miss Draven." He sighed, sticking with the simple version of the problem.

"Yeah. A problem with choosing someone utterly unavailable will be a lack of availability." She was smiling as she said it, trying to tease him into a good mood, but Niall folded his arms with a frown. He didn't want to be teased. He didn't want his friend picking holes in Draven.

"It's not his fault." He glared.

"I didn't say it was." Ellen glared back. "Though I do remember saying you'd cheer up if you got a boyfriend, and I am fully willing to eat my words on that one."

Niall huffed.

"Okay," Ellen said, drawing out the word with pointed patience. "I've tried asking you seriously about him and you blew me off. I've tried joking about the problem. What do you actually want me to say?"

Niall managed to bite back an "*I don't know.*" He wanted Ellen to get it, but how could she when he wasn't able to explain anything?

"My parents asked to meet him, and I dunno how that's gonna go." He tried to find a tangible, concrete problem.

"Your parents are great. Come on, what do you think is gonna happen?"

"I don't know. It's complicated." Why had he started this? But he had to talk to someone. He couldn't tell Draven that he was in the wrong for existing, but he needed to get all the ways he was such hard work off his chest, except he couldn't because no one would believe him and—

"How so?" Ellen pushed.

"JUST STUFF."

Ellen folded her arms at being yelled at, and Niall sunk down in his seat.

"Sorry. All the stuff where he's not from here. It's so hard sometimes. I mean, he and I work. But I don't know if he and everything else does."

"I mean, my take is always if someone makes you miserable, it's not worth it."

"I did not say he makes me miserable." Niall prickled.

"Evidence to the contrary," Ellen shot back, eyeing him up and down.

"Having to deal with all this makes me miserable. Being apart from him makes me miserable."

"Which is eighty percent of your relationship. And is that ever going to change? Are you ever going to have a real relationship?"

"Oh, so now my relationship's not real?"

"You know what I mean. Look, you know I'm down with whatever you want. You want to screw around, do that. You want to be Mr. Sensible and start planning your wedding and your family home with the little rainbow picket fence, do that. But you're not doing either."

"Oh, and those are the only two relationship models in existence? Yay binaries. Always helpful and constructive."

"Or run away and join a queer circus collective. Whatever. My point is, do what makes you happy, and this is not making you happy. You were always talking about wanting something serious. Something real and long term. Where did that go?"

"It's still what I want. I want that with him."

"Are you ever going to get it, though?"

"Why are you randomly attacking my relationship?"

"Because you literally just said that your boyfriend meeting your family will go down like an alien landing."

"I did not LITERALLY say that."

"Stop being a fucking pedant. You're the one who said it wasn't working."

"You're not supposed to agree with me. You're supposed to be my friend."

"I'm being your friend. If it isn't working, it isn't working. Maybe that's not something you like hearing, but maybe it's something you need to."

"You're always so negative! Like, all the stuff about how the world sucks—" So what if he'd been saying it and thinking it too, at the weekend? Maybe it was from spending too much time with Ellen. Maybe Draven could be right, and it wasn't so dreadful here. He would never be able to put the two of them in a room together. "You don't have to project that onto my relationship too!"

"Oh, so now it's my fault? How?!"

"If you don't have anything supportive to say, leave me alone," Niall snapped.

"Fine." Ellen picked up her bag and disappeared to the back of the bus. A moment later, Niall heard the aggressively loud thrum of heavy metal guitars turned up loud enough to leak out of headphones. He jammed his own back in, scrolling through his phone for anything as angry as he was feeling. More than anything, he found himself opening his messaging apps. He wanted someone to turn to, someone to hear his hurt. He had no idea why he was scrolling mindlessly back and forth through his contacts. The one person he wanted to be there wasn't. Even if he was, maybe he'd never understand.

Chapter Twenty-Three

It was ten fifty-seven. They'd said they would meet at eleven. Niall bounced on the balls of his feet. He ran his fingers along the shelf. He'd been there for twenty-two minutes already, and had managed to keep still for all of ten seconds. He checked his phone again, but it only reminded him of the time, and the fact that he couldn't message Ellen to distract himself. Over the course of the week, he'd almost caved repeatedly. He wasn't used to having friends, and he couldn't stand the thought that he might have messed it up. But it still wasn't like he could explain his side of things.

Ten fifty-eight. Just because Draven wasn't early didn't mean anything. Of course, if he didn't come, Niall didn't have to put Draven in the same room as his parents, or test the water-tightness of all the dos and don'ts and excuses that they'd gone through the previous week. Had he really just thought that? That was a horrible thing to think. Maybe it was a normal thing to think? Just the normal awkward nerves of introducing your boyfriend to your family. If he didn't come now, it probably meant he wasn't ever coming back. That it was too weird and too scary here. Niall didn't want that to be true.

As it clicked over to ten fifty-nine, Draven appeared around the end of the bookcase. Whilst the doubt did not fully dissolve, it was sharply and thoroughly pushed to the edges by the feeling of warmth that seeing him always produced.

"Hey! You're here!" Niall darted forward, pulling him into a too-tight hug.

"Yes," Draven said. Niall pulled back, searching for signs of whether the hesitancy he'd heard was real or just in his head.

"You look...different." He'd been torn between saying "normal" and "strange"—normal for this world, which was strange for Draven—but decided that neither of those was polite. Draven was wearing black trousers, a powder blue shirt and a tie.

"I look boring, but presentable. Right?" he added anxiously.

"You look very smart. I think I like you in a tie." He gently tugged on it to bring Draven into kissing range. "You okay?" he asked as they broke apart. It wasn't only Draven's clothes that were muted.

"Just nervous," he said. He wasn't meeting Niall's eye.

"It'll be fine." Niall forced a cheeriness into his voice that he didn't feel. It sounded fake, and he wondered whether Draven could hear it too. "Shall we?"

"Yeah." Draven reached out, taking Niall's hand for one more squeeze of reassurance. He let go, and tucked his hands in his pockets, falling into step beside Niall, but apart from him.

* * *

"How was your week?" Niall tried breaking across the awkward silence as they walked towards his house.

The pause before Draven answered was too long.

"Fine."

"What did you get up to?"

"Tell me about your week." The fact that Draven was shaking him off was so blatant that Niall frowned. He was reminded of their first conversations, where Draven hadn't known how to tell him anything about himself. It had only been a few weeks, but he thought of this as "not like Draven." Since that door had opened, Draven had been a non-stop chatterbox. Niall hadn't expected to have it suddenly closed in his face again. But what did he know? About Draven, about his world, about having a boyfriend.

He did as he'd been asked, and talked about his week. Or rather, his classes. His own conscious avoidance of the fight with Ellen only fed his feeling that Draven was hiding something too. He filled the time with physics, trying to believe it was just nerves, as Draven claimed, until the green front door of his house came into view.

"This is it." As he pushed open the gate, he watched Draven's eyes tracking methodically over the neatly trimmed window boxes, the shiny brass numbers on the door, the big bay window. All the details that were so familiar to Niall that he barely noticed them, but which came together to form the composite image of "home." Draven had that look, the one that was hungry and excited to know things about this world—in this case, about Niall.

"This is where you grew up?"

"From when I was ten, yeah. C'mon." He slipped his hand into Draven's as he stepped up to the door and put his key in the lock.

As they stepped inside, Niall thought his parents did a great impression of people who had been busy about the house and not at all waiting for the sound of the door opening. They poked their heads out of the kitchen, calling cheery hellos as Niall and Draven took off their shoes. They came bustling down the corridor to offer handshakes whilst Niall hung up his and Draven's coats.

"It's nice to meet you. Niall's—"

"Niall's told us so much about you."

It was the default thing his mum said when meeting someone and he heard it dry up on her tongue. It wasn't true this time. He suspected that any of the ways she could accurately finish that sentence weren't going to sound particularly polite.

"Niall has given us vague and confusing non-answers to all our questions about you."

"Niall has given us a strict code of subjects we're allowed to ask you about and rung various alarm bells."

"Niall's got you here in one piece then," she changed tack, smiling brightly.

"Yes."

Draven's voice was small and timid. Niall wondered how literally he was taking that comment.

"Is lunch ready?" he jumped in, making sure Draven didn't ask how many of their guests arrived needing medical attention.

"Almost. You go make yourselves comfortable and we'll bring it through."

* * *

As they sat down to eat, the air was busy with food talk. There was the hustle and bustle of laying out cheese and bread and hummus and salad. Niall's mum was telling Draven that he was free to help himself but also constantly asking whether he wanted some of this or some of that, and checking for the millionth time that he didn't have some food allergy that Niall had either kept secret or not known about.

Once everyone had something on their plates though, there was a noticeable pause as they looked for something to say.

"Niall said he's been introducing you to all kinds of books," his mum said.

"Yes! He's good at that." He shot an appreciative smile across the table at Niall.

Niall tried to smile back. Books were certainly a happy topic, and one that steered them clear of reality. However, Draven was scarcely widely read. He'd finished part one of the *Redbloom* trilogy, but he'd barely started volume two. They kept finding other things to do. Even when he was listening to Niall describe books, he still had a hard time telling fantasy apart from reality.

"The library here's a little on the small side." His dad shrugged, half apologetic.

"Have you read everything in it?" Draven asked.

Niall paused with his water halfway to his mouth, wondering whether laughing and trying to pass that off as a joke would help. But it was probably ruder if it was a joke.

"Well, no. Can't say I have."

"Or even everything that interests you, even a little bit?" Draven pressed. "People keep apologising for the library here, like it isn't any good, but if you can still find a book you want to read, there can't be that much wrong with it." He glanced over to Niall, clearly looking for moral support. Niall tried to hastily arrange his features into a more encouraging look, but Draven's confidence dimmed.

"Sorry?" Draven's apology came out like a question, turning from Niall back to his parents. "I um...grew up in this...community. It's kind of...closed off and...different to here."

They had put enough truth into the carefully refined statement that it was barely even a lie. Niall had hoped that would mean Draven could say it a little more smoothly than he was currently managing. He kept shooting Niall furtive glances over the table, like he was checking he was saying it right. Still, either his parents were writing that off as nerves or being polite enough to pretend not to notice.

"What's it like?" his mum prompted gently, her tone pleasant and conversational.

"It's...it's very nice, in a lot of ways. They would argue that it's perfect, people back home I mean."

"But you disagree?" she asked.

"I guess it is. Sort of. But I like it here too."

"Do people know you've been leaving?"

Draven toyed with a forkful of salad in a way that rather answered that question. Niall wanted to tell her to stop, wondering what part of *"He doesn't like to talk about his home life"* hadn't been clear.

"Only one. I think they might not understand," Draven admitted. "I don't like lying or sneaking about. I'm not a dishonest person, and I'm not going to be dishonest or sneaky with your son, I promise."

"I wasn't assuming that. Though I'm glad to hear it. So, your family doesn't know you have a boyfriend?"

"No." Draven's voice shrank further.

"Mum," Niall protested, in a tone that said, *"Leave him alone."*

"I'm not interrogating," she said. "But you'll be welcome here—if they find out, and they start giving you a hard time. You don't need a specific invitation to come round."

"Thank you." Draven looked up, and Niall tried to feel reassured. His mum was sweet, and there was no doubt in his mind that she would be kind to someone who needed kindness. Whether they could have a normal lunch conversation was another matter.

"I think you have a good way of looking at things," she said. Again, there was that pause while everyone tried to think of something they were allowed to ask. "Generally an optimistic sort, are you?"

"I suppose? Maybe?" He picked at the piece of bread on his plate. Niall debated whether the conversation was skating too close to home, and he needed to step in and rescue him. But they had to talk about something. By their world's standards, Draven had a bright outlook, but Niall wasn't sure it counted as optimism if you weren't aware of the possibility that things might not work out. Draven had also ended up stumbling from his world into this one because he felt so bored and out of step, which hardly fitted the definition of an optimist. Not that they could explain any of that.

"That'll be a pleasant change from all the doom and gloom this one spouts." His dad jerked his head toward Niall.

"Oh, that's hardly fair," his mum said. "It's not like any of us like the way things are going."

"I'm just saying. The way he goes on, it's like it's constantly the end of the world."

"Hey," Niall pointed out. Firstly, *I am sitting right here* was one thought that sprung to mind, but more importantly... "No politics," he reminded them.

"Why not?" Draven asked.

Niall speared a small piece of cheese as a way of avoiding eye contact.

"It's easier without." Even with the backstory he'd fed his parents, he had to admit that sometimes Draven's view of things was so simplistic it came across as naive. He knew it wasn't Draven's fault. He knew other people theoretically knew that it wasn't Draven's fault, but he didn't want them to think Draven was stupid. He'd talked to him about philosophy and literature, and he knew that Draven was incredibly intelligent. That wasn't going to come across when something as intricate as this world's politics was on the table. He wanted this to work. He wanted his family to like Draven.

He chanced a look up and found that Draven was staring at him with an odd mix of expressions on his face. He looked as lost as Niall expected him to, but he was also looking like he'd been slapped. Which wasn't fair. Niall was being considerate. He'd spent hours preparing Draven for his family and preparing his family for Draven. He had tried to put them all on the same page. It wasn't his bloody fault if people kept trying to go off-script!

"Okay." Draven's tone was flat. It wasn't actively annoyed, but Niall was used to him sounding chirpy, and the absence of that registered as cold. "What do you want us to talk about?"

Niall took a huge bite of bread, hoping that some suitable answer would occur to him by the time he finished slowly chewing it. That wasn't fair. He never knew what to say. Draven knew that about him. He'd pretty much swallowed all the bread in his mouth, but he kept pretending to chew. Most people couldn't take a silence as long as he was making this one, and riding it out worked in his favour, as his mum gave in.

"Got any hobbies?" she asked Draven.

Draven's attention switched back to her. Haltingly, the conversation got going again. Draven was naturally chatty. Niall's mum was naturally chatty. They managed to patch over the awkward silences, making a little bubble of conversation between the two of them, with Niall's dad chipping in from time to time.

Niall wasn't sure whether it was his own awkwardness, and his fear that it was all about to go wrong that kept him feeling like he was on the outside of that. But he didn't think he was imagining it when, over the rim of his water glass, the look Draven gave him was still a little cold.

Chapter Twenty-Four

"Is this tiny you?" Draven nodded to one of the pictures on the windowsill.

Lunch was finished, and whilst he had insistently helped clear a few dishes from the table, he had been equally insistently waved off. Now he was standing, trying to find things to say whilst he waited for Niall's parents to finish putting lids on pots and sliding cheeses back into their wrappers.

"Yeah." Niall took a step closer. Draven moved along the row, away from him. There were various life stages of three different boys documented along the length of the windowsill. In the earliest shots, where they were basically small lumps in blankets, it was hard to tell which ones were Niall but after a while they had the right eyes.

"Did you skip picture day on a regular basis, or are you hiding them from me?" Draven glanced along the row. There were far more pictures of Niall's brothers, but he suspected that Niall himself was the one responsible for that. His eyes flicked to the table where Mrs. Silverstein was stacking the last of the plates.

"I hit a really unfortunate ugly phase that lasted from the time I started school until the time I finished it. No one needs to see that."

"You're not ugly." It was too unkind not to say it, even if he would have put more heart into reassuring Niall on a normal day. The dining room door clicked closed. Draven waited a beat, eyeing the empty table and noting the lack of return footsteps.

"Thanks. Hey—" Niall reached for his hand.

"Are you embarrassed by me?" Draven took a step back, folding his arms across his chest.

"What? No!" Niall's tone was firm, but his words came out too quickly, too loudly.

"You wouldn't let your parents talk to me about anything real," Draven said, thoroughly unsatisfied with Niall's denial.

"I get that they can't know much about me, but you wouldn't let them talk about here. Are you worried about what I'll say?"

"No." Niall wasn't exactly meeting his eye as he said it. "It doesn't feel fair. You're not going into those conversations on a level playing field. I wanted to make it easy for you."

"That wasn't easy! That was you shutting down every conversation and making me feel like I needed to apologise for myself."

"I was trying to protect you."

"From what? Is this world ending?"

"What?"

"Your dad said you always act like it is, and your mum said that was fair."

"It was more a turn of phrase than anything."

"So... It's fine here?" He regretted going for that as soon as it was out of his mouth. "I mean..."—he threw more words into the silence before Niall could tell him what he didn't want to hear—"it's... There's maybe some things but—" But what? *They're small?* They didn't feel small. It felt like shadows were looming over him, and the only thing he knew for certain was that they were all bigger than he was. "Just tell me! I need proof this world is good, or they'll stop me coming here!"

For the first time since his parents had left the room, Niall was looking at him. *Really* looking at him. Staring, wide eyed.

"What?" Niall asked.

Draven opened and closed his mouth a couple of times, trying to find a way to take that back, even though it was true. He hadn't meant to blurt it out like that.

"Since when are those the terms and conditions?" Niall demanded.

"I meant to tell you—" *more gently.*

"But you didn't! I can't give you that, Draven. No one can. And you let me— What was the point of doing this?" He gestured at the lunch table.

Because you love me. Because you want this to work out. They were the first answers that sprung to mind, but Draven swallowed them down. He was awkward. An embarrassment. There were ways Niall thought he didn't fit into this world, only he wouldn't tell him what they were, much less give him a chance to do anything about it.

"Because I can fix it."

He strode into the hallway, retrieving his jacket. There was a stack of newspapers, waiting to be put in the recycling, and he grabbed one. There would be solid, concrete information. It would have all the things Niall wasn't telling him, but it would show all the good things that were happening too. There was never enough bad news to fill a whole paper. He could take it back to Mage Starkweather. She would help him make a plan to fix the broken bits, and everything would be fine.

He returned to the dining room, slamming the paper down.

"What are you doing?" Niall asked.

Draven ignored him, pulling books from the pockets of his jacket. Each one hit the table with a resounding thud. He almost recoiled. He had never slammed things in his life.

"Draven, what are you doing?"

"If you won't give me answers, I'll figure it out myself." He had promised. He had promised Niall he would make it all better. He had promised Mage Starkweather.

"Put those away!" Niall hissed. "My parents are gonna be back any minute with dessert."

"So?" Draven threw the books open, searching for spells.

"So, they can't see those."

"Why not? Are they going to burn me at the stake?"

"No, but—"

"You said it needed to get real. This is real, Niall. My world. Your world. I am going to make them fit together. *Right now.*"

"Draven!" Niall snatched the paper up, gesturing at the front page. "We are talking about war. Climate change.

Poverty. Social justice. You cannot fix that with…what? Nose warming spells? Glamours?"

Draven looked at the headlines Niall was indicating.

"Why are those things in a newspaper?" he asked. "They only happen in stories." And in the Other World. As it had been when they'd chosen to withdraw. If they were all in the newspaper, then none of it had changed. Niall's eyes widened, like Draven had said something out of line. Some piece of stupid wrong thinking that would embarrass Niall if he said it in front of other people.

"Not here," Niall said softly. He tried to take a step towards Draven, but Draven snatched the paper and pulled away. He had to find a limit, some sign that this was finite and contained. He turned the pages with a shaking hand but it was all bad. How many people were in the world? Were all of them suffering? Why?

"I can fix it." His voice was shaking. He wasn't convinced but there was more in these books than the small spells he'd been allowed to use at home.

"No. You can't. Put this away." Niall began snapping the books shut. Draven tried to push down the feeling that Niall was acting like every single grown-up in his life, treating him like an airhead who wanted quick fixes and shiny parties. This had been more than that. This was him doing his best. He had finally felt powerful, like he could make a difference.

"You want me to sit and eat dessert?"

"My parents are about to come back in, so yeah, I would like you to sit and be normal for five minutes." He picked up Draven's jacket, trying to cram the bulky volumes back into the pockets.

"Sitting around, accepting all of this is not normal!" Draven pulled a spellbook out of Niall's reach.

"I don't like this stuff either, but it is big and complicated, and beyond you. You think people haven't tried making this better?"

"Well, they need to try harder!" He flicked through the pages, sure he'd seen something useful before.

"Draven. Please, stop—"

"No, YOU STOP."

He meant "*Stop sweeping things under the carpet.*" "*Stop telling me to be 'normal.'*" "*Stop shouting, and being part of what is strange and frightening and not soft in the world.*"

But that wasn't what he had said. And magic listened to your words, not your intentions.

Chapter Twenty-Five

"Niall?" Draven reached out, trying to shake Niall's shoulder, but he remained rigid, a frown frozen on his face. "Niall? Unstop! UNSTOP! Come back! Please?" He tugged his sleeve urgently, the only part of him that yielded. "I'm sorry. I'm so, so sorry. Can you hear me? I didn't mean to—"

There was a shuffling of feet from the next room. The spell only affected Niall. His parents were going to come back. How could Draven explain? He couldn't. What he was could not be explained. The evidence of it would be right in front of their eyes, but it wasn't a great first impression of magic. He had frozen their son. He had attacked. He hadn't meant to. But this was a world where hatred was real, and people acted on it. What would they do to him?

He needed to not be here. The further he was from Niall, the quicker the spell would wear off, and the safer he'd be. Especially as the footsteps were getting closer. It would be better for both of them if he—

—his shoulder collided with cold hard metal. A familiar scent, musty but with a sharp tang hit his nose. The library. Had he somehow ported? His head was still spinning, but he could see the signs with their angular white letters, the books, the threadbare carpet. He ran his fingers over some book spines, their plastic covers slippery and cold. He got halfway to taking ten deep breaths before he realised that wasn't going to be enough. His sobs had been momentarily halted by his surprise, but he couldn't stop the swirling tide of images in his brain or the crashing waves of conflicting emotions—all of them bad. He had never realised there were so many horrible feelings in the world, much less that someone could feel them all at once and not simply die.

He hurried back toward the portal, scared of being exposed and alone in this unfamiliar and unfeeling world, and threw himself in.

He emerged on the other side, wiping his eyes. He threw a hurt look at the portal, like a loyal pet that had suddenly turned and bitten him. He pinched the bridge of his nose and squeezed his eyes shut. He couldn't cry like this, not here. He needed to swallow it down and get home. Except he couldn't. He let out a gasping sob, leaning against the bookcase, because everything, absolutely everything, was so wrong.

He had been so preoccupied with his misery that he hadn't noticed anything around him, except the swimming glow of the portal, its brightness and his tear-blurred eyes limiting his vision. He jumped about a mile when a voice, not rebuking, but authoritative and knowing cut across his sobs.

"Is the Other World not treating you nicely anymore, Mr. Montrose?"

Draven straightened up, his heart in his throat at being caught, and was relieved to find Mage Starkweather.

"I would ask whether you're alright. Except, well, I can see that for myself." She was not the kind of person you could imagine hugging, although he was still tempted. He wanted to throw himself into the arms of someone who understood. It hurt his heart to think that, until minutes ago, the first person who sprang to mind for that description had been someone else entirely. He turned, feeling guilty for running, half wanting to dive back in. But how could he? There was so much to be afraid of on the other side. He felt firm fingers closing around his wrist.

"I think you should come away from there now," Mage Starkweather said, "and tell me what's happened. Let's sit down, shall we?"

Draven wanted to say no. It was Sunday—it was his day with Niall, and he had made a mistake in leaving—but he couldn't do anything except let himself be quietly pulled aside, and into some chairs at the edge of the Special Collections.

"I think, given the circumstances, we can bend the rules on drinking in the library," she said, conjuring up the tea things which he recognised from the library's kitchen. The universal remedy for shock. Niall's go to for everything. Niall, who he'd abandoned in a world full of horrible things.

The cup that she set down in front of him only made him cry harder.

"I'm sorry, Draven," she said, watching him sob. He looked up. Droplets of water clung to his lashes, but when he blinked, clearing them for a moment, he saw her peering at him with genuine concern. "I never meant for it to end up like this."

"It's not your fault," he managed. She'd only known for a week. He had set this whole thing in motion far longer ago than that.

"Isn't it?" she asked sadly. "I gave you permission, didn't I? I swear, I only had good intentions." She paused, and he made an effort to process what exactly she had said. He tried to reign in his tears enough to focus on her.

"You...you let me find the portal?" he asked. "You've known all along that I'm going?" He almost laughed. It seemed silly. This serious woman, the head of his guild, whom he had looked up to and admired, but with whom he thought he so fundamentally disagreed—it didn't tally with any of the conversations they'd had. It wasn't in line with how things were done here. "Why?"

"Because something was missing. Most people are happy to live here. They're content with the knowledge that we're plugging away at the problem, bit by bit. You wanted more. You're not the first. Every now and then there's a restless spirit, one who's looking for the big answer, and who isn't happy with the one that we provide—that this really is as good as it gets. So, I gave you more. I let you see for yourself. I knew you'd have to, to be satisfied."

"But I'm not satisfied. Now everything hurts."

"An unfortunate consequence of getting what you want. What you thought you wanted, I should say. Maybe that's where I misjudged things. I wanted you to realise that we can't ever belong there, so that you'd be happier here. I forgot how much learning that could hurt."

"Can't we?" he asked, plaintively.

"Can't we what?" she asked.

"Belong there?"

"I'm a little confused. What did you see? I assumed something there badly upset you."

"It did. But we could try to make it better?" He didn't know how. It was beyond him. But she would know. She was a real grown-up who made plans. If she would help him work out how, that was a drum he was more than willing to march to the beat of.

"You know that isn't possible. Magic no longer—"

"Magic works there!" he stated breathlessly.

"You used magic in the Other World? When there isn't enough to go around here?" For the first time her tone became unfriendly.

"Only twice," he said, deciding it was easier to count today as one incident. He was sure he hadn't done any harm to people here, and if she understood that, she'd be willing to help. "The first time...the first time was on purpose, and was maybe a little bit selfish," he admitted. "Except it's a spell I'd use back here, nothing forbidden. Niall, my boyfriend, he's always believed so much in magic. He wanted to see."

"You shouldn't need to buy people's trust. That's very symptomatic of what the Others are like, and why we can never get along."

"It wasn't to buy his trust. He believed me anyway. But he'd always wanted to see, and it was only one tiny spell, to try to make him happy. Today, it was an accident. But I don't think I'm taking from people here. I wouldn't want to do that, but the first spell didn't even show up on my records here. I think it works differently."

"Why did magic just come out today?" She arched her eyebrows in a way that suggested she already knew. "You were upset. So shaken by what you saw that you lost control." She supplied the answer for him when he didn't do it himself. "I was sceptical when you told me things had changed there, but I wanted to believe. But everything you're telling me is exactly how the Others have always been. Harsh, hurtful. Even the ones who aren't, the ones you'd like to improve things for, are too stubborn to let you help them."

"No. No, that..." His voice faded, the protest dying in his throat. Because wasn't that exactly the point he and Niall had hit in their conversation? He wanted to say that it didn't mean anything, that she knew nothing about him and Niall, and yet she was describing almost everything that had happened. Like she'd seen or heard it before. Like instead of blazing some brilliant new path, they were just a little bit of history repeating itself.

"I notice that when his world hurt you, you came running back here. Where was he? Didn't he look after you?"

"He tried," said Draven.

"Clearly, he didn't succeed. He knows where you come from, and what you can do, but does he understand anything about who you are?" she asked, and he could feel her eyes penetrating him, like that was a loaded question. Perhaps another rhetorical one.

"I think so," he choked out, not meeting her eyes. Because it had been one fight, just one, and they'd both been stressed. They...they shared what? A love of reading. Suddenly the ways they'd always been on the same page didn't seem to count for much. They had been, when it had been easy, but Niall's world was full of sharp edges, which wanted to cut him, cut them both, and Niall couldn't see what was wrong with it.

"He values the things that are important to you?"

Draven looked down. He neither wanted to defame Niall, nor to tell lies. It hurt that it wasn't possible to open his mouth without doing one of those things.

"Let me guess, it was all exciting at first. He was so impressed with what you could do. Now he's turned on you. It's not so cute anymore, is it? The way you see his world doesn't fit in. Even though you're right and he's wrong, he's never going to see it because he's surrounded by other wrong people—people who think that a poisoned mind is a normal thing to have."

"It doesn't— He's... He might change."

"They don't. I told you, you're not the first. This is what happens, every time. The more likely outcome is that you change. Either you exhaust yourself trying to fix a world that doesn't care about you, or you give up and become like them. Hatred is catching. I want you to promise me you won't go back." She rested a hand on his arm, looking concerned.

"But I—"

"Draven, the first big fear you came to me with was having no direction in life. Maybe I played this wrong—maybe I played this all wrong—but I wanted to show you how that happens. I wanted you to be content with the answers you could find here. Please, don't make me risk you in that way."

"Is that what's going to happen?"

"How you're feeling now, does it feel good for you?"

"Well, no."

"You're a bright boy. You could do amazing things here. I don't want you throwing your life and your talents away on a world that doesn't appreciate or take care of you."

"It's not the whole world though. It's him. He's worth saving. Or, it's worth trying."

"Even if he won't let you? Even if you have to beg and cajole him into understanding anything about you?" The motherly concern was replaced by frank disbelief.

"I can't give up on him, just because we had one fight."

"Draven, we can monitor your merit scores this week if you need further convincing, but I think you already know what they're going to show. I can't let you risk yourself that way."

"I'm willing to take the risk."

"I'm sorry," she said, although this time she didn't look it. "But I cannot let you act in a way that endangers you or the community. I will be rescinding my permission—"

"No. No, please. I can't leave like this. He'll think it's his fault. Or he'll wonder forever if I'm coming back. I have to see him again."

"I can give you one more trip. You will say goodbye, and I will take back my permission."

"Can I have time to think about this?"

"It's this, or I take it back now."

"Okay." His shoulders slumped. If a stay of execution was the best he could manage, he would have to take it. Take it, and find another way.

"I'm going to need more than an 'okay.'" A parchment and a silver-nibbed quill appeared on the table in front of them. "We're going to have to make a binding agreement."

Chapter Twenty-Six

"Niall? Earth to Niall? Hello?"

The world swam back into focus with his mum waving a hand at him from across the table as she set down bowls of meringue and fresh fruit.

"Draven?" Draven's jacket was still clutched in his hand. Niall's head snapped round. There was one remaining spellbook on the table, which he hastily gathered up, but no sign of his boyfriend. "Where is he?"

"I assumed he went to the loo— Niall?"

Niall sprung to the door of the dining room. He knew they had fought. Then something strange had happened. One second Draven had been standing there, yelling, the next his mum was back. Reality itself had disjointed, in a way that made him fairly sure magic was involved, but what kind? What had Draven done? Had he tried to fix something, and made the world around him glitch? Where was he now?

"Niall? What's going on? Did you two fight?"

He ignored his mum, and the awkward hint that she had heard their raised voices. He tore around the house—as if, if he turned a corner sharply enough, or caught the world off guard, there would be magic to be found. But there wasn't. Draven was gone.

"We should check the library," he said, coming back to where his parents stood in the doorway of the dining room, looking baffled.

"What? Did he walk out? His shoes are still here. What happened?"

"We should check. It's the only other place he knows. It's the only place he could have gone."

His mum didn't hesitate long. Draven was demonstrably not in the house, and asking what was happening was not going to help find him. That appeared to be her priority. Niall noticed that she bit her lip as she picked up Draven's shoes, and he was sure she was imagining Draven walking barefoot down the street. Niall couldn't say he didn't think that was what was happening.

He also couldn't insist they drive to the library at breakneck speed. They crawled along, keeping an eye out, even though that wasn't what Niall had meant. He was sure if Draven wasn't in their house, he was at the library, and all the time they wasted looking for him like a normal runaway gave him time to get further away or more lost and scared.

Eventually, his mum's tires scraped against the gravel of the car park. Niall didn't wait for her to fully stop before he unbuckled his seatbelt and opened the door, running towards the automatic doors of the library, which swished back to admit him.

He dashed across the well-worn carpet without noticing it. The spines of the books blurred. He was looking for one particular place, even though it didn't make sense. His brain fabricated reasons to hope—maybe Draven had worried about the spell he'd cast, maybe he'd gone to get help, maybe he'd left a note. Niall pulled the bookend off the shelf, turning it over twice, running his hands inside the space he'd already seen was empty. He tried it with the rest of the ones on that shelf. Maybe he'd got the wrong one, maybe Draven had—he wondered how much of the library he could pull apart, looking for a message that clearly wasn't there.

He rounded the end of Draven's aisle, willing something in his senses to find the portal that Draven always told him was right there.

"I don't think he's here, love. Let's go home," his mum said. "You can explain, and we can—"

Niall shook his head and sat down on the floor, Draven's jacket still clutched in his hands. Draven couldn't have vanished beyond reach. It was one thing to walk out, to need some space but he couldn't be gone to where Niall couldn't reach him, not on that note. It was Sunday. It was their day.

As the minutes slipped by, the voice telling him that Draven was gone was getting louder and louder. But so was the panic-fuelled hope. He couldn't be. He would reappear. Draven would come back. It wouldn't get to four PM. That was always the time Draven had to leave, and he wouldn't go, wouldn't waste the rest of their day, without coming back, not when it would be a whole week—was it going to be? A week felt like an eternity to wait, which was why Draven had to come back and sort things out now, but then a worse possibility dawned. Hadn't Niall practically told him to give up? Maybe he wouldn't come back. Niall didn't want to believe that Draven would do that. But he had. Draven could literally vanish from his life and Niall was powerless to stop him.

As the minutes crept onwards, his brain turned over and over what had happened.

The limited amount of the world that he could see looked normal. His parents didn't seem to have registered anything as being wrong or strange, and he wasn't sure whether that was because they didn't know well enough to look for it, or because that strange trance-like state hadn't passed over them too. Maybe it had just been him. Perhaps Draven hadn't tried to fix the world, at least not all of it, not at once, and had settled for fixing the problems right in front of him.

Niall wasn't proud of himself. He wasn't proud of raising his voice or shoving the paper in Draven's face. But people made mistakes. Or rather, people in his world did. How many was he allowed before Draven stopped wanting to come back, or started seeing him as part of what needed fixing? Or did he already?

It was hard to analyse whether he felt any different, when nothing felt normal right now. But did it matter whether he did or didn't? The point wasn't whether it had worked, it was that Draven had cast a spell on Niall, and now he had disappeared.

Chapter Twenty-Seven

Four o'clock hit, and Niall didn't know how to move. A lead weight had settled over him while he waited. The gradual creeping confirmation that he had been abandoned. He didn't even want to cry. He didn't want to move either. He felt stuck.

"Come on." His mum had seemed to accept that he wasn't going to leave until closing time, but now her arm gently tugged under his. He let himself be pulled to his feet, though his shoulders remained hunched. "Let's go home and put the kettle on. How about you message Ellen, see if she wants to come over?"

Niall slumped, if it was possible, even further.

"We kind of had an argument too. She's only going to say, 'I told you so.'"

"Okay." She took a deep breath. "Friends fight. People fight. If she's a good friend, she is going to put that aside and be willing to be there for you right now. Do you want me to call her?"

"Up to you." Niall wasn't sure whether he meant "*yes but I don't want to admit it*" or "*I lack the capacity to make any decisions right now.*"

"I'll give it a try. Let's go."

He allowed himself to be taken back to the car, and back home, where he crumpled onto the sofa in a tearful heap. He hugged Draven's jacket to his chest and picked up the remote control, idly flicking, wondering what could possibly suit his mood right now. He wanted distraction. He wanted someone who felt exactly what he was feeling. He wanted to escape from everything. He wanted something that felt like a fuzzy blanket, familiar enough that he didn't have to concentrate. There was, actually, something that ticked all those boxes. He was loading it up as his mum returned.

"Ellen will be over in a bit," she informed him.

"Right. Okay." He wasn't sure how to feel about this. Initially he'd felt a little jab of hope. He wasn't sure if that was real or if it was just the fact that his friend's name usually evoked a positive response, and he had momentarily forgotten to be miserable about how things were between them. He could perhaps worry about how horribly this was going to go, and pretend that all his worrying was about that—condense it down and focus it on a person who was going to walk through the door in about thirty minutes instead of one who he didn't know when he would see again. If he told himself the twisting knots of anxiety in his stomach were all down to this, maybe they would loosen when Ellen arrived and they hopefully had a chance to resolve things. "Thanks," he added, deciding that, on the whole, he felt glad about this visit. "What did you tell her?"

"That you had boy trouble, and you wanted a friend."

"What did she say?"

"Just that she'd come over."

"Thanks."

"You want company?"

"No. Got the Doctor." He nodded at the screen where he had selected "The Parting of the Ways." An episode about separation, about not being able to go back to a life of just eating chips after you'd seen something more, and of stopping short at nothing, not even scattering words through space and time, to get back to the stupid, grumpy Northerner who you loved. He wasn't sure if he was Rose or the Doctor in that metaphor, and thought he might have switched halfway through that train of thought. He'd first discovered the episode when back-watching it all in his primary school years, and it had always been one of his favourites. It was also the first time he'd ever seen two guys kiss on screen. Even if it was just a crumb, a tiny, almost meaningless moment, it had meant something to him.

He wanted to enjoy his misery viewing in peace without risk of judgement or question. Not that he thought his mum would do either of those things but it was so much harder to be utterly unselfconsciously miserable with another person present, and he needed to do that for a bit.

He was most of the way through the episode when the doorbell rang. He let his mum let Ellen in but paused his viewing. He scooped the proliferation of soggy tissues into the bin and sat up, so Ellen would be able to join him on the sofa. If she wanted to.

"Hey. So, do I need to break the bastard's kneecaps?" she asked, taking a seat beside Niall.

"You'll have to find him first," he said. It was meant to be a joke. Because that was what people always said, and it was especially true in this case. But apparently, he wasn't up to joking about it yet because this reminder caused fresh tears to spring to his eyes and he flopped onto Ellen's shoulder with a sob.

"You wanna talk about it, or you wanna go back to whatever that is?" She gestured at the screen, where Rose was turning the Dalek's beam back on it. "I see you're of the school that believes watching mindless violence is the solution to these things. I approve. I thought I was in for an evening of questionable gay romcoms."

"It's Doctor Who," he informed her, still snuffling. "And it's actually really emotional."

"Naturally," she replied to both statements, as Niall rearranged himself over the arm of the sofa, clicking the remote to let the last five minutes of the episode play.

"So..." he began once it was over, glancing sideways at Ellen. "I think I might be like, a complete butthead."

"I'd be tempted to agree." She smiled, clearly joking. "But right now it feels like kicking a puppy. What makes you say that?"

"I feel like I owe you an apology. I guess...you might be right, in some ways? I don't know. I still want— Everything's so— I want...I think I know what I want, but I don't know."

"Well, that's good and clear." Ellen poked him in the ribs. "Don't worry about us. What happened today?"

"He was here for lunch, and I was just trying to keep the conversation away from things he doesn't know about. I thought it would be easier, but he got all annoyed about it."

"Okay." Ellen pursed her lips, but more like she was trying not to jump in than like she was annoyed.

"And I was kind of right about that, because the second he saw a newspaper, he freaked out. I don't think he's ever seen a source of information from outside his community before. He thought hatred was a fictional emotion. It all blew up from there. He was talking about fixing things, and I was trying to make him see that he couldn't."

"And?" Ellen pressed.

"We got in this whole big fight."

"But..." She scrutinised him, and Niall used blowing his nose as an excuse to avoid eye contact. She was giving him that look again, seeing the missing parts in his story. "I mean, he must see that's not possible. How was he planning on doing anything about all the problems in the world?"

Niall waited for any other answer to come to him. None did. "Magic."

"Okay, so he's a fantasy nerd like you but—"

"No. He can do magic. For real."

"Like 'I am vaccinated using rose quartz'? Cos if so—"

"No. Like he comes from another world, and magic is real there."

"I am eighty percent sure you're attempting to be funny, and I don't get it."

"Not really in a laughing mood. I don't think he's all that powerful, but even if he could manipulate things on a small scale—"

"You're serious?"

"Okay. I know you're probably not gonna believe me, but can you pretend you do. Roll with it. Or, here." He fished in Draven's pockets, pulling the spellbooks out, and dropped a couple onto Ellen's lap.

"These aren't elaborate film props?" She thumbed through a few pages.

"How'd they fit in the pockets?"

"Your boyfriend...is from another world, and wants to fix this one with magic?" Ellen repeated, still looking sceptical.

"Yeah. I think he already started. Or tried to. With me. We were having this fight, and then everything stopped and when it started again, he was gone. I think he used a spell on me." Niall decided to keep going as if she believed him unless he hit a bump that said otherwise. If she could roll with it enough to deal with the relationship side of things, that would be enough for now.

"What? That's messed up."

"I don't know why he did it. Whether he thinks I'm part of the problem or it was an accident or..."

"You do know that's bullshit, don't you?" Ellen leant in, peering intently, trying to look him in the eye. He evaded her gaze, not sure she'd find the sparkling well of self-confidence and determination she was looking for.

"Yeah?" His voice was small and full of doubt. "I mean...maybe? I don't want him to think that about me." He curled inwards, thinking of all the things he hated about himself. Chest acne. Awkward. Unlovable. Given that he felt that way, why didn't he want them to be magicked better? It surprised him how little he desired it. If Draven had been able to produce a potion or a spell to rid him of his chest acne, then sure (though preferably without Draven having to know it existed in the first place somehow). But even the idea of the glamours had scared rather than enticed him. Did he want to radiate confidence and charisma? He couldn't imagine doing that and still being anything like himself. He hadn't needed to. When Draven looked at him, it was like he saw a completely different person to the one that Niall saw in the mirror. What if that illusion had been shattered? Did Draven now see him as he was? He didn't want Draven to feel like he needed to reach inside and transform him to make him worthy of love. It felt like Draven's thoughts were running beyond confidence, and into what made someone good. In spite of his many, many flaws he'd always considered himself a broadly decent person. "I mean, I'm not perfect. I'm really, really, REALLY a long way from perfect. People need to change and grow and recognise when they have flaws and do things about it. So, I'm not saying he shouldn't expect me to change sometimes or something..." He trailed off.

"But?" Ellen prompted.

"But I deserve better than someone who thinks I'm a broken thing they need to fix. I'm not?" It came out as a question, and she only raised her eyebrows and crossed her arms, waiting. "I'm not." He only said it to the sofa cushions, but the intonation lay flat and level.

"You're not." Ellen wrapped him in a hug. "You deserve someone who loves all the weird stupid shit that makes you you."

"Maybe he does. I might be reading way too much into this. But everything's so messed up right now. He must be so freaked out. I hate that I can't even talk to him or find out what's going on. How do I deal with this?"

"The not knowing?"

"All of it. I want him to come back. I want us to fix it all."

"Careful, you're sounding like him."

"But this is different. It's our relationship, not the whole world. It's ours to fix."

"Yeah... If I say something you're not gonna like, promise not to bite my head off?" she asked.

"What?" Niall asked. His eyes narrowed, waiting for the punch but he tried to wipe that look off his face. She was giving him a choice to hear it or not, and the fact that he couldn't walk away from a remark like that was on him. "Hit me with it."

"You said it's your relationship—it's 'ours to fix.' And yeah, it is. You plural, yours and his. Not just you."

"I know! I'm saying I want to patch it up, talk it out with him."

"What are you willing to compromise on? Look, if he thinks he needs to fix you, he's out. But weren't you kind of doing the same to him? You can't control him, and your parents, and everything around you until he fits in."

"But otherwise, he won't! I'm just trying to make it easy!"

"For you. It sounds like he'd be perfectly happy to walk into your house, announce he's a clueless wizard and get your parents to fill him in on world politics."

"Mage."

"What?"

"He's a mage."

Ellen gave him a long hard stare which communicated "*Is that really the point?*" far more effectively than words ever could.

"I can't just let him! He'll get hurt. Or in trouble. Or things won't work."

"I'm not saying you can let him go...uh, blasting spells around," Ellen said, with only a slight look of incredulity before she managed to utter it, "or that you shouldn't prepare him, cos yeah, that sounds kinda dangerous. But you're not preparing him, you're shielding him, and then being mad at him for not understanding. If he wants to be part of this world, he needs to get educated, and he needs to get a say in what he does with that information."

"You're the one who's always saying you don't believe anything can make a difference."

"Yeah, I say we're probably all doomed. But what do you think?" she asked. Niall swallowed. He'd never confronted Ellen about her point of view. He wasn't sure whether it was because he agreed with her or didn't want to fight with her.

"I don't want to think that? Even if it might be true?"

"Okay," she said, as if disagreeing was the most natural thing in the world. "You don't have to come down and wallow with me. If he's got some fighting spirit, or he's given you some, then go for it. Someone has to. I don't promise that, if I get to meet him, I won't have a strong urge to smack him because honestly, he sounds annoying. He is not my cup of tea. But you said he was yours. That's the point I've been trying to get through your skull. If you don't like him, move on. If you like him, start acting like it. Saying you like him but expecting him to be something other than what or who he is isn't fair. He doesn't get to change you, but you can't hold him back either. If he wants to take on the world, well, good bloody luck to him. But if you want to be his boyfriend, you need to back his plays. If he wants to be yours, he needs to respect your comfort zone. If there's no place where those overlap, then you don't get to be together. I'm sorry, and I know that's not what you want to hear but I'm not going to sit here and tell you it's all going to be alright when—unless you both start being more realistic—it isn't going to be."

Niall paused to process. He couldn't find a flaw in what Ellen was saying, other than *"But I don't want that to be true."* Which wasn't a good answer. He was definitely Rose, except he was nowhere near that brave yet. Her chip shop speech about standing up for what was right had stung. It wasn't because it was just like him and Draven—it was because she was right, like Ellen was now, and he hadn't lived up to that ideal.

"I want him," he concluded. "I should have handled it better. I wish I had."

Chapter Twenty-Eight

The radio clicked on. Draven didn't want to open his eyes. He slid down, pulling the covers up over his head, and considered throwing the radio against the wall. The presenters were chirpy, the sun was shining. His whole life was ruined, and the radio didn't care, the weather didn't care—the world was having the nerve to continue spinning in spite of his broken heart.

He hit it off. He didn't care what kind of day it was. He didn't want to take a shower. He didn't want to move. Every single day that he hadn't wanted to go to the Energy Makers' Guild felt like it had been combined, the weight of all of them simultaneously pressing down on him. Shirking your duty was not community-minded of him though. It was how Others behaved. Selfishness was one of their traits. The sheer force of wanting to prove Mage Starkweather wrong compelled him out from under the covers. He could go there. He could go and come back. Maybe if he could be himself this week, put in a stellar merit session on Wednesday... They had made a binding agreement though. It would take something big to change her mind. Still, it had to be possible. *If he even wants you when you go back.*

He was out of bed though. He let inertia carry him through getting dressed and out of the house. This was the same routine he'd had every day. If he changed it, there would be questions. Questions he did not know how to answer. He could keep putting one foot in front of the other though, until something big enough to throw him off course happened. He could follow along.

For the first fifteen minutes of his journey, he assumed the feeling that life was moving with all the speed and thrill of drying paint was just him. But as he glanced at his watch, comparing it with the view outside, he was sure they were moving more slowly than usual. There was something off, something on the edge of his perception. As the passengers thinned, he realised that it sounded like the hum of electricity. There were more than ten people still on—it felt to him like the sound had been present from the start of the journey, disguised by the presence of morning chatter. That was odd. That was very odd, given that Mage Starweather had outright rejected the concept of running things this way.

He stepped off at the Energy Makers' Guild. As he made his way into the atrium, he crossed paths with Rowan. Her brows were knitted together in concern, and she pointed him away from the usual corridor towards the conference room.

"Emergency meeting," she said.

"Those are two words that don't sound great." Draven grimaced. Independently, each of them was uninviting. Combined, they were deeply worrying. He followed Rowan in, taking a seat next to her.

"Good morning." Mage Starkweather surveyed the assembled company. She looked grim. "Although the ambient magic level reported on the radio this morning was low amber, this was actually untrue. Today is a red day." She didn't stop at the collective gasp that went up, ploughing on before muttering could start. "We have chosen not to report this for fear of inciting panic. Instead, we are deploying the emergency reserves and making several switches to electric where we think this will be least detectable. Guild heads are being made aware in order to strategically vary their workloads. However, in order to not raise alarm, a larger burden of power saving will fall on us. It goes without saying that this information is strictly confidential and not to be communicated to anyone outside this building. You will receive a revised work schedule from your head of department."

She swept from the room without taking questions.

* * *

Draven sat in the data lab, which was currently lit by candles. Beyond the new atmospheric lighting arrangements, the revised schedule hadn't affected him too much, seeing as his entire day was built out of menial dross work anyway. Or rather, had not affected the content of his work. It was hard not to feel affected by a red day. It was objectively bloody terrible as a turn of events. As far as he was concerned, it was the smaller of his current problems. He could only see Niall once more. He put his head down on the desk. It fitted with the prevalent mood well enough that no one was going to question it. After a moment, a piece of paper slid over to him from Yvette's side of the table.

Reasons to be cheerful:
1) It's spooky! Kinda like we're having a seance/weird pyjama party
2) Good excuse to do less work

He looked up, finding she was leaning over her candle to up-light her face, her eyes wide and dramatic. He managed a weak smile and tried to return to the data in front of him. It was hard to focus on the meaningless numbers when it felt like the issue was personal. Why had this happened after he was in Niall's world? This and the green day both had. It was hard not to feel like he was the destabilising effect, even if it didn't make sense. It was two times. Twice out of the five times he had visited. Was that a pattern? One up, one down. The other guilty and traitorous thought that kept crossing his mind was *Would it be so bad if it was?* He'd come up against that question before—was it better to have highs and lows than a constant middling nothingness? He wasn't sure what the answer to that question was, but he knew the answer to another one. Would he give up Niall, if it was? He looked at the stony faces around him. The shutdown was affecting the higher-level mages more than them. They had been shifted to data collection, and there was a lot of unhappy murmuring about it. Around him, almost everyone was miserable, and he knew that, if it was his fault, he should feel bad about it. He did. He didn't want to make other people miserable. But he cared about Niall more.

They had been asked again to report anything unusual from the day before. Mage Starkweather already knew the details of his day, so perhaps he didn't have to. He worried she was going to blame him, after all, he had used illegal magic—

He had used magic.

He stood up so sharply that everyone stared.

"Draven?" He ignored Rowan, and she was forced to pursue him into the corridor, Yvette hot on her heels. "Draven, where are you going?"

"Mage Starkweather."

"What? Draven, she's incredibly busy. If you've got an idea—"

"I have to talk to her."

"What's going on?" Yvette asked.

"You can tell me." Rowan was losing her breath at the pace she was having to follow him up the stairs.

"No. Sorry. It has to be her."

"I think she's out," Rowan said.

"Okay. I'm going to wait there." He strode off up the stairs.

"Draven, come back!" Rowan followed him for a stair or two but gave him up as a lost cause. Yvette was more persistent.

"Hey, what are you doing?" She continued to trail him up the stairs.

"Going to talk to Mage Starkweather," he repeated.

"About what?"

"This." He gestured vaguely, encompassing the whole world.

"Hey!" The sharpness of Yvette's voice snapped his attention back to her. "You are acting super weird, and you have been for weeks! Tell me what's going on!"

Draven managed to slow his spinning thoughts enough to focus on the here and now. She was right. He owed her an explanation. He probably should have told her a lot further back in all this. It was a little like telling Niall about magic. It wasn't the kind of thing you brought up straight away, but then you found you had stepped directly from there to the point where it was too far gone, and you should have said something a long time ago.

Well, it was all going to come out soon anyway.

"I've been going somewhere. The Other World. It's real, and there's access—"

"You met someone there." Yvette was quick to put the pieces together. Her face was neutral as she assembled the evidence.

"Yes. His name's Niall. He's my boyfriend. He's—"

"How could you keep all that from me?" she asked sharply, her cheeks flushing.

"I wanted to tell you—"

"So, why didn't you?" She crossed her arms.

"I don't know. It was complicated, and confusing, and things kept sort of happening. I'm sorry."

She looked for a moment like she wanted to stay mad, and like she had not given up on it completely. Her arms stayed crossed over her chest, but there was an undeniable curiosity in her eyes. For now, her desire to know things seemed to outweigh being in a huff with him, though he wasn't ruling out the possibility of the balance shifting.

"What's it like there?" she asked.

"It's wonderful!" He thought of his first impressions of the library; the sharp smell that stung his nose, and of everything he'd learnt that was dangerous or frightening. He wanted to be honest. "It's big. And messy. And complicated."

"Sounds great," Yvette deadpanned.

"It's different to here." That piece of information was enough to bring a big, soppy smile to his face. The world wasn't the tiny sliver they had always been shown. Wasn't that enough? She wasn't looking as excited.

"It sounds dangerous," she said.

"You sound like my mother," he teased.

"Screw you! This is serious." The anger flared up again. She kept pushing it below the surface, in service of the conversation and her curiosity, but it was clearly still there. "You said it's big and messy—I don't want anything bad happening to you."

Draven knew she meant the dangers of the Other World, but he couldn't think of anything worse for himself than being stuck here forever. Not now that he knew the truth. Not when Niall was there.

"It's not like they always said. It's not like here either," he said. "But for the most part, they're just people. Good people, trying to live their lives, and do the right thing."

She floundered for a moment, trying to find a response, but no new questions about the world came to her. Anger and betrayal flickered behind her eyes as it filled up the space her curiosity had carved out.

"You know what? It doesn't matter. It's your dream, not mine, and well…good for you, I guess. You got a whole new world, and a whole new life that you didn't even need to make me part of."

"You're still a huge part of my life. I want it to work. His world and this world coming together, and it can. There are so many problems to solve there. You know what happens when you solve problems and do good."

"The green day? That was connected?" In spite of herself, Yvette looked excited. He imagined her, her hair piled high, radiating a glamour as she set painted stars in motion. Her eyes lit up. They were on the same page again.

"What's good for me is good for you. For everyone. She doesn't want me going back anymore, but as soon as she hears this, she'll have to! All of us! I can take you there. Maybe I can bring him here."

"Maybe things will change?" she asked. "I don't want a whole new world. I want this one to be a little bit brighter."

"It will be," he promised, pulling her into a hug.

* * *

Mage Starkweather came back mid-morning, thankfully alone. Yvette had returned to work, as there was no sense in both of them being in trouble. Draven felt his heart lifting as the guild head turned the corner.

"Mr. Montrose, should I be worried as to why you're pacing up and down outside my office?"

"No. You should be excited."

His good mood, infectious though he thought it should be, did not catch her. In fact, her brow furrowed at this pronouncement, as if it deepened her concern about his presence. "Very well," she replied. "Let's talk." She opened the office door, gesturing him inside.

"I've solved it," he declared. "I know what caused the green day to happen. We were asked last time to document anything out of the ordinary we'd done. And I—well, I didn't. I wasn't sure where my visits were coming from, and who I could tell. But the green day happened when I used magic in the other world."

"And the red day?"

"The red day happened when I did something wrong. Something unkind. When I used magic in a positive way, we got green. That's how it works—we do good, we get more energy. We've always known that, and there's so, so many bad things there. It feeds the magic here instead of diminishing it."

"I see. Mr. Montrose, if that were true, why would it be something to get so excited about?"

"Because the energy crisis would be solved."

"How? We live here. They live there. You're only going back one more time. You made an agreement."

"But this changes everything. A binding spell can be undone if both parties agree—"

"But I don't agree, Mr. Montrose," she replied. Draven stared at her in confusion, wondering which of them had missed a step in this conversation. He was presenting the answers to everything they'd been looking for, and she seemed more annoyed than excited. "This is not what you were supposed to learn about the Other World. Not at all."

"What I was...?"

"This was supposed to bring you back into line with the rest of us. It's barbaric there. We cannot continue to associate with them, whatever the cost to us."

"But it doesn't cost us. It helps us, and it helps them. That world deserves magic, it's crying out for it, and it would fix everything—that sounds like a perfect harmony."

"Except that they don't deserve it." Mage Starkweather's lip curled. Draven stared, uncomprehending. That didn't make sense. They were taught all the time about balance and doing good. It all fitted. Them being cut off—no wonder they were stunted and failing to flourish. He had heard so many times that they had been running out of magic. That they'd had to do it. Except, that made no sense. Not if they'd kept the worlds working in harmony. Mage Starkweather wasn't talking at all regretfully about splitting themselves off.

"This is what caused it, isn't it?" he asked. "It used to be fine, when we were connected. Things were different. There was enough magic. The separation wasn't because we were running out—it's what caused the crisis. We brought this on our own heads by being selfish, and now you won't let me fix it by helping them!"

"Selfish? You want to talk about selfishness—look at the Others. Did you know they could solve all their own problems? A few of them hoard money and resources. There's no need for Others to be homeless, or starving, and yet they are. What kind of person can look at that and not feel sick?"

"What kind of person can stop feeling sick about it by turning their back and pretending it isn't happening?" He surveyed the woman in front of him, searching for some indication that he was wrong about all of this, but she merely stared back, cold and calculating, looking disappointed in him. He was desperate to find something of the person he had thought he'd known—the one who had told him he reminded her of a younger version of herself. He wondered what that meant. It no longer sounded like a compliment, not to him. Why wasn't she shocked by anything? Why wasn't she jumping for joy that they could change the fate of not one world but two? "You knew. You knew all of this, all along. Why would you send me there, to find this out, only to tell me that it doesn't matter?"

"Oh, but it does matter. It matters a great deal."

Draven looked up, feeling a surge of hope.

"Now you understand the problem. Properly, and completely. You had so much spark, so much drive for this. I could see you rising to the top of this guild. To do that, you needed to understand, truly, what had happened. You also had that restless streak—the kind that wasn't going to be satisfied unless you saw with your own eyes. I made it so you could get all your questions answered."

"I thought you cared about me."

"I do! I think you're an excellent mage with a lot of potential."

"You want me to turn my back on an answer—one that helps us, but also solves problems for other people—and keep chipping away in vain at a problem we inflicted on ourselves. What would be the point?"

"Safety. Safety and stability. No one else is going to follow your lead. How long before you tank out, Mr. Montrose?"

"You're just trying to scare me."

"What do you do with an infinite amount of problems and a finite amount of energy? I thought you liked things that can be solved."

"I thought you said it was worth making the world a little bit better, even if you can't fix everything."

"I meant this world! What are you going to do when all the flaws of that place start taking hold of you? The hatred, the cruelty, the selfishness. It made you angry once already. It'll keep doing that, until you're just like them."

"Maybe some things are worth being angry about! You want to build a world without cruelty or selfishness by simply ignoring everywhere it happens? I think I'll take fighting problems I can't solve over pretending they don't exist, thanks." He sounded braver than he felt. It was easy to sound brave when it was all hypothetical.

"Good thing you don't get to decide then," she said. "You may go back to work now, Mr. Montrose."

* * *

Yvette was waiting for him. She must have heard that Mage Starkweather was back. She was sitting on the floor outside the office, with her knees pulled to her chest. He wondered if their voices had been loud enough that she already knew, and he wouldn't have to tell her. Judging by the way she looked up, with huge, expectant eyes, she had not. His own face must have betrayed him, because hers fell.

"What happened?" she asked.

His first instinct was to say *"I don't want to talk about it"* but he'd been doing a lot of that lately. He'd brought her in on this. He'd promised. Again. When was he going to learn to stop telling people he could make their lives better? He only ever let them down.

"She wouldn't listen."

He watched Yvette swallow down the disappointment. "Well. That's that then."

"No, it isn't!" Draven said. "I have to keep going back. If she'd change her mind—"

"But she isn't going to! We're stuck with this world, and the way it is," Yvette snapped.

"We can't give up!"

"We? When it comes to this problem, there is no 'we' here." Her anger pulsed through every word, and tears sprung to her eyes. "You lied to me. You snuck around behind my back. This is your dream, and I was only part of it as of five minutes ago when you filled me in!"

"But it could be yours too. It would mean more green days. All the magic you've ever wanted, right at your fingertips!"

"Don't. What you want is being dangled just out of your reach and look how it's making you feel. Don't do the same to me. Don't tell me it could happen but it's not going to."

"Yvette—"

"I'm going back to work, Draven. We have an energy crisis to solve. Thanks to you, we don't even have working lights. Way to save the world."

Chapter Twenty-Nine

Draven trailed home, utterly defeated. It was the prevalent mood. Even without the red day being officially announced, the atmosphere of sluggishness had seeped its way into the population. Funny how, for the first time in his life, he fitted in, whilst feeling like he was never going to belong here again. In some ways, the weekend couldn't come fast enough. He needed to see Niall again and make everything right. In other ways, he wanted time to slow down. He needed a plan.

As he walked from the tram stop, he dug his hands into his pockets. They brushed against something large and solid. Something square. He pulled out the photo album he and Niall had bought at the market. He'd forgotten to hand it over at the end of their date, and he hadn't worn these trousers since. He traced a hand over the faded pattern of the cover and clutched it to his chest as he walked.

No one was in when he arrived, and he put the kettle on. He pulled two cups from the cupboard, his own favourite, and the blue guest cup, and when the tea was brewed added milk and sugar to the second cup. He took both cups and the photo album upstairs, shutting out the rest of the world. He considered for a moment. He usually slept in the middle of the bed, but he often woke up rolled over to the right. He placed Niall's cup on the nightstand on the left, and settled down, consciously only taking up half the space. He closed his eyes, letting the smell of Niall's tea wash over the space. The strange sourness of the milk tempered by the sugar. He tried to imagine all the other ways that Niall smelt and pretend they were there too.

He opened the photo album, drinking in each page. They were mostly people, posed alongside inconsequential backgrounds of anonymous concrete bollards or village halls. He savoured each one. This was Niall's world. He was going to know it and understand it. He refused to believe that he was only going back to it one more time. He would find a way. The fashions and the style of the shots were outdated, he could tell that much. He thought they looked 1960s-ish, but that was basing it on the styles of here. Which, as he could tell from the sidelong looks Niall didn't think Draven noticed him giving him, were not aligned with the trends in the Other World. They looked similar to things he'd seen in old photos of his grandma, and the hairstyles weren't dissimilar either.

He turned a page and almost spat out his tea. He stared. It was because he had been thinking how much they reminded him of his grandma. Surely. That was it. But he knew those clothes. He'd seen that exact outfit in other pictures. It wasn't that this woman resembled his grandma. It was her. He stared at it, brain racing, not quite daring to believe this was real. But it was. He leapt from the bed, shoving the album into his pocket. Maybe there was someone else who could give him answers—different ones, the ones he wanted to hear—about Niall's world.

* * *

"Yes, this is me," his grandma confirmed, handing him back the photo.

"Where are you?" he asked, breathless.

"I think, if you've got hold of this, you already know that. I think it's me who should be asking you a few things." She didn't sound angry. More curious. Curious and perhaps a little proud.

Draven was torn, wanting to ask her a million things, and also realising the chance he had to ramble happily about Niall, about his adventures, which he had been missing out on for so long. He was half convinced his grandma could fix this. He couldn't see a way out of this, but he usually couldn't when he was mixed up in the middle of something. She was always able to see what he couldn't.

"I found a way!" It all came tumbling out; the excitement of finding the portal, of finding Niall, the fact that Mage

Starkweather had set him up but that he hadn't learnt at all what she wanted. "How did you get there?" he asked.

She answered with a tilt of her head, gesturing him to follow, and led him upstairs. They made their way into the spare bedroom, where he had stayed for sleepovers. Where he still did sometimes. It wasn't necessary—his house was a short walk down the road—but that had never been the point. He sat down on the bed, its orange fleecy cover soft beneath his fingers, as his grandma opened the wardrobe. There was a box, approximately the size of a shoebox, but covered in a polka dot fabric, from which several toys smiled at him—a doll in a hand-knitted yellow cap, a rabbit with bandaged legs to keep the stuffing in, and an ancient bear who had no hair left on his nose but still had the kindest eyes. They'd belonged to his mother and her siblings and it had always been one of his Sunday treats to play with them, so long as he was exceedingly gentle.

His grandma removed the box, placing it gently on the bed, and he scooped up the rabbit, holding him carefully, turning him so his black button eyes could watch what was coming out next. It was a small stack of books, along with several pamphlets. He was quite sure these had not been stored in the wardrobe during his childhood.

"I did a bit of rearranging." His grandma, as usual, answered his unspoken question. "These used to live in my room."

"Were you trying to get me to find them when you told me to go looking for what I'd lost?" he asked.

"I think there's more than one corner of this house that could have poked your mind into action." She handed him the pile. Along with the books, which he recognised as more old-fashioned spells, there were two slips of paper—an article clipped from a newspaper, and a green sheet which had been folded into a pamphlet. The newspaper clipping was faded and yellowed with age.

He lifted it and read.

New Year's Day was ushered in with all the usual fanfare. The traditional magical spectacular continues to outdo itself year on year. For the three hours up to midnight, the stage was filled with everything from choreographed fountains to full sensory illusions that transported the audience to a tropical paradise.

As has become customary, the show was not only on stage but in the audience too. Colour changing gowns are a perennial favourite, though garments with added movement effects are starting to encroach on their territory. A few of the most notable garments were—

The article was torn off, but Draven had read enough to get the gist. For New Year, they took picnics. They sat on the lawn, waiting for the fireworks at midnight. There was no gala, no three-hour display of magical prowess—the fireworks put enough of a dent in the power reserves. Some of his clothes had magical effects, sure. Most things he owned were lined with warming charms. He got enough grief for those being a frivolous use of magic, when he could have just worn more layers. The clothes described in the article were things he'd only glimpsed on the green day. The lifestyle and the world described in the article were too. He glanced at the date in the article headline. It was from the 1970s. In some ways, that fitted with what he knew. He knew that things hadn't always been the way they were now. There had once been more magic. His grandma often spoke of how things were better before in a way that implied she remembered it. But it was so different, seeing it down in black and white. Having real, solid evidence, and a description of that life. Whenever he had asked about the past, it had felt unwanted. Like he was stirring up ghosts and asking awkward questions. He had never had a solid answer on when things had changed or why. He supposed he still didn't. It was creeping closer though. The past so distant it might as well be another land. It was what he thought whenever he looked at the castle. Now part of that past was in living memory, but still so foreign to him. Was it in touching distance or not?

He picked up the leaflet which looked like it was from the 1960s and was entitled *Portal Travel: The Dos and Don'ts!*

He opened it, eyes skimming the first page.

Getting to the Other World is as easy as a hop, step or jump through any one of Galdorsfarne's networked portals! With links to destinations around Northeast England, it couldn't be easier or safer to travel. You may have heard negative press about portal travel. We're here to reassure you, and give the ins and outs of going in and out!

The pamphlet's style was relentlessly jaunty, and he couldn't help but smile as he read it, though with a slight heartache. How casually they talked about hopping between worlds. How easy it had been. Why had they given that up?

"It was like this for you." He gestured at the newspaper article, vaguely at the pamphlet too. "You used to have all this?"

"We did," she confirmed quietly.

"They always make mixing with the Other World sound like ancient history."

"Yes. They do like to give that impression. As far as I can tell, the portals have always existed. We're from here, but we belong there too. That must be why they had such a job closing them up. When you know where to look, you see the maintenance crew all the time, patching over the cracks in the world."

"Like the castle?" Draven said, touching the spot on the map that showed the link with Niall's priory.

"That was always one of my favourites."

"Why did you never tell me?" he asked. "You always knew I wanted adventures."

"More or less what I told you during the green day. I was worried about filling your head with nonsense. I thought about it, after you got so low with the Energy Makers' Guild. I wanted you to always have something to dream about, and when you gave up on that, I wondered if it might help. But I had no idea there was still a way through. I didn't want to dangle something in front of you that you might never be able to experience."

Draven ran a hand over the pamphlet again, trying to reconcile its tone with his understanding of the world.

"It talks about it like it was a holiday. Like something you'd do for fun in the afternoons." He tried not to sound critical. A corner of his brain still tugged at the hope that maybe Mage Starkweather didn't understand that he was suggesting something different.

"I wouldn't say that exactly. It wasn't a hobby or a holiday. It just...was. There have been different attitudes over the years about how involved we should be, what it means to help, how far we could stretch ourselves." Her fingers traced the map of Northeast England. "But there never used to be any doubt that helping was the right choice. Our world is part of that one, and each needs the other to survive. We need to do good, and every place needs magic, or else it dulls and falls apart. I'm glad to know it still has its heart, its soft spots and its good. I've always worried about what happened to it since we cut ourselves off."

"How...when...why did that happen?" Draven asked.

"When your mother was small. As for why, it's hard to say. We'd weathered so much with them. Two World Wars, some of the darkest times of humanity. That didn't do it. If anything, that brought people together, gave them a reason to look after one another. Or at least showed us what hatred looks like well enough that we didn't want to be guilty of the same. Then... Not out of nowhere—these things are never from nowhere—but without any one real reason, there was this ugly attitude rearing its head. The idea of us for ourselves. That letting them in was bad for us, and we'd be stronger on our own. I don't know whether they knew that breaking ourselves off from the Others would be like hexing our own noses. Whether they knew but they didn't care, or whether they really were deluded enough to believe their own lies. But they did it anyway. Stirred up enough hatred and resentment, if you can imagine such a thing, and said it was leaking through—that it was what we got for mixing. Never mind that we always had. I'm not saying things were perfect. You needed a thicker skin in those days, to mix with them, to manage what went on there. But I'd say we were better off in than out. After all, look at us now, barely scraping by. Before the split, that was their big promise—we're wasting our energy on them. More for all of us when they go. They stopped saying that pretty sharpish. Made it disappear from any records of the time, as far as they could. They closed up the portals. Or said they did. We tried to move on. You've seen how well magic works when you can't get behind what's going on. So those of us who were against it—well, we had to try to make the most of it. Do good by other people. Keep the world ticking along."

"So it's all a lie? All the compassion and consideration we show?"

"That, I don't know. I think mages are more inclined to tolerance on the whole. Even when we were more entwined, I didn't always understand the Others, or how they could get things so backwards. But it's needed for the energy. If you're getting a reward, is there any such thing as a selfless act?"

"I'm not sure. So, you're saying I wouldn't be able to help over there?"

"I'm saying it gets complicated fast. First off, there's wanting to be rewarded. I suppose that's not so different from our merit sessions, and they work, somewhat. Hard to tell how much, seeing as it wasn't a thing before. But the problems themselves and applying magic as a solution. Let's say the library's window is broken in the Other World. Let's say you fix it. How do you explain it getting fixed to everyone there? You have to use magic to make people think they saw something they didn't. Now, is that still selfless and good? Maybe it is, but when you start trying to balance the books like that, manipulating people as part of what you're doing, it can go downhill fast. What about why it got broken in the first place—you haven't fixed the fact that kids chuck rocks at windows. So, you go out to fix that, but that's where things get even more complicated. Because the reasons those kids are chucking rocks are big and deep and complex. Sweeping social changes. Things you can't do by yourself. Things that involve knowing the best thing to do and getting that idea into enough heads that it gets done. So, do you still want to go? Do you want to fix things, knowing you'll have to pick your battles and never be done?"

No. He wanted it to be easy and obvious. Where was he supposed to start with problems like those? Except, he'd had some good advice once, on starting to untangle a complicated problem.

"*'The things we have to do are pretty simple. Find the thing that's missing. Do the thing that's right. It's working out how to do them that's the tricky part.'*" Draven replied, with a smile. "I found it. I found what was missing, for me and for him. And it's the right thing to do, so I have to. I don't see how I can live here now—everything about it feels so wrong. But if you and Mage Starkweather are right, I'm never going to belong there either."

"Belonging is a complicated thing." She sighed. "You have your family here. We understand where you came from and what you grew up with. But that's not the same as being able to give you what you want."

"I want to make Niall's life better. I want to make his world better. I don't care that there are people who should be doing it—well, I do, I want to go over there and sort them out. But the fact that there are shitty people in charge doesn't mean that I should stop wanting to help Niall. He didn't do anything wrong. Saying I should leave it to everyone else is like saying he doesn't deserve to be loved and taken care of, and that doesn't make any sense to me. Not that it matters anyway. She made me sign a binding agreement."

"Well, as you know, magic's only as solid as the words it's made of. Numbers were always her strong suit. I'm surprised she managed to set you up so casually in the first place. I'd almost be tempted to think that was an accident if the rest of it didn't line up so well with what's typical of her. Let's have a look at this. See if we can't find a loophole."

Draven pulled the parchment from his satchel. He watched intently as his grandma studied it, his hands gripping the sides of his chair. He wanted to believe there was a way out of this. If anyone could find it, it would be her. He felt his heart stop as a look of anguish passed over her face.

"What?" he asked. "It's not possible?"

"It's not that." But whatever it was, she didn't look happy about it. "Read it again yourself. Carefully. Exactly what it says. Also, what it doesn't say. I don't think it's easy, what it's going to take. But you have my support. If that's what you choose."

Draven took the paper, trying to curb his sense of frustration that she wouldn't just tell him. He got that there were some things he had to figure out for himself. He stared at the message, feeling it stab at his heart, his brain clouded by the panicked fog that this was the end. His grandma hadn't seemed happy with the solution she'd found. His brain wouldn't budge, like when you'd been staring at the same puzzle too long, and had made the same connections again and again, so that all you could do was lead yourself around in well-trodden circles. He tried applying his grandma's advice. What didn't it say? Oh.

Oh.

For a second, it felt like the world had been pulled out from underneath him. His first instinct was to think that he could not possibly do it. Except, couldn't he? There was something behind the cavernous feeling of loss that had opened up in his chest. It was the whole of his worldview readjusting to the fact that he had hope. Yes, it was a lot to take in. It meant some pretty big sacrifices. He didn't even know if Niall was going to want him. But he had hope. That was a pretty good sign that sticking his neck out was worth trying.

Chapter Thirty

Niall rolled over, burying his face in Draven's jacket. After a week, it was losing its scent, but the faint trace of herbs, almond, and all the smells he now categorised as "magical" still lingered if he pressed his face deep into the folds. On his bedside table sat the collection of items he'd pulled from its pockets—a stack of spellbooks, crumpled shopping lists for surprisingly mundane items, and a small number of pebbles he suspected served no real purpose other than Draven liking how they felt in his fingers. Niall stroked a finger over each of them, over the books, and over the most solid reminder he had of Draven: the flask of tea. He'd tried not to get swallowed up in the afternoon Draven might have had planned for them after they'd left Niall's parents' house. He had failed and had imagined all the places they could have gone and drunk the flask of tea, or ignored it in favour of being distracted by each other.

His week had been semi-functional. His mum had managed to make him go to college every day. Maybe being partly distracted by his studies and his friends was better than being fully undistracted at home. It didn't feel like he'd listened in class or done much other than sit with his head on a table during his breaks.

Niall had told himself any number of things during the week. First and foremost, that Draven's absence did not mean he was never coming back. Draven not being there during the week was normal. He had told himself a few times that it wasn't his fault, and a few that it was, and a few that it didn't matter whose fault it was, it just needed to be made better.

Right now, he was telling himself he believed in magic. Or rather, since its existence had been categorically demonstrated to him, in his own ability to do it. Because it was Sunday morning. It was time for Draven to come back to him.

He made his way down to the kitchen, fetching one of the guest cups from the cupboard and took it back up to his room. He set the cup precisely on a coaster and took a deep breath, staring at it intently. He had no idea how magic worked. There was a little voice at the back of his head that said he couldn't do it, even though it was real, and there was the voice arguing back that he still believed—the voice which he was never quite sure whether he was faking or not. It didn't matter. Even if he was pretending to believe in magic—in his own ability to do it—he decided that counted. He had something that belonged to Draven. That meant something. Objects had power. Something from Draven's world being in this world mattered. He had watched the intricate gestures Draven made and knew he would be making things up to try and copy one of those, so instead he crossed his fingers as he tipped some tea from the flask into the cup.

One week on, it was still piping hot. He added that to the list of things he would tell Draven when he saw him. It really was magic. Better than they could do. He would tell him that the world was not okay. It was not fair, and that he didn't like the way it was. With no "but." The world, and the people in it, sucked sometimes. It wasn't like he thought it ought to be that way, but it wasn't the first time he'd been disappointed. He wasn't sure if he remembered, specifically, when that was. Niall had always known hatred existed. He had always known he risked having it targeted at him. He had had to deal with it alone, and he'd got scared and small. So, it was going to be different for Draven. That was what he should have said.

But we can make it better. We can find a way to take it on, me and you. He would tell Draven that, and it would be true.

He inhaled the tea's scent. It smelt bitter, but not unpleasant. It reminded him of tea as it steeped in the pot, and it had a freshness and a purity to it. He took a sip, finding that it made him grimace, but he was determined.

You're my cup of tea, he told himself. *Just as you are. I will not try to add milk and sugar. So long as you want me, just the way I am too.*

Niall finished it—every last sip of strange, otherworldly tea—and told himself firmly that his boyfriend was coming back.

That was all the magic he could do on Draven. The rest was stuff he would have to do on himself. He pulled open the drawer, shifting aside the pile of trousers to find his pile of treasures. He slipped on the necklace from Draven's world, running a thumb over the runes and wishing for a little goodness, but that wasn't the only magic that was in here. There was all the kitschy jewellery and stupid shit that had the power to make him himself. He snapped the little bracelet of plastic stars around his wrist, knowing that it meant he was brave. He pulled on the kitten sweater, in all its tacky glory, wondering if he could be bright and brilliant. He rolled up the sleeves so that the bracelet wasn't hidden and turned to look in the mirror.

He looked ridiculous.

He was still gawky, and added to that was the fact that his hair wouldn't lie flat, and that he hadn't slept well for a week.

But he didn't hate it.

* * *

Draven stood by the portal. Alone. Mage Starkweather didn't need to follow him. She had his word, bound across time and space. Her permission would be withdrawn once he had done as she said, and his access to the portal would be closed off. He fidgeted with the strap of his satchel. He had checked and double checked all the things he was bringing, just in case. He was worried Niall wouldn't show up, but he had his phone number and his address. He would find him.

He hesitated on the verge of taking the final step. It felt bigger than it ever had done; bigger even than when he had been plunging into the unknown. He took a deep breath. Goodbyes had to be some of the hardest, saddest things in the world. He tried to tell himself this wasn't one, and that gave him the strength to put one foot in front of the other, and step into the swirling green mass before him.

He was barely out the other side when he felt someone grabbing hold of him, and he automatically pulled backwards, alarmed, until he saw who it was.

"Niall." He breathed a sigh of relief, glad that he had found him even though everything was a long way from being right.

"Can you do the vanishing thing if I'm holding onto you?" Niall demanded. "Or whatever it was you did?"

"I'm not sure," Draven said. "People don't tend to grab where I'm from."

"Well, people don't tend to vanish into thin air where I'm from and not be reachable for a week! That wasn't fair!" Niall was keeping his voice low, but Draven thought that might have more to do with their setting than Niall's mood.

"I'm sorry. You can let go, and I promise I'm not going to run away mid-conversation."

"What did you do to me?"

Draven stared at the floor. He had done plenty of feeling bad about the incident, but it had never occurred to him that Niall might not even know what had happened.

"I froze you," Draven admitted. "I—"

"I don't need fixing. I...I'm not saying I'm perfect or anything. But I'd say I'm actually...fine as I am."

"What?" Draven blinked at him in utter confusion.

"I think I'm okay. I don't need to be put on your list of things to fix."

"I think that's selling yourself short. Why would I want to change you? You're the best darn thing this world's got going for it." He almost laughed at the look on Niall's face—he might have if the whole thing hadn't been so serious. Niall was looking like he always did when he was complimented, like he was about to start fighting back against it.

"I...I'm okay." Niall shrugged. Draven didn't correct him. He could heap hyperbole on Niall as much as he liked, but that small word was a big deal coming from Niall's own mouth, and he didn't want to undermine it.

"Yes. You are." He paused, clearly floundering in the space between him and Niall. Niall seemed to be softening up, but everything still felt messy.

"Hey. We hug, don't we?" Niall offered, holding out his arms. Draven leant into them, grateful for the harsh, blue smell that greeted him as he lay his head on Niall's chest.

"I got scared," Draven told him. "I didn't mean to magic you without your permission. It was an accident, and I am so, so sorry. But I freaked out, and I thought the best thing I could do was get out of the way. It was a stupid decision, but when I got back, Mage Starkweather was waiting for me. It was, as I believe you would say, a whole big thing."

"That doesn't sound like a good thing." Little wrinkles of concern creased Niall's forehead.

"It's a complicated thing. Can we talk about us first? I missed you. I mean, I always miss you, but I hate everything that happened last week and—does it change things?"

"I..." Niall faltered. "I guess it means that this time, when I say it should get real, I have to mean it. I'm sorry. I didn't mean to be controlling, I was freaking out that something would go wrong. Way to shoot myself in the foot."

Draven tensed. He stayed put in Niall's arms, partly so he wouldn't have to see his face as he said this, and partly because he didn't want to be anywhere else.

"I want to belong here. With you."

"I want that too."

They had said that before, and it hadn't been enough.

"Is that possible?" Draven asked.

"Let's make it possible. You be you, and I'll back you up. Unless I think you're about to do something cataclysmically dangerous?"

"Yeah. I don't know what I'm doing," he admitted. "It's complicated, and bigger than me, and I can't fix it all. I just want to do some good."

"You already did. I never needed you to fix the whole world, y'know."

Draven pulled back, finally searching Niall's face, finding that he looked like he meant everything he was saying.

Draven traced a hand down his cheek, and Niall's came to rest on it, half holding him in return, half pausing him.

"So, what happened when you got home?" Niall asked.

Draven knew there was still more to deal with, but he would have been happy to melt into Niall and ignore it, at least for a little while.

"Me coming here wasn't an accident. It was Mage Starkweather's idea all along, to try to scare me off, pull me back into line. She finally came out and said as much. It didn't work though, because instead of all the big, bad things in this world, I met you. Niall?" he asked, before Niall could push with follow up questions that he wasn't ready to answer yet. Not until they'd talked through some other things. "Would you love me, even if I wasn't magical?"

"You mean if you weren't a mage? You'll always be magical to me. It's awesome that you're a mage. I love that about you, but it's not why I love you. Is that some kind of cost for you coming here? Are they going to strip you of your powers? Or did they?" he asked.

"No. Not exactly." The binding agreement would strip him of his powers if he broke it. He had thought long and hard about what to do. His commitment was firm; he wanted to help. If he did it by magic, it would be a lot more effective. It would also have the benefit of helping people back in Galdorsfarne—solving the original problem he'd set out to solve. It would give Yvette the life she wanted. That was the best-case scenario. He could still be of value here though, even without powers. He wasn't sure he'd be as effective at changing things, but he could try, and he would still matter to Niall. He hoped he was right about what was going to happen, but even if he wasn't, he'd be okay. Assuming the next part of this went according to plan too.

"How would you feel about having me around more?" he asked.

"Good," Niall answered instantly. "Very good. You know that. But it comes at a price, doesn't it?" he asked.

"Yes."

"Your powers?" Niall asked.

"Not exactly. There's a risk there. I might be reading it wrong. But that's a gamble I'm willing to take. She promised me one more time, then she's taking away my access to the portal."

"What?" His hands, which had been resting lightly on Draven's arms, gripped them forcefully again. There was panic in Niall's eyes for a second, before Draven's request caught up to him. "Wait, did you...so, have you...run away?"

"Not exactly. But I think I might be about to. She said I could have one more trip. I'm supposed to explain things, and to say goodbye. Except, words are tricky things. You have to be precise. She never said return trip. She never said which side I have to be on when she takes away my access. So, I think I've upheld my end of the bargain. I've made one more trip, and I will allow her to cut off my access to the portal. Behind me."

"What are you saying?" Niall checked.

"I guess I'm saying...can I stay with you?"

"Of course," Niall agreed. The answer came immediately, even though he still looked like he was reeling from what Draven had said. "But are you sure about this? You're going to leave your family, and...everything. And if it goes wrong, you lose your powers? I can't ask you to do that for me."

"You didn't," Draven pointed out. "Those are things that would happen for now. My grandma knows how to find me. It's not goodbye forever." He had to believe that. "But if I left you, it might be. You need me more. For now, I belong here. If you want me?"

"I want you. I want this to be your choice though. You're giving up a lot, and— None of that means I'm lukewarm about you being here, but I need to know I'm not pressuring you." Niall's grip relaxed, even if he looked like he was having to force himself, finger by finger, to not hold on.

"You're not the kind of person who'd do that. It's one of the things I love about you." Draven reached out, squeezing Niall's arms firmly. If that had been a gesture of farewell, he didn't think he could ever have let go. That had to mean this was the right choice.

He turned to the portal, thinking about the letters he'd left with his grandma—one for his parents, one for Yvette. It was a crummy way to tell them, he knew that. But there was no way his mother would have let him go, and if she didn't get a face-to-face goodbye, then it wasn't fair for Yvette to have one. At least this way, they had a little piece of him to hold onto, until he next saw them. His stomach squeezed with regret, wanting to go back and do those goodbyes differently—to make sure they understood, and to know his reasons were accepted. But he still wanted to say them.

He traced the air in front of the portal with his fingers, mimicking the symbol that was on the paper he'd signed.

"Agreement completed." He felt something, like a hot wind rippling over him, pulling something away. The portal hovered in front of him, but it was dull. He reached out a hand and it pushed him back. He did not have permission to be in the Special Collections. That kind of answered his question about whether, if he took a book through the portal, it was technically still in its own library. They could have fun bending their heads around the physics of that. When they got...home.

"What happened?" Niall asked.

"It's still there. But it's not for me anymore." He wasn't sure whether that meant the agreement agreed with him or something else. But one thing was certain, he had made his choice, and now he was going to have to live with it. "I'm scared." Now that it was done, now that Niall couldn't try to talk him out of it, it was safe to admit that.

"Me too," Niall said.

"What of? You're used to this world."

"Now I have you. I have to keep you safe and help you understand." He held out his arms. "And at some point, I have to let go and let you make choices about it yourself."

"No, that's my job. I've come here to look after you," Draven mumbled, leaning into the hug.

"I think I might return the favour from time to time." Niall stroked Draven's hair. "You can do— You can make the world a better place, and I'll teach you how to use a microwave. Fair trade?"

"You were going to say 'do spells,'" Draven said. But Niall had changed tack, and believed that Draven was still going to make the world a better place regardless. "Let's see if I still can." It hadn't felt like anything was being torn out of him. He thought he would know if his magic had left him, and he still felt whole. "Is your nose cold?"

"A little."

Draven hesitated, his fingers fumbling, even though it was so familiar. It felt slow and difficult, like he was pulling on a part of himself that was far away. But it was still there. He pressed a finger to Niall's nose.

"Feels like magic," Niall confirmed, reaching down to touch his warm nose to Draven's. "Let's go?"

Draven nodded, fiddling with the strap of his satchel. He took a deep breath, gearing himself up to step out into a brand new, big and complicated, thoroughly imperfect world. Niall reached out a hand, pulling Draven's away from its nervous fiddling, and twining their fingers together. Draven could feel Niall's hand shaking too, just a little, but he didn't let go as he marched them across the well-worn carpet, out into the world beyond.

Chapter Thirty-One

One month later

Niall set the mugs down as carefully as possible, but there was a soft clunk of china hitting slate. Twice. Draven opened his eyes.

"Presumptuous," he muttered sleepily.

"May I join you for tea?" Niall asked. Draven was already flicking the covers back, and Niall slid into bed next to him. "You awake yet?"

"No. Shh," Draven replied, cuddling up against him. Niall stroked his hair gently.

They were in Draven's room. Niall's parents weren't naive enough to think that the two of them weren't going to find every excuse to end up behind closed doors together and had made limited attempts to stop that happening. They had made the guest bedroom into Draven's room more from a point of maintaining everyone's sanity than anyone's innocence. *"Much as you think you want to spend every second together, there will be times when you want or need some space. It's healthy to have that."* His mum had felt that Draven might need it more than Niall did. Everything here belonged to Niall. Draven couldn't be expected to move in and take half of Niall's space and feel comfortable with that. He needed somewhere that belonged to him too.

The idea of Draven moving in had been accepted remarkably easily by Niall's parents. He supposed it helped that there wasn't any other option, and they were hardly going to turn him out with nowhere to go.

It was weird to go from having a boyfriend he saw once a week to a boyfriend who lived with him, and had to learn to co-exist with his family. And to live in this world. It was hard not to get on with Draven, he was sweet, polite and helpful—something that ticked a lot of parental boxes. It hadn't taken long for Niall's mum to point out that his boyfriend pulled more weight with the chores than he did. Family-wise, that was the easy part. Life-wise, everything here was so new to Draven. Sometimes they forgot what he didn't know. The news regularly terrified him, and even what Niall thought of as cosy comfort shows exposed him to previously unknown issues.

Sometimes, the problems were much more trivial, but more direct in terms of how Draven was, or was not, gelling with the world. Like when, after a week of living with them, Draven had tearfully confessed to Niall that Niall's parents frequently flat out ignored him when he tried to talk to them. Or when Niall's parents had pulled Niall aside to ask why their coat pockets were being filled with sage and salt. The answers had turned out to be "earbuds" and... And he wasn't sure they'd fully dealt with the other thing. For now, Niall's parents seemed to be willing to believe that Draven believed in magic, and thought he was helping. They didn't want to take that away from him and had only made one attempt at a follow-up conversation with Niall about his own grip on reality for believing it too. It would have been easier to side with his parents, to join the game of smiling and appeasing, and pretending that he was pretending for Draven's sake. But he'd stuck to his boyfriend's side of the story—this was real.

It scared Niall to think how much trouble Draven could get into outside if he could manage such giant misunderstandings in their own home. One of the hardest things to watch was that Draven knew it too. A lot of the gentle unpicking Niall had thought he might have to do had already been done rather sharply by Mage Starkweather; Draven knew people lied and didn't always have your best interests at heart. Niall wasn't having to teach him that, but to comfort him through the repercussions of learning it. He had become the one who argued that it was worth stepping outside and taking on the world.

Gradually, they were finding things for Draven to do. This was another point where the scales tipped unfairly in Niall's favour. He had a full, complete life here, one which kept him out of the house for most of the day. Draven needed things to do other than sit at home waiting, but without the risk of getting himself into trouble. Magic-wise, he had started small. He cleared the graffiti from the library chairs, and unsquashed flowers that, by accident or deliberate malice, had been crushed. He found tiny little corners of the world that had been damaged and smoothed them back out. He also volunteered a couple of times a week at the charity bookshop in town, because kindness was its own form of magic.

Today though, it was Saturday. They had a whole glorious weekend stretching ahead to spend together. Maybe they would save the world. Maybe they would go to the library. Maybe one led to the other. Before that though, there was going to be tea and snuggling, and the kind of delicious, unhurried making out that weekends were built for. Niall looked down at the dark head that had settled itself on his shoulder, eagerly anticipating when Draven would wake up. It was tempting to accidentally shift his shoulder too abruptly, or to "need" to cough. Anticipation could be fun, but a fully conscious and snuggly boyfriend was even better.

That was mean though, and there was no being mean allowed. Small acts of selfishness stopped the world from turning as it should. He let his mind wander over those thoughts. It was easier to see it in Draven's world, where everything was so black and white—where there was a direct punishment from above for failing to be considerate. But deliberately waking his sleeping boyfriend to try and get kisses sooner did make him a jerk, and somewhat undeserving of those kisses. And, if Draven suspected him, he might even be grumpy enough to hold out on kissing Niall for several extra minutes. On the micro level, the theory worked. It was when you tried to apply it to something as big and messy as his whole world that it got complicated.

Niall occupied himself instead by looking around the room. It had not changed a huge amount since Draven moved in. Almost everything here was something Niall recognised from his own life. The coasters that their tea was on were souvenirs from some slate mines in Wales. It felt like they had been in the guest bedroom for his entire life, even though he dimly remembered the trip—there had been a train and, in his mind, the possibility of seeing a dragon, both of which were deeply cool and had thus left a lasting, if hazy impression. The covers that he and Draven were snuggled under were the same "guest set" that he'd seen got out for visiting friends and relatives over the years. His parents had offered to buy Draven things of his own, but he had refused it as wasteful.

In one corner, was a heap of books, which had formed the majority of the contents of Draven's satchel. On top of them sat a very old stuffed rabbit with bandaged legs, keeping his buttony eyes on them. Most of the books were spellbooks, though there was one family photo album, which Draven was still taking him through, doing a few pages at a time until it got too much. The tea on the nightstand was in a pink earthenware mug with chipped gold trim.

The other major change to the room was the blackboard. Draven had compulsively written lists when he first arrived. He had been told he would lose sight of who he was, and what he valued. With that warning in place, he had set to making sure he didn't. He had covered pages and pages, writing with a furious energy, then crossing bits out. Niall had been concerned by this franticness, and had eventually purchased a tin of blackboard paint, and covered the wall opposite the bed, so that Draven could write and revise to his heart's content. He had boiled his thoughts down to a few key points. The dust of discarded ideas lingered in the outer columns. In the middle, Draven had written a large message to himself, its swirling calligraphy belying the heaviness of its content.

"This is not normal."

Under this, in Niall's scrappier writing, was the subheading "Draven's Agenda for World Domination."

Beneath this, in Ellen's writing, "Aka The Gay Agenda."

Finally, below all this unworthy vandalism Draven had listed the points he wanted to stay focussed on:

1) I want to hold your hand whenever I damn please, with no fear of repercussions.
2) Be kind, expect kindness.
3) Other people are directly responsible via their inaction and should be held accountable.

The fourth point switched back to Niall's hand.

4) Remember that I love you, and you are never facing the world alone.

ACKNOWLEDGEMENTS

As per the dedication, my first thanks go to my parents for surrounding me with love and books. You support me from half a world away and support me being half a world away. You have always made it clear that I can strive for anything I want to, and that my life is mine to live however makes me happy, so long as I'm not hurting myself or others. Draven would approve of you.

Niall would approve of my sister for constantly pebbling my DMs with interesting facts and amusing memes, and I enjoy it too.

Jiji, who kept me company and made sure I spent very many hours sitting at my computer—you were an excellent cat.

I have been blessed to be a member of several fantastic writing communities, all of which have played a part in shaping me into the person who was capable of making this book.

Firstly, my online gang of RPG wizards—you let me give myself the label of "writer" long before I considered myself capable of something like this, and were a ready audience for my stories, while providing me with joy, entertainment, screaming frustration and fits of sobbing from your own. Particular love and thanks to Savanna—partly for reading an early draft and offering feedback, but also for just being you.

To Inkwell Shanghai and the indomitable Dr. Ryan Thorpe, for giving me a space to grow from rookie writer to workshop leader, in a safe and validating community. Special shout out to Elena, for being there when I was so proud and excited that I'd somehow cobbled something resembling a novel into existence and I decided I had to show someone. Thank you for meeting me where I was at and giving me constructive feedback but also enthusiasm and encouragement when, in retrospect, what I gave you was a flaming heap of garbage, and also wildly outside your usual wheelhouse.

To Team Tea and Books, the writing squad I found through the positive power of social media, who query together, commiserate together, and have vicious debates on scone topping order*. Thank you for holding my hand through the heartaches, giving me fun distractions, offering feedback on everything from mood boards to query letters, and being ready to shout from the rooftops about my book. Particular thanks to Teapot Sarah, who read a not-so-rough draft of the book and has been the boys' biggest fan and cheerleader ever since.

In spite of being chronically online or in my own head, it turns out I do have some real world and three-dimensional friends. Probably too many to actually thank, which is a lovely problem to have. Magnus, you have been around since before this began and always offer steady belief and enthusiasm for what I do. B, I'm not sure which group to put you in, seeing as you're in so many—I'm ecstatic that we've gone from daydreamers to debut siblings together. And to everyone I work with, for making my day job a lovely place to be, and for being the kind of colleagues who I can talk to about my weird side hustle in writing gay magical things.

Thank you to the many content creators who make writing advice free. So many of you have helped without knowing it. Ditto the many people who build positive spaces for writers to connect on social media, and the many chums, passing acquaintances, and generally friendly people I have on there.

There are several people who turned this from dreams and data on my drive to an actual book. Firstly, thanks to SmallPitch, for the event that turned into a like that turned into a full request that turned into an offer.

To Space Wizard, which is basically to Bill and Heather. Bill, thank you for taking a chance on me, for being a helpful and uplifting collaborator, and for your genuine warmth and enthusiasm for my story. I know I am biased and have a limited sample size, but I truly believe I have the best publisher with the coolest hat. Heather, thank you for your copy edits. I'm sure it's a mind-bending job trying to correct typos while not altering British spellings. I recognise and realise that it was a colourful experience and hope you can go travelling or spend time in your pyjamas to recover.

I feel so lucky to have found my amazing cover artist, Jess Montz. It takes my breath away every time I see how you took things that existed in my head and got them exactly right—from people who don't exist to buildings that you've never seen for real, but which mean the world to me.

Finally, a massive thanks to my readers, especially if you're like me and enjoy having a peek at the acknowledgements too—it's wild to believe you exist, and I hope you enjoyed this.

*jam then cream, obviously

ABOUT THE AUTHOR

P.S.C. Willis (they/them) is a queer British writer, and graduate of both Newcastle University and Reading University. They currently live in Shanghai, where they have quit any number of hobbies (ukulele, roller-skating, drag) but stuck fairly well to writing. Their work spans everything from flash fiction to novel length, mostly in sci-fi and fantasy. Community is a huge part of their writing process, and they run a local workshop and writing meetups, as well as connecting with fellow writers in many online spaces.

P likes to create stories that allow others to believe in good people, in magic, or both. Their work can be found in *DreamForge* and various anthologies. Links to this and social media can be found at https://pscwillis.com

Please take a moment to review this book at your favorite retailer's website, Goodreads, or simply tell your friends!